Silently
Blessed

I0637674

LUEMISHER
"MIMI" JAMES

James Publishing

ISBN: 978-0-9857826-3-4

Publisher: James Publishing (Virginia Beach, Virginia)

VISIT US AT:

www.SilentlyBlessed.com
Twitter: @SilentlyBlessed
Silentlyblessedbooks@gmail.com
FaceBook: SilentlyBlessedBooks&More

Printed in the United States of America.

ACKNOWLEDGEMENTS

First and above all, I would like to thank our Heavenly Father for giving me a gift that allows me to commune with Him at all times. Through my heart, spirit and finger tips, God has been with me from the very first word until the very last word of *Silently Blessed*. He has also been there from the very first thought to the very last thought. Our Father's hands are continuously in my life and transferred into the characters of *Silently Blessed*.

A special thanks to my husband, Bernard James. The support that you have given me throughout the entire process has been essential for the completeness of *Silently Blessed*. I cannot thank my husband without thanking his parents, Thomas James Sr. and the late Tablue James. I appreciate the outstanding upbringing of your son. Thank you to my sons, Ki-Jana and Ra-Jon James, for allowing me to concentrate when needed. Thank you for your hard work and great behavior in school and at home. The two of you are two of the most well-mannered young men and that just doesn't come from your parents, it comes from strangers as well. Thank you to my God son, Jonathan Cooper. Keep up your hard work in school. God bless all of you. Don't look right and don't look left. Keep doing YOUR best. Our Heavenly Father will do the rest!

However none of this would be possible without my parents, the late Lowman "Sonny Boy" Steverson and Jestine Steverson. I truly thank my parents for raising me the right way and keeping me grounded in church. Thank you to my Daddy for being the ultimate disciplinary. Even though my Dad has gone on to be with the Lord, I know he is looking down and smiling now. I love you Daddy and miss you. I appreciate my dear Mother for being such a Godly woman. Thank you for taking us to church and Sunday school. I remember sitting on the choir with you, Mother, because I wasn't old enough to sit on my own. Mom and Dad, I will always cherish the fond memories.

Many thanks to my brothers and sisters, Norma Williams, Sammie Lee Steverson, Leon Steverson, Steve McQueen Steverson and Claire Steverson-Smith. Thank you for your love. Everybody needs brothers and sisters like you all.

Many thanks to Lisa Domme for editing and Yvette Rouse for proof reading *Silently Blessed*. Lisa and Yvette, the both of you were truly blessings as you shared your God given gifts. I appreciate every moment of your time that you so kindly devoted to *Silently Blessed*. A special thanks to Douglas Mlyn for the professional graphic designing and the typesetting of the book. I would also like to give thanks to Bernard James, for the outstanding pictures taken for the cover design. Many thanks to Charles Tubbs for taking the author's photo.

Additionally, I would like to thank Star Bucks on Nimmo Parkway in Virginia Beach, VA. Your store's atmosphere was heavenly. When I sat down in that beautiful atmosphere, it was like heaven meeting earth.

I would also like to thank Master Cielo at King Tiger Martial Arts in Virginia Beach, VA. God gave me many ideas while my children trained. While they trained, I wrote as if no one else was there. King Tiger Martial Arts is family oriented and a gift for those who happen to be a part of the school.

I would like to express my gratitude to Turkey Branch Baptist Church in Neeses, SC. Thank you to Mrs. Erthella Milhouse for being my choir director on the children's choir. I would also like to thank the late Jewell Inabinette for being my Deacon. I also want to extend a thank you to Clara Inabinette for being his devoted wife. I must thank you for being another woman of God that I can emulate. I truly looked up to the both of you throughout my childhood.

Many thanks to my neighbor, Sandra Borror and her family, you all are just like family. I am grateful to God for the love that you have shown for me and my family.

I would like to send out a special thanks to my Piney Grove family for embracing my family. God bless you all for the utmost encouragement.

God bless all of you for allowing Him to use your gifts and life.

There were six wealthy families who were close friends. They resided in Atlanta Georgia. Out of these six families, there were five Christian families and one family who were atheists. These upper-class individuals lived in a prestigious, gated community called "Ridgeland Towers of Atlanta." All who were Christians attended Faith Deliverance Church of Atlanta and they, of course, were well known in Atlanta. They struggled with strongholds in their everyday lives. God spoke through their children, their nannies, their chefs, and yes even their atheist friends. Through all of their tribulations, there was one couple who was amongst them who were always there to inspire and remind them of the true word of God.

There was John and Rachel Richardson. John was a lawyer who owned his law firm. They had two children and their names were Charles and Charlotte. They were God sent for the other families. There was Ronald Ivy, he was the top physician for one of the local hospitals and his wife, Tressie Ivy, owned a boutique in the heart of Atlanta. They had three children and their names were Steward, Melinda, and Stacey. Howard and Joanne Stone owned an Audi dealership and they too had three children. Their names were Ashley, Ashton and Amira. Reese and Melody Ford owned several fitness centers and they shared three children together. Their names were Tremaine, Samone and Nia. There was Paul and Sasha Jones. Paul was a gifted artist and Sasha owned the most elegant, high- in salon in Atlanta. The couple had one daughter and her name was Sehara. There was Ridge and Scarlette Crane and they owned several gas stations throughout Atlanta. They shared one daughter together and her name was Cassidy Arnasia. Ridge had a daughter from a previous relationship and her name was Meriah, she did not care for her step-mom. The Cranes were self- proclaim atheists. Five of the families attended Faith Deliverance Church of Atlanta. Their Pastor name was Jeffrey E. Patterson and he was an anointed man of God. The couples struggled with putting God first, even though they attended church Sunday after Sunday. Through their trials and tribulations, God used their children, nannies, and their chefs to get their attention.

Rachel Richardson's heart went out for everyone. She found herself praying silently anywhere and at anytime. Rachel and her two children were in traffic one day. She felt the need to pray for the people in the car next to them. Before long, Rachel, Charles and Charlotte were holding hands interceding for the strangers that sat in the car next to them. When they finished, it looked as though a load had been lifted from the people's lives in the car next to them. All of the people in the other cars who surrounded Rachel's car, hearts reflected and connected to Rachel, Charles and Charlotte.

God used "The After Holiday Party" to touch and turn! All the couples were at Ronald Ivy's work party, "The After Holiday Party." The ladies found themselves in the ladies' room sharing their problems with one another. Ultimately, Rachel adheres to the Holy Spirit and ministered to them. She did not realize she touched another soul while ministering to the other ladies. At the end of the night, the DJ played a beautiful song that all the couples absolutely loved. This particular song seemed to bring the couples closer to one another.

God used Little Cassidy Arnasia to speak to her parents, Ridge and Scarlette Crane. The Crane family was eating one morning. A disagreement between Scarlette and her step-daughter, Meriah occurred. This incident stirred Little Cassidy Arnasia's spirit. Although she was only four years old, she was the wisest in the household. She told her family she wanted what Mrs. Rachel had in her house. Little Cassidy Arnasia said to her family, "It not right in dis house." God orchestrated the entire situation. The Cranes chef, Chef Fisher, was a born again Christian. He confirmed what the little four-year-old was saying. Little did they know, experience after experience, the Cranes who were atheists, were getting closer to God.

One Saturday, Rachel treated her friend, Trina, who was a regular at the homeless shelter where she volunteered, to a hair makeover at Sasha's upscale salon. Sasha's salon clientele was not welcoming to Rachel's friend, Trina's appearance. Needless to say, God swept through the salon touching any and everyone who was there through a song that popped up at the right time in Trina's life.

Anytime Pastor Jeffrey E. Patterson got a chance, he poured into his people. Faith Deliverance Church of Atlanta had a spring barbeque every year, which was always open to members and the community. Pastor Patterson message for that day was "Accepting Everyone." Pastor Patterson's message spoke to many hearts. God showed up on time and on point. Although the atmosphere was touched by the glory of God, several hours later, Pastor Patterson counseled a couple that was going through trying times.

Howard Stone invited one of his employees and her family over for dinner. Carol, Jim, Chelsey and Kerry had dinner at the Stones. Nanny Nora could not work this particular night, of all nights. Ashton, Ashley and Amira were misbehaving, out of nowhere Carol's thirteen-year-old daughter Chelsey stepped in for Howard and Joanne. By the end of the dinner, Howard and Joanne's eyes were opened. Chef Meg was enlightened and affected just by being on her job.

The Richardsons visited Rachel's family in South Carolina. She had three sisters and three brothers and their names were Sharon, Terri, Patricia, Byron, Raymond and Sammie. The Richardsons stayed at Rachel's parents' home, Mama Lula and Papa Ray's. They showed their love to everyone in South Carolina. But, sadly many of Rachel's family members did not care for them because of the life God had given them. Although negative comments and attitudes were thrown towards them, they showed love in spite of the situation. Needless to say, God is always on time. God dropped a memory moment while everyone ate dinner and stirred up hearts.

Stacey's dance recital was a mountain to climb for the entire family. Tressie just could not bring herself to be happy about the recital because she could not accept her daughter's disability. She was devastated and would have done anything to get out of attending the recital. Little Stacey felt her Mother's rejection towards her and this led to Little Stacey's episode in the midst of the dance recital. Due to Little Stacey's episode, Tressie had a meltdown as well. Of course, Rachel showed up on the scene willing to do God's work. By the end of the night God planted individuals exactly where they were supposed to be at the right time. There were many people that were touched by Tressie and Little Stacey's episodes.

Joanne Stone had a "Ladies Night Out Party" in her home, but Rachel was the host. There were several women from church that Joanne invited. Every lady gave somewhat of a testimony. Corrine Bay was a powerful business woman who thrived on competitiveness. Another young lady by the name of Lois Ferguson worshipped the ground Corrine Bay walked upon. Maranda Hickory was a housewife who was grateful for the husband that God put into her life. She not only loved being a housewife, but she loved being a housewife of a construction worker. There was Alice Truman who was another successful business woman who was married for years, but didn't appreciate her husband. Deborah Niles was a woman married to a big time lawyer who everyone knew was a womanizer. Deborah knew it as well, but chose to turn a blind eye. She was addicted to a lavish lifestyle. Scarlette, Tressie, Sasha and Melody were there as well and gave their testimonies. Throughout the night the women were being blessed by each others' testimonies.

Ridge and Scarlette Crane visited Ridge's childhood friend. Their friends were atheists as well. Little Cassidy Arnasia didn't want to be there from the start. She didn't like the atmosphere; Little Cassidy couldn't shake this nagging feeling. Although she expressed her feelings to her parents, they chose to stay a little while longer. Ridge and Scarlette felt strange amongst other fellow atheists. On the way back home, they were touched by a beautiful song.

Cousin BJ and his family visited John, Rachel and the kids. They were in awe of the way their cousins lived. Cousin BJ and the family felt God's welcoming presence while they stayed in John and Rachel's guest home. When they walked in John and Rachel's home, they could tell Jesus resided there as well. Cousin BJ and Memphis was so moved by the atmosphere of John and Rachel's home, they were compelled to get saved that Sunday at church. After church that Sunday, John and Rachel had their friends over. Cousin BJ shared his story with people he just met for the first time. From Cousin BJ's release, others shared some of their burdens.

The ladies visited New York City at Christmas time. On the plane to New York, God used His touch through magazine articles and the people that surrounded them. It was as though everything the ladies came in contact with helped them in some way or another.

The morning after they arrived in New York, they met a distinguished gentleman name Mr. Steadford Grey. All of the ladies were attracted to Mr. Grey's powerful anointing. He was like no other they'd ever met.

Rachel made arrangements for the ladies to volunteer at one of the homeless shelters there. The other ladies were not eager at first, but once they gave in, the ladies' hearts were filled with gratification. After the feeding that night, Rachel prayed for all the people who were homeless. Through Rachel's prayer, the Holy Spirit touched everyone there. Pastor Leon Wolfe was the overseer for this particular shelter. He joined in the prayer with the homeless for the first time that night and was moved to change his ways.

The ladies were walking back to their hotel and somehow they ended up in an alley. Needless to say they were about to be robbed by a gang. Out of nowhere, Mr. Steadford Grey showed up to save them all. The next day, the ladies went shopping. Rachel was trying on a dress then discovered something that would alter her life. Most of all, it would be the greatest test of FAITH for our most precious family ever! Now the journey is exemplified in Silently Blessed.

CHAPTER 1

Psalm 55:17 Evening, morning and noon I cry out in distress, and he hears my voice. (N.I.V.)

On a Wednesday night in January, John and Rachel Richardson and their children arrived home from bible study. Rachel's heart was as heavy as ever.

Rachel commented, "Bible study was outstanding tonight."

John felt the same. "I agree, bible study is especially good at different moments and times in a person's life. Honey, I pray our friends and neighbors will try to work on their attitudes towards people who are less fortunate than they are."

"I agree whole, heartedly. I am still praying and believing that God is truly working on their hearts. Although I am still praying and believing, at times it is discouraging to hear some of the words that come out of their mouths."

John responded, "You and I know God is in control. Don't worry about the things you cannot control."

"Sweetheart you are definitely right."

As Rachel walked upstairs behind John, disappointed by her friends' comments, she looked toward John.

"Sweetheart, we are going to say a special prayer tonight."

John concurred, "Yes, of course."

Before Rachel began to pray she said to John, "Why do we continuously socialize with our circle of friends?"

"I believe God sends people in our lives for a reason and a season." Rachel looked up at John with a look of concern.

"Thank God for you, our family and yes, of course, our friends as well."

John and Rachel thanked God for an awesome bible study, but also proceeded to pray about the disappointment and distractions that occurred in bible study due to their friends.

The next day Rachel ran into one of her neighbors. Tressie Ivy, a snooty business woman who owned a clothing boutique in the heart of Atlanta.

Rachel asked, "Did you enjoy bible study last night?"

Tressie replied, "Yes, it is always great to attend bible study."

Rachel sounded very concerned and her heart was full of guidance.

"You are certainly right, but it means nothing if we don't apply it to our lives."

Tressie seemed clueless. "Oh yes of course. You have a blessed day. I have to get to the boutique and I have to go shopping as well. The hospital is having their extravagant party this weekend. Rachel, I am so excited. You know the hospital big parties are always lavish. I have to be the best dressed woman there."

Rachel kindly ignored her. "Be blessed and God willing I'll see you at church."

Rachel and Tressie embraced before going their separate ways, but Rachel prayed silently.

Rachel volunteered most of the day as usual. After volunteering that day, Rachel ran into one of her other friends, Mrs. Joanne Stone. Joanne was a stay home wife and mother. Her husband Howard owned one of the top car dealerships in Atlanta. Rachel and Joanne greeted each other with a friendly hug.

Rachel asked, "Did you have a wonderful day?"

Joanne replied, "I have been shopping most of the day. You know Ronald's hospital party is this weekend. I had a great time shopping for the dress for the party this weekend. Oh, honey it is so frustrating shopping for a dress when you are my size. It is hard when you are a size 16."

Rachel gently smiled. "Yes, I know I talked to Tressie this morning. Joanne, why do you torture yourself with the words that you use against yourself?"

"Rachel, you are always giving everyone encouraging words, but it is up to that person to believe it themselves. That is the reason why I love you Sister. You don't find women like you every day."

As Joanne spoke, her eyes filled with tears. Joanne quickly changed the subject.

"So, Rachel, are you coming from the homeless shelter?"

"Yes, and we were busy all day; you know Joanne I would not give up serving for the world."

"Oh, Rachel, if everyone could be as caring as you. I just got back from shopping for my dress for this weekend."

Rachel said, "Tressie was excited as well. So where is the party this year?"

"I don't know, but I know it will be as grand as ever. All the ritzy people are going to be there. Rachel, I just can't get enough of those parties and our lifestyle."

Rachel replied, "Do you mean the neighborhood that we live in and the jobs our husbands hold? Joanne it is nice to go to the extravagant parties and to have the pleasure of not worrying about money, but tell me where is God in that lifestyle?"

Joanne asked, "What do you mean? We attend church every Sunday and we attend bible study."

Rachel explained, "Joanne just because you attend church does not mean you are a servant for Christ. When you go to these parties make sure you tell someone about the goodness of Jesus Christ and who He is in your life."

Joanne answered, "Pastor Patterson always preaches about how we should let our light shine, but I feel so uncomfortable in that situation."

Rachel further explained, "Joanne, imagine how Christ felt on the cross when he died for our sins? That was just food for thought."

Joanne replied, "God knows I am a work in progress."

"Joanne, I will keep you in my prayers."

"Thank you Rachel, I need it. Well, I will see you later, God Bless. Oh I'll see you at The Unity Gazebo Courtyard on Wednesday for bible study.

"Yes, I'll see you at bible study. Oh, the hospital's party on Saturday."

Joanne remembered, and smiled, "Yes, of course, everybody who is anybody will be at the Hospital's party. Oh Rachel don't you just love it."

Rachel gently smiled and went her way.

Rachel picked her children Charles and Charlotte up from school, and afterwards she went to the supermarket.

Rachel asked her children, "How was your day?"

Charlotte answered, "Mom it was a busy, busy day, but Mommy it was so much fun; you know how much I love school."

Rachel replied, "Great job, sweetheart!"

Rachel asked, "What about you Charles? How was your day, honey?"

Charles slowly answered, and it was clear to Rachel that he was not happy. "Mom you know I think school is a drag."

Rachel explained, "Charles, you have no choice you have to go to school, besides you are always making the principal's list. One day, son your hard work in school is going to pay off. You are blessed, Charles, because there are lots of children that wish they could do better in school."

Charles replied "Mom, you always say that."

"There are children who have problems that affect the way they learn in school. I know if they could change the way they learn, they would in a heartbeat. Charles, I am just trying to make you understand, good grades don't come easy to everyone. I am proud of both of you. Keep up the great work. May God bless you two and all of the other children who are doing well in school and trying their very best that they can."

Her heart melted for children who were not doing as good in school as her children.

As Rachel drove on she silently prayed, *"Lord, God at this moment give the precious children of this world the ability to do their very best in school. Lord, I'm praying for the children whose parents have no idea how to pray or have no desire to pray and just can't find it in their hearts to pray. Keep your precious children close to you and their parents who are your children as well. In Jesus's name, Amen."*

Rachel shed a tear or two and looked up to the "Father"

quickly and silently said, "Thank You." As soon as Rachel finished her prayer, Charlotte and Charles looked at her as though they knew exactly what she prayed about.

As she continued to drive to the supermarket, she ran into a traffic jam. A song came on the radio that reminded Rachel of the love Jesus have for our precious children of the world. As the song was playing, Rachel noticed the family in the car next to them. The Mom and Dad looked as though they were stressed out and they also appeared to be arguing. On top of it all both of them were smoking. Their car appeared to have, had a built in chimney due to all the smoke that was accumulating in the car. The children were packed into the car like sardines. The children were silent and holding on to each other for dear life, not knowing what the next moment is going to bring. Rachel felt both the parents' frustration and the children's fear. It was as if her discerning spirit connected with the family in the car next to them. As she listened to the words of the song, the more she thought about the family in the car next to her and she was overwhelmed. She cried out to God for the family. Charles knew why she was crying without saying a word to her about the family in the car next to them.

Charles out of the blue and out of character suggested, "Mom let's pray for them."

Little Charlotte agreed, "Yeah, Mommy let's pray now."

The people in the cars around them respectfully watched as they held each others' hands and prayed. The family that they were actually praying for respectfully watched as well. As they watched, the smoke decreased, the parents seem to mellow out and the children all looked as though a burden had been lifted off of their sweet, innocent little shoulders and faces.

Rachel and her family found themselves praying anywhere for anybody at anytime. To say the least, they always prayed for their friends. John and Rachel had a set of friends that did not believe in God. They knew their atheist friends were sent by God.

Ridge and Scarlette Crane came into fortune by winning Mega Millions. They bought several service stations throughout Atlanta. Ridge managed all the service stations. Although this was the only thing he had to do, it was still stressful at times. Ridge and Scarlette Crane was a couple who chose "not" to believe in God, but their "Little Cassidy Arnasia" was intuitive and sensitive to the revelations that surrounded her atmosphere. Ridge had a ten-year-old daughter, Meriah from a previous marriage that felt every unwanted feeling from stepmom, Scarlette. These unwanted feelings reverted to a rebellious spirit.

Ridge was coming home from a stressful day at work. As he walked in the door, Little Cassidy Arnasia ran to him hysterical. "Daddy, why they fight so, Daddy?"

Scarlette said loudly and angrily, "Ridge, she needs to go back to her Mom! I cannot take the disrespect. I will not take any more, Ridge! You need to do something with your daughter!"

Meriah said loudly and helplessly, "Dad, I hate her for making me feel like I'm nobody."

Meriah turned to her stepmom Scarlette and looked her square in her eyes. With all the insecurity of a child, she said, "I'm only a kid."

Meriah ran upstairs to her room. Scarlette immediately felt extreme guilt. As Little Cassidy said her peace, Scarlette noted everything she was saying in her heart. Of course she cringed as her five-year-old spoke.

Little Cassidy Arnasia commented, "Mommy, Daddy, we need somethin' up in the sky. Somethin' high Mommy, Daddy. My heart hurt fo' my big sista. Mommy, you got to be bigga than big sista, Mommy. Why can't yall hold hands?"

At this point, she was in tears. Ridge picked Little Cassidy up and she held on for dear life.

She whispered in her dad's ear while crying, "Daddy, we need Mrs. Rachel "Jesus" Daddy."

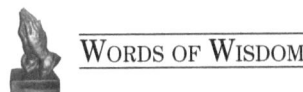

*Brothers and Sisters, think of our neighbors when they
are bound and cannot dig deep enough. We must be our
brother's keepers. When we see or sense in our spirits that
there might be a problem, we should pray immediately.
We may never know the urgency at hand. A prayer from
one family to another is priceless. Imagine how this could
affect the world.*

CHAPTER 2

Isaiah 55: 6-7 Seek the Lord while he may be found; call on him while he is near. Let the wicked forsake his way and the evil man his thoughts. Let him turn to the Lord, and he will have mercy on him, and to our God, for he will freely pardon. (N.I.V.)

Mrs. Tressie Ivy just arrived home from a day of shopping. Steward concerned and a little aggravated said, "Stacey has an I.E.P. (Individualize Education Plan) meeting coming soon. Mom, are you going to be able to be there?"

Tressie replied, "Honey, it depends on what day it is on and what time."

Steward was annoyed, "Mom, just make the time."

Tressie suggested, "Oh Steward sweetheart, I'll just get Nanny Nellie to attend. Besides she is always there for me."

Steward was greatly concerned, "Mom, just remember you are Stacey's Mother not Nanny Nellie."

Tressie tried to take a stand with nothing to stand upon, "Yes I am Stacey's Mother, but that doesn't mean I have to be there."

Steward commented, "I only wish that I could be there for Stacey, but I am always in school when her I.E.P. meetings are held."

Tressie replied, "Oh Steward, don't be silly. You are only a kid as well as Stacey."

Steward tried with all that he had as a teenage boy, "Mom you should just be there because this is what Moms should do."

Tressie chose to be a Mom at a convenient time, "Nanny Nellie will stand in my place and that is final, son."

Tressie gathered up her shopping bags and hurried upstairs. On her way upstairs, she ran into her other daughter Melinda. She showed Melinda her outfit for the hospital's extravagant party.

Melinda asked, "Mom, are you going to Stacey's I.E.P. meeting?"

Tressie replied, "I'll tell you just like I told your brother, Nanny Nellie is going in my place. She always informs me of everything that has to do with Stacey's education."

Melinda replied, "OK Mom maybe one day you will take out some of your precious time to go to Stacey's I.E.P. meetings. Mom, what would Jesus do?"

Tressie chose yet again to be clueless, "Oh Melinda, don't be silly. Honey, it is not that serious as long as I have someone to be there in my place. What do you mean what would Jesus do?"

Melinda was annoyed, "Mom just to answer my question- Jesus would have been there for Stacey's I.E.P. meetomg. As a matter of fact, I take that back. He is always present even when you are not. Mom, you are Stacey's Mom, not Nanny Nellie. I will continue to pray for you. Oh Mom, nice dress."

Tressie smiled nonchalantly and said, "Oh thank you honey for your continuous prayers." Melinda proceeded downstairs to the kitchen. She shook her head in disbelief and Tressie proceeded upstairs to her master suite.

When Melinda entered the kitchen, she and Steward looked at each other somehow knowing what conversations each one of them had with their Mother. Both Melinda and Steward had a spirit of sadness upon them. Their spirits immediately connected. Melinda grabbed a snack out of the refrigerator and Steward finished his.

Steward asked, "Melinda, you talked to Mom already haven't you?"

Melinda said with a sad tone, "Yes, Steward it is so frustrating talking to Mom because she acts as though she has no clue that it is vital for her to be active in Stacey's life and education. All she cares about is her boutique, vacationing, shopping and going to extravagant parties, Steward."

Steward shared the same opinion, "Melinda, I understand your frustration, but Mom is hurting and she does not want to face up to Stacey's disabilities. She loves Stacey just as much as we do and this is the way she chooses to handle the situation."

Melinda replied, "Steward, I love Mom and there is no excuse for the way she acts when it comes to our baby sister Stacey. Our little sister is a blessing and Mom should recognize that. Mom is a grown woman and claims to be a born again Christian. Steward, Mom needs to walk the walk. I told Mom I will continue praying for her. God knows I will."

Steward assured, "Melinda, the most powerful actions we can take are praying and fasting. God hears our prayers and He will answer them in His time. Just you wait and see. When God moves we will know it is Him for sure. Melinda, God is moving even when we think He's not. Mom will come around."

Melinda and Steward embraced. Melinda finished her snack and Steward went upstairs to his room to study.

Later on that night Mr. Ronald Ivy, Tressie's husband arrived home. He was the head physician of the local hospital, and he looked exhausted. Tressie met him at the door excited about her new outfit she bought for the party.

Tressie asked, "Hi honey how was your day? I had an exciting and fantastic day. Oh, Ronald I bought my beautiful red, form fitting dress just fit for a queen. I'm glad it arrived at the boutique in time. It looks spectacular on me, honey."

Ronald finally got a chance to answer. "My day was busy, but blessed as well. Sweetheart, isn't it time for Stacey's I.E.P. meeting?"

Tressie was a little annoyed, "Yes and Nanny Nellie is going to stand in my place as always. I so appreciate her and she is such a lovely lady."

Ronald was annoyed and frustrated yet again, "Sweetheart don't you think you ought to go this time?"

Tressie knew she won the battle again, "Oh honey she's got it. Besides I wouldn't know what to do anyhow."

Ronald asked, "How are you ever going to learn if you never attend, sweetheart?"

Tressie answered boldly, "Nanny Nellie has it covered

honey, besides you have gone before. Why don't you try to make the meeting?"

Calm, cool and collected, Ronald looked at his wife with sadness in his eyes. He sighed, "I will go with Nanny Nellie, sweetheart."

Tressie as happy as ever said, "Great, everything is taking care of. I love you and let me know everything that is discussed, sweetheart."

Ronald immediately got in his normal routine and went upstairs and took his evening shower. Afterwards, he went to Melinda's room for his first stop. At the door, he said "Knock knock, is there anyone in here?"

Melinda replied, "Yes Dad, come in. How was your day?"

Ronald sighed, "It was busy, but blessed as well. You know sweetheart we are going to have to continue praying for your Mother. We all want her to do right by our precious little Stacey."

Melinda said, "Dad, both Steward and I are always talking to Mom about not being active in Stacey's education and life. Steward always say God will answer our prayers in due time."

Ronald agreed, "Yes he is right. We are going to have to be patient. In the meanwhile we will love Stacey and your Mom with all of our hearts. Our precious Stacey is a gift from God. The sooner your Mother realizes it, the sooner she will have peace. Your Mother seems to think this extravagant life is all it takes to get into the kingdom of heaven. She feels like if she goes to church every Sunday and gives to the less fortunate, she has a ticket in."

Mr. Ivy looked at Melinda with sadness and frustration in his voice and eyes. With a crack in his voice Ronald continued. "She has to get it together, be a true child of God and be a true servant for Christ." Melinda looked at her Dad with a sense of peace because her hero was in the room.

Melinda was overwhelmed with sadness, "Dad, deep down inside Mom knows that these materialistic things mean nothing when you are not relying on God for everything. Yes, we are tremendously blessed and I thank God for that, but we would not have any of this if it had not been for the Lord."

Ronald agreed, "You are so right. I love you and God bless you."

Ronald proceeded to go to Steward's room. *Knock, knock.* Steward answered, "Come in Dad."

Ronald replied, "How are you son? I know you have talked to your Mom and I know one day everything will be alright. God said, he will never leave us or forsake us."

Steward replied, "Yes we all know this is what the "Word" says, but if you don't believe it is just a statement. I believe Dad!"

Ronald agreed, "I hear you son. Do you know if your Mom asked Nanny Nellie?"

Steward replied, "Dad I honestly don't know. Mom just has a way of telling Nanny Nellie what she wants done."

Ronald said respectfully, "I'll make sure Nanny Nellie is asked properly. I will also be there. You always give an individual respect no matter what the circumstances are. Son, I am going to let you get back to your studying. Good night and I love you."

Ronald went to Stacey's room and knocked on the door. Stacey always got excited when her Dad came to see her. "How was your day sweetheart? Did you enjoy school? What did you learn?"

Although Stacey was twelve years old, she was very small in stature and she had the understanding and intelligence of a five-year old. She also had a speech impediment. Stacey was a happy, little twelve-year old whom everyone loved. Her spirit was like a breath of fresh air.

Stacey replied excitedly and it was clear that she was very hyper. "Thaddy I write my name. I read bookth thaddy, oh oh and we go to grocstherie store today. I got you new wallet thaddy. I got Mommy a flowa cause I know Mommy love flowa thaddy. It's a fink flowa thaddy. Do you think Mommy will lack it thaddy?"

Ronald lovingly smiled, "Sweetheart, did your Mommy come to see you tonight?"

She held her head down with sadness, "No thaddy, why not?"

Ronald comforted her, "Sweetheart, I don't know, but I bet she will be happy for her flower when you give it to her."

At that point Stacey was drowsy. "I ready to say prathers to God and go thu bed." Ronald prayed with Stacey and she fell asleep.

Ronald and Tressie were in their master bedroom suite. Tressie was reminded of how great a husband she had. She looked him in his eyes and appreciated every moment with him because there was no doubt in her mind, Ronald was sent from God.

Tressie said, "Honey, I appreciate you for everything that you do for our family. I love you so much for the man that you are."

Ronald replied, "All I want is for my family to be truly happy. Did everything fit?"

Mrs. Ivy excited, "Yes, everything fits perfect. I can't wait until the weekend. Ronald, I ordered your tuxedo as well. Oh, honey we are going to be the sharpest couple there."

Ronald smiled and at the same time lovingly concerned, "Sweetheart, everything always turns out nice for everyone."

Late at night, around midnight, Tressie woke up suddenly with thoughts of her youngest daughter heavy on her heart. This was a sad routine for Tressie because of the relationship she had with her youngest daughter Stacey. When Tressie prayed she almost became a child again because of the role she played in her daughter Stacey's life. Although she appeared very happy, she certainly wasn't. Owning her boutique and shopping all the time gave her temporary happiness. This was a bandage because she was in denial about her daughter's disability.

Tressie quietly went in Stacey's room and prayed quietly and wholeheartedly. She gently stroked Stacey's hair and started crying uncontrollably.

She prayed. *"God it's me again Tressie Ivy. Tell me what to do when it comes to Stacey. Lord, I don't know what to do when it comes to my baby girl. Lord, I am so afraid to admit this to anyone, not even my precious Ronald. Continuously wiping her tears Lord, why am I so ashamed of my Stacey? Please guide me and show me the way. When I see Mothers with their children who have disabilities, and to see that it doesn't bother them, absolutely drives me crazy. Lord, it tears me apart inside. The only time I feel peace is when I am spending money. Forgive me Lord for not being a light for you, but you know I am a work in progress. Lord, hear my cry. In Jesus' name, Amen."*

Tressie got herself together quietly, then went back to bed.

 WORDS OF WISDOM

Mothers are precious jewels that are God sent. Sometimes everything is not perfect when we receive our children. When or if that time comes, Mothers and Fathers "Jesus" is the answer not materialistic things. Materialistic things gives you a temporary fix, God gives you an everlasting fix.

CHAPTER 3

Haggai 1: 5-6 Now this is what the Lord Almighty says: "Give careful thought to your ways. You have planted much, but have harvested little. You eat, but never have enough. You drink, but never have your fill. You put on clothes, but are not warm. You earn wages, only to put them in a purse with holes in it."(N.I.V.)

It was the morning of the big "After Holiday Party." Melody and Reese Ford were work-out fanatics. They owned several fitness centers throughout Atlanta. Some Saturdays, some of their friends and church family would come and work out with them. They always encouraged church family and friends to get physically fit and join their gym. They always got up early on Saturdays to prepare to train. When they thought about training people it really ignited something in them. But, can this really compare to a revelation from God?

The chef and the nanny usually arrived around six a.m. The chef cooked breakfast and made their nutritional drinks. The nanny was there to care for the children. Their children usually got up when the Fords were at the gym. Nanny Abby was a sweet old lady who had lots of children and grandchildren of her own. The children loved Nanny Abby because she always tried to instill great manners, and most of all, she instilled God's word into them. Every now and then Nanny Abby teared up. She thought, "*Lord, God I love these babies, but my grandchildren and children need me as well. Lord, if one day I could spend precious time like this with them, it would make me a lot happier. Lord, my babies Nia, Samone, and Tremaine need me as well. One of these good old days I will not have to work. Maybe one day Lord.*"

Chef Spin and Nanny Abby usually spoke to one another, but this particular Saturday morning both were drawn to each other longing to have a conversation. Chef Spin was twenty-nine years old and wanted to be a "Super Rap Star." He always thought being a rapper would be a guaranteed ticket to being rich and famous.

Nanny Abby and the children were eating their breakfast. Out of the corner of Nanny Abby's eye she saw Chef Spin watching them. Meanwhile, he cleaned the dishes and ate. Nanny Abby thought, *"Now Lord I know that little fellow isn't watching me. Lord I think he wants to talk to me. Use me Lord and help me be a blessing to this young man."*

Chef Spin nervously said, "Mrs. Nanny Abby, right?"

Nanny Abby and the children looked at Chef Spin as though he just broke the law. The children didn't know what to think. They were not used to seeing Nanny Abby and Chef Spin having a conversation. All of the children were in shock. It was as if the children wanted to see and hear them have a conversation.

Nanny Abby kindly answered, "Yes, baby. I feel like you have something that is bothering you. Spit it out son."

Chef Spin nervously reacted, "Nanny Abby have you always wanted to be a nanny?"

Little Nia was excited, "Yeah, my Nanny Abby love me and all my brotha and sista. She never leave us." Nanny Abby smiled; got out of her chair and gave Little Nia a kiss on the cheek.

Immediately afterwards Nanny Abby went over to where Chef Spin was and with a low tone said, "Son, I love these babies like they're mine, but if I could I would be home being a Grandma. Who signs up to be a nanny all their life? My life hasn't been a bowl of cherries. Now as I think about it my decisions had a lot to do with what I am today. That's why I always tell my grandbabies and children... Make the best of your life. Strive to be all that the Almighty Father wants you to be."

Soon after the children finished their breakfast Samone and Tremaine went upstairs. Little Nia stayed in her chair so Nanny Abby could keep an eye on her.

Chef Spin was encouraged, "Nanny Abby, I have always wanted to be a Rap Star. Yeah Nanny Abby I'm always very excited when I am writing my own rap songs." He started rapping and dancing all over the place. Little Nia and Nanny Abby started laughing hysterically.

"So, what do you think Nanny Abby?" Chef Spin was anxious to know.

Nanny Abby quickly got herself together with the biggest smile on her face, "Son, the message was alright, but did you clean it up for Little Old Nanny Abby?"

Chef Spin feeling like someone punched him in the gut, "You are so wise Ma'am. How did you know?"

Nanny Abby smiled, "Baby, somehow I just know these things. Son you are a great cook. Have you ever thought about someday running your own business?"

"Ma'am I have, but Nanny I want to get rich quick. That's how everyone else is doing it." He was a little discouraged at that point.

Nanny Abby asked as kindly as she knew how, "Son, have you ever ask God about what He wants for your life?"

He answered, "Ma'am, my Mom always gets on me about going to church. I just don't have the time. Nanny Abby I am always working and if I am off, I sleep the day away."

Nanny Abby said with her Mother's gloves on, "Son, what if Jesus did not have time for you. Where would you be? Baby, we can't breathe without our Almighty Father. Make time for Jesus. You make time for everything else in your life. *Nanny Abby grinned.* You make time to write and rap. Why not include Jesus? Son you will find life much more bearable. As long as you live, Son, you will have mountains to climb."

Chef Spin was a little frightened, "You sound so much like my Mom. She scares me when she says things like that. Nanny Abby, why does God allow his children to bare pain?"

She answered, "Son, for one we wouldn't recognize Him. *She smiled.* "Believe it or not, there are a lot of things that I don't know. But I do know this there are things that we're not supposed to know."

Soon after, Nanny Abby heard Tremaine and Samone arguing upstairs. Nanny Abby strongly suggested, "Son, listen to what Old Nanny Abby said."

She grabbed Little Nia and ran upstairs with the older children. As Nanny Abby and Little Nia went upstairs Chef Spin watched with admiration and respect in his eyes.

Reese and Melody arrived at the fitness center 30 minutes earlier than anyone else. Everyone else started to arrive at the fitness center soon afterwards. John and Rachel Richardson arrived; a match made in heaven. Ronald and Tressie Ivy, a couple who seem to have everything from the outside, arrived right afterwards. The only thing Ronald really wanted for his wife was for her to be happy. Then Howard and Joanne Stone made their way in. They were a couple that grew apart over the years and lacked wisdom. Ridge and Scarlette Crane was a couple who always made it clear that they did not believe there was a God. Were they certain about their reigning title? Sasha and Paul was the last couple to arrive. They both had promising and successful careers.

The ladies and men split up in groups. The women walked to the cardio machines, Rachel looked up at Melody and said, "I have been working hard on my abs throughout the week and I have been watching what I eat. I have noticed a huge difference and I actually see some results."

Melody responded, "Yes, your abs are more defined."

Melody looked to Rachel with great excitement. "Great job Rachel; I love when my clients are working hard and getting results. Rachel, as I always say our bodies are our temples and besides whom do we represent?"

"Christ! there is no one who I would want to represent more," Rachel was convinced.

Rachel, Melody and all the other ladies started to workout. Melody was on the cross trainer next to Joanne. Joanne was clueless, "I know I have asked you this before, but how can I get my abs tight and smaller?"

Melody replied, "You have to eat a well balanced diet along with regular exercising. You also have to do cardio at least four times a week. Joanne, that's your bread and butter. You have to do cardio more than once a week. That's just not enough."

Joanne searched for excuses to smooth things over. "Well, Melody you know I am a busy woman and I have a family as well. The kids keep me in knots. Honey, they keep me on my toes."

"We all are busy women with families. You are going to have to get serious and start exercising on a regular basis, Melody commented.

Joanne was sweating and breathing heavily, tried to crack a joke. "Melody, maybe I should get you to do my schedule."

Melody was very annoyed, "You will make the time for your body if you really want the best for your body. Besides your body is your temple."

Joanne thought, *"Yes, it is easy for you to say and do because you own the gym. You are here all the time."*

Melody thought, *"God give me peace and patience."*

When Melody looked back up; she gave Joanne a smile.

Sasha, Scarlette, Rachel and Tressie were having a conversation as they exercised.

Sasha asked, "Rachel, do you see that lady over there?"

When Rachel looked at the lady, she immediately recognized her from the church and the homeless shelter.

Sasha said, "Rachel, that lady is always with a different man and she has a bunch of children. I am surprise she can afford this particular fitness center. She just doesn't look like the type."

Tressie eagerly jumped in, "Yes, she is always up at that altar praying. I wonder why."

Rachel was a little annoyed, "Now Sasha how did you figure that? Honey, you don't know what she can or cannot afford. And Tressie the altar is where she needs to be. If the truth be told all of us need to be at the altar every Sunday. Prayer is powerful."

Scarlette felt compelled to jump into the conversation. She grinned as she spoke. "Look at her Rachel. She needs to be at the "Y" or one of those other fitness centers that are inexpensive."

Rachel got aggravated and disgusted, "You ladies have got to stop judging people. So what if, in your eyes, she doesn't look as though she belongs here. Who are you to say whether she has the finances to be a part of this fitness center? Ladies, you all need to put yourselves in her shoes. How would you like it if someone was to think negative about you?"

Sasha was a little bothered, *"Oh my goodness. Why does she always have to take up for everyone?"*

Scarlette was bold as ever, "Rachel, I know you mean well, but that lady is not a saint." Tressie, Rachel and Sasha laughed hysterically when they realized what Scarlette just said.

"Oh, I'm certainly not a saint either."

When Scarlette caught herself, she could not help, but laugh along with the other ladies.

Scarlette corrected herself. "Let me rephrase that statement. Rachel, I heard she sleeps with any and everybody. I have heard she's broken up a few marriages."

Sasha agreed, "Yes Rachel, I have heard the same thing."

Tressie agreed as well, "Rachel, haven't you notice, she goes to the altar every time Pastor Patterson does an altar call. I'll bet any money it is true."

"Ladies, you all know that you can't believe everything you hear. Now, I don't mean to be rude. I am going to end this conversation because you all know I hate gossip. We need to pray for her whether what you all say is true or not."

Sasha was discontented and bothered, "Rachel you always give your heart. I can be that way at times, but this is not one of those times."

Rachel looked over to Sasha and smiled.

Tressie thought, *"Maybe I need to be at that altar every time."* As soon as Tressie looked up, Rachel watched her as though she knew what she thought about.

Scarlette immediately said, "Rachel you shut that gossiping down like no other. Most of the time, I know if I have something to say about anybody, I don't come your way or call you. *She smiled.* Rachel if your Jesus is anything like you.... um who knows maybe one day I will join you.

Rachel responded, "Scarlette, to hear you say that means I am going in the right direction. Ladies, why waste your time on negative energy and thoughts? What a waste of time." All the other ladies felt conviction immediately.

Meanwhile the men were on the other side of the gym exercising. Reese always trained the men as if they were his "Cadets" and he was their "Sergeant."

Reese shouted, "Guys, are you ready?"

As Reese spoke and trained the men, he continuously checked himself out in the mirror.

Surprisingly, Reese fits into the gym with an ego that size. All the other men looked at Reese and said, "Yes." The only reason they would answer is to satisfy Reese and his ego for that moment. All the other guys would look at each other and laugh. As long as Reese got his satisfaction the men did not care.

Howard struck up a conversation with Reese as always. Howard said, "Reese I have been working out everyday brother and my physique is still just big and round; not muscular. I see how my wife looks at young men who are cut up through and through. I don't blame her because when I see a beautiful lady, I am going to look. You know Brother I can't help, but stare sometimes. I know Pastor Patterson always say we shouldn't stare and it allows the enemy to come in. I just can't help myself. Do you know what I am talking about my brother?"

Reese looked at Howard a little concerned, but could also relate.

Reese expounded, "Howard, Pastor Patterson always said, "There is nothing wrong with looking at the opposite sex. The problem arises when a man or woman lust over the opposite sex."

Howard got overly anxious. "I know brother and I have been praying for deliverance. Lust is a big concern for lots of men who claim to be Christians."

"Howard, we have to pray daily that our flesh dies. But do we really want our flesh to die Bro?" Reese sighed.

While all the other men worked on their biceps, triceps and legs, Howard shared more concerns about his body with Reese.

Howard said, "Reese I work out every day for about twenty minutes. Why can I have a body like you young brothers? You know I am a lot older."

Reese pointed out, "Howard I have told you this before, you need more cardio in your workout plan and you have to watch what you eat. You can't eat any and everything. If you do at least forty minutes of cardio five days a week, do your weight training, and watch what you eat, you will see a big difference in your weight and muscle definition."

Reese got a little disturbed. He saw an older guy that was in the gym often.

He turned to Howard and commented, "Howard that guy is your age and you can be as fit as he is. You see age has nothing to do with it. Besides Howard you're not that old. Your body is your temple and you should treat it with respect. *Reese ran his fingers through his hair and checked out himself in the mirror.* If you haven't noticed I love my body."

Howard laughed. "Everyone knows YOU love your body, Brother."

Reese made sure he brought it to Howard's attention. "Yeah Bro, but I am not the one complaining."

Howard smiled, "Bro, I just wish I had one fourth of that self esteem. Man, what a blessing when you have a healthy self-esteem. Continue praying for me and Joanne."

Ridge, John, Ronald and Paul walked up to Reese and Howard. Howard felt the need to ask the other guys about looking at the opposite sex.

Howard restlessly asked, "Guys have you ever felt guilty for looking at another woman besides your wife?"

John immediately answered, "Howard, there is nothing wrong with looking. When you start lusting over the opposite sex, that is when it becomes a sin. All of us are human and so are our wives."

Ridge laughed and jokingly commented, "Howard you're always checking those females out. Watch yourself." He laughed hysterically.

All the other men smiled and one of the other men commented immediately.

Paul hesitated, "I don't have problems with looking at other women because…look at Sasha. She is drop dead gorgeous. I think all men should feel that way about their wives. Your wives are also stunning."

Reese proudly agreed, "Yeah, I know what you mean. I love my Barbie Doll. She is definitely a "10.""

Howard said with all honesty, "Guys, what if you don't think your wife is a "10"? Is there something wrong with you because you feel that way? *He smiled.* Joanne has gained over ninety pounds since we got married, but I still think she is a beautiful woman."

Ridge felt proud. "You guys know I love the way my wife looks. What is more attractive than anything else is the pride that she takes when she takes care of herself."

John humbly said, "Well you Brothers know me. *He paused then smiled.* Rachel is the apple of my eye. My prayer is that God grant us many more years together."

Ridge was astonished, "Now John, explain to me how something or someone you clearly can't see grant you and Rachel years together."

Everyone knew Ridge was an atheist. Nevertheless, he would sometimes throw a monkey wrench in a conversation without warning. John was a very respectful Christian Brother who always wanted everyone around him to know Jesus.

John immediately smiled, "Ridge, one of these days before you know it your soul is going to cry out."

Ridge was a little taken. "Do you really think that my soul will cry out?" He laughed. John was as confident as ever. He responded in such Godly manner. "No, man I know."

John gave insight to Howard, "Brother, when it comes to your relationship with your wife or anything else for that matter, it all boils down to the relationship you have with Christ. When you truly put Christ first, everything falls in place."

Everyone met in the Fitness Center's lounge, except, Sasha because she had to go to the salon for a few hours. The ladies sat together and the men sat together for fellowship and conversation. Everyone was excited about the hospital's lavish "After Holiday Party" that was going to take place on that night.

Joanne was excited, "Have you ladies got your dresses for the party yet? Of course you all have your dresses! The party is tonight. I have mine and it is tailor made. It is absolutely gorgeous and it fits beautifully with my figure."

Tressie immediately responded, "Yes, of course I have mine. How sleek and elegant! My Jimmy Choo's go perfectly."

Joanne gave Tressie a competitive look then a big smile that was faker than a three dollar bill.

Joanne sarcastically, "My shoes arrived last week and they are also Jimmy Choo. Howard loves to see me in Jimmy Choo's."

At times Joanne and Tressie carried this urge of competition with one another which was so juvenile. They just didn't seem to realize, every time they allow themselves to fall into the pit of competition. The other women would try their best to ignore the two of them. When they became blind to their reactions toward one another, others automatically noticed. The distasteful spirit of competition made the atmosphere tainted.

Rachel was so uncomfortable; she stepped into relieve the tension in the room. Rachel looked to Joanne and then she looked to Tressie with uplifting words for both ladies.

"Ladies, both of you are always dressed beautifully. I know all of the other ladies are going to be beautiful as well. What lady wouldn't like to dress up and go to nice parties? Ladies we all should always thank God for everything that we have because without the Father, none of this is possible."

Joanne finally settled down a bit. "Girls, I just get so excited."

Tressie was still a little on edge. "Ladies, it's always great to prepare for the fantastic parties that my husband's hospital throws."

Rachel concluded, "Tressie, all of us enjoy preparing for parties. We should enjoy and realize how blessed we all are. You know God is not pleased when His children are not happy for one another."

Tressie agreed with her egotistic attitude. "I know that we are blessed. Anyone would want to live this lifestyle."

Melody was also excited. "Tressie, I got my dress from your boutique a couple of weeks ago and it is candy apple red."

Tressie looked as though she just sucked on a piece of lemon. She looked over to Melody and thought, *My God forgive me, but my dress is red and my figure is not half as beautiful as Melody's. Oh God everyone's going to compare me with her.*"

Tressie finally said, "Oh great so everyone should have a wonderful time. Scarlette and Rachel, what about you two have you all got your dresses?" Scarlette was in a careless mood. "I am going to wear one of the dresses I already have." Tressie and Joanne quickly look at each other with a shared thought, *"Oh my, she didn't go and get a new dress."*

Tressie looked over to Rachel searching for an answer. She asked, "What about you Rachel, are you wearing something that you already have as well?"

Rachel proudly responded, "Yes, I am wearing a dress that I have had a while, but I haven't yet worn it. Besides it really doesn't matter whether a dress is new or old as long as a woman feels great in it." All the ladies smiled.

Tressie nosily asked, "Does anyone know what Sasha is wearing?"

Rachel quickly replied, "It doesn't matter. I am sure she is going to look stunning."

Melody agreed, "You are so right Rachel. Sasha can wear

a paper bag and look stunning."

"We are going to have a great time tonight girls." Tressie laughed and started dancing in her seat. All the ladies giggled.

 WORDS OF WISDOM

Brothers and Sisters, the spirit of competition can eat away at your soul without he or she having a clue. We should all realize our friends deserve our love. Adding competition to a friendship or any other relationship is like adding ammonia to one's precious skin. Don't fall into the pit of deception. Brothers and Sisters, how do we react when there is gossip presented in our ears? Will our ears receive it or will we put up a wall of prayer immediately? We must remember the power our tongues possess. We must love one another as God loves us.

CHAPTER 4

Exodus 23:20 See, I am sending an angel ahead of you to guard you along the way and bring you to the place I have prepared. (N.I.V.)

Ronald and Tressie was the first couple who arrived at the party. Since Ronald was the head doctor at the hospital, he made a point to go around and made sure everything was done properly. He always got a V.I.P. table for themselves and their dear friends.

Everything in the room was decorated with gold and silver. All the furnishings were glass oval tables decked out with fine china and silverware. All of the tables were decorated with a different set of colors, but all included silver and gold. Each guest name was written on his or her napkin and everyone received a beautiful complimentary gift which included crystal. Every person who walked through the door felt important because of the atmosphere that they embodied.

There were worldly, successful people everywhere in the room. Everyone looked as though they did not have a care in the world. Only a handful knew Jesus. Yet others glorified them because they were well known. Jesus should be the only one worthy of glorifying and idolizing.

Tressie was alone at her table. She thought, *"Everyone should be able to experience being in this sort of atmosphere."*

When everyone came in, she got up and greeted them. Tressie had to be sure that everyone noticed her in her dress. Finally her friends started arriving. Nothing could excite Tressie more. As everyone entered the party, their pictures were taken. Joanne and Howard walked in decked out. Joanne wore a beautiful form fitting dress that hugged her curves perfectly. Howard wore a sharp custom made black tux. His shoes were shining so bright, they sparkled like gold.

Reese and Melody were constantly stopped by people continuously giving compliments. Melody had on this beautiful red gown that had an embellished train fit for a queen. She looked like a live Barbie doll. Reese wore a handsome midnight blue tux with a red vest. The vest had the same embellishment as Melody's dress. To top everything off he had on the midnight blue Gators to match and not a hair out of place.

Heads turned as Sasha and Paul entered the building. Sasha resembled an Asian goddess with a dark complexion. Her long jet black beautiful wavy hair cascaded down a backless, white, knee length ball gown that fitted her exquisitely. It looked as though someone painted it on her body. Paul sported a sharp fade. Paul wore a black tux with a white vest which was embroidered in black. His leather, embroidered, diagonal pointed shoes were straight from Italy.

People watched with a certain respect when John and Rachel entered the party. If people had alcoholic drinks in their hands, they sat them down when John and Rachel walked through. They exuded the attributes of Christ. Rachel wore a wine, one shoulder sequined gown. To set the look off, Rachel rocked a sharp, short hair cut with highlights all the way through. John sported a black tux with a wine vest. The vest had a unique design that caught everyone's attention.

Scarlette and Ridge arrived, catching everyone's eye. Scarlette elegantly wore an ivory backless little number fit for a princess. Ridge rocked an ivory tux with the ivory shoes to carry it all off. If they weren't married, one would have thought they were going to tie the knot afterwards.

All the couples finally sat down. John and Rachel ordered their usual sweet pineapple juice and sweet-ice tea. Tressie ordered her usual screwdriver and Ronald ordered a sweet ice tea as well. Howard and Joanne ordered red wine. Reese and Melody ordered a light beer. Paul and Sasha ordered white wine. Ridge and Scarlette ordered their usual beer.

Tressie started a conversation with Rachel.

Tressie asked, "Rachel, why don't you and John ever drink or at least try a drink?"

Rachel, with much humility answered, "Tressie we have

no desire to drink alcoholic beverages. *Then she smiled.* John never orders alcohol either. It's obvious he doesn't need alcohol either."

Everyone looked at Tressie then watched Rachel.

Rachel with her calm, cool spirit responded to the question. "You know Tressie we are truly one at this point in our marriage. It comes naturally. We always have a great time anywhere we go. We are always looking for ways to witness and spread the Gospel. Now if we are drinking alcohol, how will we be able to minister properly?"

Tressie insecurely tried to justify, "Oh yes of course. I know what you mean because I always try to tell the less fortunate that they can have what I have as long as they work hard."

Rachel yet again tried to give insight, "Tressie, honey in order to witness and spread the Gospel, you have to tell people about salvation. They must know how to get saved because some people don't know that you have to be saved in order to go to heaven. Spreading the Gospel does not mean tell people about your multimillion dollar home, because they can have the same and not be truly happy. Tressie, sometimes you are the only bible some people will ever see. If you are not living your life as Christ lived, you can very well be a stumbling block for that person."

Tressie responded, "Of course, Rachel, I know that we are blessed. Everyone can look at us and immediately figure the equation out. Honey how hard is it? Rachel, I don't mean any harm, but I can't understand how I can be a stumbling block. Just like I said before I always tell people how blessed we are."

The drinks and food arrived. Tressie and Rachel's conversation struck up questions about their marriages. The other couples started looking at one another; not saying anything and thought, *"Am I witnessing for Christ? When is the last time I told someone about Jesus? How is our marriage? Are we really as one?"*

Ridge and Scarlette looked as though they were confused, but on other hand so curious. Rachel and John were the head of the marriage ministry at church. Everyone gave them the utmost respect because they were not only readers of the Word, but doers of the Word… Ridge and Scarlette refused to believe that there is a God, but were so curious about why their friends were always at church on Sundays and bible study on Wednesdays.

Ridge captured everyone's attention when he asked, "John, so how do you guys keep your marriage together all the time?"

John replied, "First of all, there is no marriage that is perfect. Trust me we have our moments." *Rachel shook her head in agreement.* "Ridge, it takes time and effort from man and woman. We've come a long way and have had good times and bad times."

Ridge responded, "Man, I need just a little bit of what you and Rachel have."

John strongly suggested, "No man, try Jesus and sit back and watch how your life changes."

Ridge answered immediately, "Why does everyone keep saying the same thing? Besides some of the ones who tell me what you are telling me, are doing the same things that I am doing. There is nothing different about them, but you and your family… *He paused.* He looked at John in a peculiar way. Ridge could not help it. "You both really stand out."

All the other couples got very uncomfortable sipping on their drinks. The men started wondering whether they were guiding their families in the right direction. The women started wondering whether they were Godly wives and Godly Mothers.

The ladies sometimes had conversations excluding Rachel. It's not like they intended to exclude Rachel, but it was something that happened naturally. Joanne, Sasha, Melody, Tressie, and Scarlette started a conversation.

Sasha posed a question. "Ladies, do you ever wonder why we have the lives that we have? All of us are very successful."

Melody was excited and full of herself at that moment. "Yes, all the time. Who wouldn't want to live a lavish lifestyle?"

Joanne was boastful as she looked around, "Well, everyone can't have it all. Of course I am a housewife." *She laughed.* "I just shop until I drop."

Sasha replied, "Everyone can't have it all. What do you mean? Do you think living big equals happiness? How much does one need in order to consider him or herself happy?"

Joanne answered, "Well honey, I can't imagine not having the things that make me happy. Oh and thank God for my nanny!"

Sasha commented, "Wow, Joanne have you ever realized there are people that have what we consider as nothing who are actually happy."

Scarlette was convinced, "I am happier now than ever before and I know it is because of being a multimillionaire. If I want anything, I can go out and buy it without thinking about how much it cost. There's not too many people, I know, that can say that boldly."

Sasha was a little annoyed, "Scarlette, do you really think you know what true happiness feels like?"

"Yes of course, I know everyone always tell me that you can't have true happiness without being saved, but I strongly disagree." Scarlette was convinced at the moment.

Sasha asked, "How can you strongly disagree and you've never tested the waters before. I believe you will be saved one of these days and then you will find true happiness."

Scarlette was curiously wondering, "Are you ladies sure you know what true happiness is? As Christians, aren't you all suppose to be focusing on your Jesus?"

Melody interrupted and jumped back into the conversation feeling strongly convicted. "Yes, Scarlette we should be focusing on Jesus. But we let this sort of lifestyle rule us. It's a terrible addiction that you don't want to break. Scarlette, I know God is not pleased. God knows our hearts and He knows that we are a work in progress."

Scarlette was as sarcastic as ever, "Melody when you say God knows we are a work in progress, I know I am not a Christian, but that statement sounds like a cop out to me.

Melody was a little annoyed, "Scarlette, just like I said, "God knows our hearts."

Joanne and Tressie looked at one another both lost and confused; they seem to let the conversation go in one ear and out the other.

The entire time the other ladies were having their conversation Rachel thought when she battled with her flesh, *"Why do I bother? Why would you leave just one friend out of the conversation?"* Then she thought, *"Oh I know, Father, this is what I have to endure at times."*

All the ladies excused themselves from the table to go to the ladies room. On the way to the ladies room Rachel thought, *"How can you get the glory through my words? Give me the words to say to encourage my sisters in Christ."* They entered carrying burdens on their shoulders.

Scarlette said anxiously and frustratingly, "Ladies I don't know how much of this girl I can take?"

Tressie inappropriately commented, "Oh, is this your tween that doesn't respect you as a Mother?"

"Yes of course, that one. I know that she is just a child, but sometimes I forget. I know this is wrong, but I resent her at times. If it wasn't for her our family would be perfect."

Rachel felt the need to give Godly advice.

"Why do you feel that way? What did the child ever do to you?"

Scarlette got a little annoyed as she always seem to get when Rachel gave her advice. "Yes, that's easy to say when you are not in that situation or position. As a matter of a fact, that's not what I need to hear right now."

Rachel responded immediately, "I will definitely pray for you although you don't believe. Scarlette, I respect your feelings, but I will not apologize for being a child of God."

By the time Rachel was done talking, Scarlette was in tears and could not help herself. She appeared to have forgotten her strong belief and allowed Rachel to minister to her.

Tressie's heart was heavy as well. "Steward and Melinda

are doing great in school. They are both still on the honor roll. They think that they are Stacey's parents. They are such wonderful children."

Joanne commented without thinking, "I haven't seen Stacey in a while. How is she doing in school?"

Suddenly all the ladies were in shock, including Joanne. Tressie always tried to avoid talking about Stacey and her schooling. All of a sudden Tressie's eyes filled up with tears.

Joanne started desperately apologizing. "I'm sorry Tressie, but I haven't seen little Stacey in a while. I didn't mean…."

Rachel interrupted to smooth things over. "Sometimes these things happen for a reason at certain times. Maybe we need to pray with you in this moment. Tressie looked up like a little lost child helplessly. All of the women except Scarlette immediately gathered around Tressie, hand in hand, touching and agreeing as Rachel prayed. They put themselves in Tressie's position and realized this could have easily been one of their problems. After Rachel prayed for Tressie and all the other ladies and their families, Tressie's spirit and soul was relieved at that moment without saying a word about what was deeply disturbing her.

Immediately after Rachel prayed, Sasha said anxiously, "I needed that prayer as much as the other ladies. Rachel I am so paranoid and uneasy when Paul leaves town on assignments. To be honest, I feel like he is being unfaithful. Maybe it's because I cannot get pregnant with our second child. He is always telling me how beautiful he thinks that I am."

Rachel replied, "He is exactly right. Honey, you know our mind is the devil's playground. Talk to Paul about how you have been feeling. Then maybe you all can set up an appointment with Pastor Patterson or one of the other ministers in the church. Certainly, you don't want a misunderstanding and mind games become pitfalls for your marriage."

Sasha asked, "Rachel, who wants to tell everyone their business?"

Rachel gently takes her hand, "Honey, that is the problem

with Christians today. We want everyone to think everything is always fine. We have to get help when needed."

Immediately afterwards, Rachel and Sasha embraced.

Melody came up to Rachel afterwards. "I also needed that prayer. I feel like I just don't spend enough time with my children. Nia, Samone, and Tremaine are going to think that Nanny Abby is their Mother. You know Rachel, it takes time to run the fitness centers. I don't know what I am going to do if the school calls again. I feel so guilty to have to always send Nanny Abby to clean up my problems."

"Maybe you and Reese need to get together and figure out a time schedule. Maybe you all can hire managers for the fitness centers," Rachel suggested.

Melody responded, "We thought about that before. Rachel you can't trust just anyone to manage your businesses."

Rachel assured Melody, "That would allow so much more time to spend with the children. It may take a little more, but at least you will have more time with your children and they don't stay children forever."

Rachel gave Melody a gentle touch and continued.

Joanne came up to Rachel. "Rachel, I thank you also for praying for me and my family. Ashley and Ashton grades are almost always border line and my children seem to respect our nanny more than they respect me and Howard."

Rachel was as kind and honest as she knew how. "Sister, maybe you need to get your priorities in order. You know our children are worth it. If your children are having so many problems in school, why not hire tutors?"

Joanne thought about all the outings she does without the children.

She looked at Rachel in agreement. Her eyes were full and her heart heavy. "Sister, I do things to occupy my mind and things to make me happy for the time being. Is that selfish?"

Rachel asked, "Do you really have to ask that question?"

She looked at Joanne then embraced her.

Rachel whispered, "It's time for that change."

Joanne nodded her head "Yes."

All of the ladies shared a big group hug then headed back to the party except Rachel.

Rachel's cup was always full after following God's commands. She looked in the mirror to adjust her necklace and noticed this beautiful young lady staring at her in the mirror. She felt this young woman's spirit crying out and she looked towards her.

Rachel took the initiative, "What's your name?"

The young lady appeared very shy and anxious.

She slowly answered, "Peppi, my name is Peppi Long. My husband is one of the doctors at the hospital. His name is Tyler Long. Do you know him?"

Rachel smiled and responded, "No, honey I can't say that I do."

Peppi slowly asked, "Do you always pray for everyone? I'm sorry, I didn't mean to be nosy, but I could not help but hear you and your friends. Tell me, how do you begin to pray the way that you do? Where does it come from? Where do you attend church?"

Rachel looked at Peppi and smiled like an angel. "Peppi I'm so sorry. How rude of me. My name is Rachel Richardson."

Rachel shook Peppi's hand.

"Peppi, prayer is simply talking to God. It's just like you and I are doing now. Oh and I attend Faith Deliverance Church of Atlanta. My Pastor's name is Jeffrey E. Patterson."

Peppi commented, "Rachel your energy is pleasing and angelical. Even though we just met I feel like I can tell you anything and it would not go anywhere."

Rachel explained, "Peppi, I love the Lord. You're right, it stays here."

Peppi said, "Rachel, if I told you my story, we would not have enough time tonight. I have so many problems and no one to talk to. My family and friends thinks that I have fallen off my rocker when I complain. All they see is the money that my husband makes and all the materialistic advantages that are upon us. They don't see that my husband speaks down to me. He's always gone out of town on "hospital emergencies." He never spends time with me or the children. Rachel it seems like I am sleeping with my enemy."

Rachel heart cried out for Peppi and her family.

Rachel gave encouragement. "Peppi don't you worry everything will be alright. If you don't mind, I would love to pray for you and your family."

As Rachel prayed for Peppi, streams of tears flow down Peppi's face.

Peppi thought, *"Where did this angel come from? I did not think we had people in the world today that takes out time to pray for someone else and their problems, especially in this setting. Wow! Thank you God."*

Peppi knew she was getting a touch of what those other women just received. The two exchanged phone numbers and promised each other that they would stay in contact.

When Rachel arrived back to the table, the other ladies were so uplifted that they did not have the desire for their alcohol beverages. The women ordered tea and coffee for the rest of the night. The men noticed the women had been crying, but they also noticed their spirits were lifted as well. The women's spirits flowed into the atmosphere amongst their husbands. The wives were so pleasing to their husbands' eyes. Somehow Ridge and Scarlette blended right in with the other couples. They were entertained watching others on the dance floor. The music slowed down, a beautiful, moving song all the couples related to played. As soon as they heard the song, all of the ladies immediately slid closer to their husbands. Their husbands naturally gravitated closer to them. Not a moment later, all the men got up at the same time. They were all gentlemen like and asked their wives for their hand for a dance. All the ladies got up at the same time. They grabbed their husband's hands at the same time.

How God must smile upon this heaven on earth scenery of husbands and wives admiring one another.

The couples were all on the dance floor slow dancing to this song just for couples.

John whispered in Rachel's ear, "Honey this song does something to couples. It is the perfect song for our friends. It brings out the best in a man and woman."

Rachel answered so eloquently, "Every couple needs this every now and then."

Reese and Melody was swaying perfectly to the music.

Reese romantically spoke to Melody, "Baby you know this song always remind me of you."

Melody smiled and directly whispered back, "Honey, that's why I always feel moved to dance with you when it comes on."

Howard had not smiled like this in forever.

While he and Joanne danced sort of offbeat, "Joanne whispered to Howard, "This song should play all night."

Howard whispered back rather flirtatiously, "I wouldn't mind that, but what I would truly love is if we went home right after this song."

They both laughed hysterically, something that they had not done in a long while with just the two of them.

Paul held Sasha as though she was a precious jewel. As he held her, she smiled as though she could read his mind.

Paul charmingly whispered, "Baby you know this song reminds me of when we first met and how in love we were. Of course, we are still in love."

Sasha whispered back in a sweet, loving tone, "I knew you were thinking that. You have that look in your eye, Baby."

Ridge and Scarlette was lost in the music as they slow danced.

Ridge charmingly whispered in Scarlette's ear. "Honey you and I have always loved this song. It seems like when this song comes on everything is renewed again."

Scarlette whispered with the softest tone. "Ridge, everything is renewed. What time is it again?"

Ridge and Scarlette were ready to go home right after the dance.

Ronald and Tressie were laughing like two teenagers.

Ronald spoke in a low tone. "Honey you look so beautiful tonight. You look just as good as the day I met you."

Tressie smiled and whispered, "What is it about this song that stirs the both of us up? Ronald you always say that when you hear this song."

 WORDS OF WISDOM

How many of you will represent God at any cost? Sometimes it will take a bold spirit to stand firm on God's word, and to follow his commands. Yes it is easier said than done. Imagine one of the ultimate goals, which is that peace that God gives you when you humble yourself and be obedient. Remember God's touch is like no other touch. Will you be the odd one out? "How is your light shining? We should always be aware that there is someone watching when we think they are not watching. We should always try and be like Jesus. Is your life encouraging or discouraging? How are we entertaining our friends who are not saved? Brothers and Sisters, what will our neighbors say about us?

CHAPTER 5 CHAPTER 5

Proverbs 21:24-26 The proud and arrogant man "Mocker" is his name; he behaves with over weening pride. The sluggard's craving will be the death of him, because his hands refuse to work. All day long he craves for more, but the righteous give without sparing. (N.I.V.)

It was a Sunday morning worship service in March at Faith Deliverance Church of Atlanta with the residing Pastor Jeffrey E. Patterson. There were families entering throughout the sanctuary. Some families appeared to want to be there; others appeared as though they didn't. There were couples very well dressed, others casually dressed; some looked as if they just made it in. There were people that were in turmoil with one another. Although these situations were going on, the ushers were very friendly, and gave great directions.

Everyone knew the families who lived in this prestigious neighborhood called Ridgeland Towers of Atlanta. Members who were spiritually immature thought if they got a little closer to them, they could somehow have a happy and fulfilling life. For this reason they treated these families as though they were gold. On the other hand, there were other members who were spiritually mature and could not understand why these particular members got special attention because they knew having millions of dollars was not going to get anyone into heaven.

Ronald and Tressie walked in the sanctuary looking as sharp as ever. Steward, Melinda, Nanny Nellie and Little Stacey walked behind. Tressie appeared to be on top of the world as usual and Ronald behind supporting her. Ronald was always happy as long as Tressie appeared to be happy. Ronald was one of the top physicians at the hospital; therefore everyone knew his status within the community. Some people spoke to Tressie and some didn't because of her personality. A few were all over her because they knew her from her boutique. Little Stacey spoke to everyone as usual. Tressie pretended as if she was busy having a conversation.

Nanny Nellie murmured, "God continue to work on Tressie's spirit and continue to allow Stacey to be a light in her family's life."

Howard and Joanne walked in the sanctuary with their three children: Ashley, Ashton, Amira and, of course, Nanny Nora. As they proceeded to walk through the sanctuary, the children appeared to be irritated with one another. Nanny Nora tried to chastise the children, but it did not work for whatever reason that day; she was forced to take the kids out of the sanctuary. While Nanny Nora took the kids out of the sanctuary, Howard and Joanne felt embarrassed, not just because the kids were misbehaving, but because their nanny had to chastise the children in their presence. This situation also made Howard and Joanne feel guilty about Nanny Nora not spending time with her own family. Instead, Nanny Nora was working because she had to take care of their children in their presence. While Nanny Nora took care of the children, Joanne and Howard went over to speak to Tressie and Ronald.

Tressie asked, "Joanne, where are the children?"

She cringed, paused then answered, "Nanny Nora had to take the children in one of the conference rooms for a minute."

"Oh, are they alright?" Tressie wondered.

She quickly answered, "They will be."

Joanne and Howard went back to their seats.

Reese and Melody walked in as attractive as ever. When they walked in, Reese held Melody as they entered the sanctuary. He had no shame in showing off his wife. Nia, Samone, and Tremaine, and, of course, Nanny Abby followed behind. While Reese and Melody walked people's heads naturally turned. Many of the members had memberships at their fitness centers. Several people spoke to them in a friendly manner. Some of the members who did not speak just whispered to one another. When Nanny Abby and the children took a seat, Reese and Melody took time out to speak to the Ivys and the Stones. Afterwards, they took their usual seats.

John and Rachel walked in with their children Charles and Charlotte. When they walked in, people's eyes lit up. John and Rachel did not believe in having a nanny at church with them. They believed nannies should be with their own families on Sundays. Of course, they had to make their rounds before they took their seats. The two went over to as many people in the church as possible just to give them a word of encouragement. A few needed someone to acknowledge them. There were others that needed something as simple as a beautiful, sincere smile.

Paul and Sasha held hands as they walked in with their child Sehara and their nanny, Nanny May. Sasha looked as if she just stepped out of a glamour magazine and Paul looked as though he just stepped out of a GQ magazine. Everyone could always tell that he was proud of Sasha and the way she carried herself. It was just the way he watched his wife. Sasha went in one direction and Paul went in another. They proceeded to speak to their clients and associates. They finally went back to their seats to prepare for service.

John whispered, "Rachel, do you think Scarlette and Ridge are ever going to come to church?"

"Yes, of course, honey, it is just a matter of time. You and I know this."

He said, "I know they will come around, but hopefully sooner than later. Baby, the hospital party was beautiful. It seems like the whole atmosphere changed after you ladies came out of the ladies room."

He looked into Rachel's eyes and saw that she was in tears.

He said, "I understand, you don't have to say anything."

John and Rachel held hands afterwards.

Praise and worship was always a blessing for whoever opened their hearts to receive. Many members and visitors stood up the entire time of praise and worship. Others looked around as if they didn't know what was going on around them. There were people that truly worshipped God and did not care who was around; and there were members that were slain in the spirit and when this happened, those who were not used to it looked as though they were confused. But these same people came back Sunday after Sunday. The saints who truly wanted to be blessed were blessed. Following praise and worship, the nannies and children left when they announced the dismissal of children's church.

Pastor Patterson walked in the sanctuary with some of the associate Ministers. The congregation always stood up as Pastor Patterson walked in to give honor to the Shepherd of this particular house. He had such a powerful anointing; everyone felt it even if they didn't realize what was going on. This particular Sunday Pastor Patterson preached on "Prospering Spiritually." When the Pastor gave the title, Tressie automatically thought he was speaking of money. She received one part of the title as usual.

She whispered to Ronald, "Honey, we could have stayed home. We are already prosperous. We could literally get up there and preach this message for him."

Ronald replied in a very low tone. "Sweetheart, he also said spiritually."

Tressie honestly asked, "Are you sure, honey?"

He whispered as though he was speaking to one of his children, "Listen carefully, sweetheart."

He gently patted Tressie on her legs to allow her to focus on the Pastor.

Meanwhile, Howard seemed to be in another world. Joanne was truly listening to the message. She started thinking of her children and their situation. Suddenly she started to cry uncontrollably. As Nanny Nora returned to her seat, Howard finally noticed Joanne crying.

Nanny Nora asked, "Why is Mrs. Stone crying?"

He answered, "I have no idea."

Howard proceeded to comfort Joanne. Even though Howard was trying to comfort Joanne, Nanny Nora was still concerned for her.

Nanny Nora whispered, "The children are okay now."

Joanne looked up with extreme guilt. "I am sorry the children were out of hand."

"You know how they are. I don't mind taking care of them. Honey, that's what you pay me for."

She gave Joanne a friendly smile.

To smooth things over and to ease the guilt Nanny Nora added, "Besides, you know I need the money."

Meanwhile, every now and again, Reese was brushing his hair back with his fingers to make sure every hair was in place. This was a habit for Reese. Everyone had no choice; they felt his arrogance. Melody smiled the whole time, occasionally flicked her hair out of her eyes. A couple sitting next to them just happened to miss the Scripture. When they asked Melody and Reese about the scripture; they could not tell them anything. All they could say was they were sorry. After this Melody and Reese looked at each other with conviction and embarrassment. Melody slowly got her small Bible out of her purse. Reese started paying more attention to the sermon. He stopped brushing through his hair with his fingers.

Meanwhile Sasha and Paul appeared to be somewhat uncomfortable. Paul was desperately squeezing Sasha. Sasha noticed several women with their newborn babies. She started staring at the women one by one. Paul noticed her reaction toward the women. At the same time, Pastor Patterson continuously repeated, prospering spiritually. Sasha got very upset the more he said prospering spiritually. Paul squeezed Sasha more as she got more upset.

Sasha rocked back and forth thinking, *Why can't I have another baby? Why is it so hard to get pregnant? God! Those women appeared to be without a husband. They have a baby! God, Pastor Patterson is preaching on "Prospering spiritually." I don't feel like I'm at that point. Lord, it is so hard waiting for you. I want so badly to have my husband's next child. It feels like I am less than a woman because we can't get pregnant again. I know I have my beautiful Sehara. Don't you think she needs a brother or sister? Lord, please keep me*

*strong in patience and allow me to have peace when I see
other Mothers with their new born babies. In Jesus's name,
amen."*

Paul whispered to Sasha, "Sweetie, it is all in God's timing." She stared at Paul with tears streaming down her face,
helplessly and still hopefully shook her head up and down.

After Pastor Patterson finished preaching the choir sang.
Not long after the choir started singing, many choir members
started praising God and thanking Him for everything. John and
Rachel praised God for their family and friends. They thought
of their family and friends' trials and tribulations. What a self-
less couple! They always felt they should pray for others while
they were in the church service. Their friends didn't find it in
their hearts to stand up in God's presence, but John and Rachel
stood in the gap for them. As they stood up, the spirit flowed
through them. The unity that this incredible couple possessed
attracted people's spirits. When they stood up together with
their hands held high reaching for heaven; many more united.

 WORDS OF WISDOM

*My brothers and sisters, it is amazing what conviction
will do. When we are attending church we are to make sure
we are following along in the church service. We are doing
God a disservice when we are not in tune to what is being
read and said. Listening and hearing a sermon is just as
important as your "nine to five." We might as well stay
home if we are not going to listen to what God has for us at
that moment. Brothers and sisters, it is amazing what God
does when we apply messages that are truly from Him into
our lives. Try it and see!*

CHAPTER 6

Proverbs 20: 3-5 It is to a man's honor to avoid strife, but every fool is quick to quarrel. A sluggard does not plow in season; so at harvest time he looks but finds nothing. The purposes of a man's heart are deep waters, but a man of understanding draws them out. (N.I.V.)

It was Friday morning, the middle of March. Rachel was on her way to volunteer at the shelter. Suddenly she stopped at Burger World. As she stood waiting in line, she noticed the cashier's attitude. The cashier's appearance said everything. She looked as if she just woke up and threw on her clothes. Her hair was so matted, very similar to a very bad hair extension that was way overdue.

Rachel wondered and prayed silently, "Lord what is her story? Where is the sad attitude coming from?"

The gentleman in front of her was very nice.

Rachel thought, *"Lord there was no need for the cashier to act nasty at all. She really hurts inside. Her eyes say it all. I pray that you give her peace throughout the day. In Jesus's name, Amen."*

Oh how Rachel hurt for the cashier. She knew things could be better for this woman; whatever she was going through. She wondered whether the cashier knew Jesus. When Rachel moved up to place her order, the cashier did not greet her. She immediately started taking Rachel's order. Rachel kindly ignored her and smiled while she gave her order. Her pleasant personality seemed to irritate the cashier even more.

With that charming, heavenly smile Rachel asked, "Good morning, how are you?"

The cashier looked at Rachel with intense anger in her eyes.

Rachel proceeded to give her order. "I would like a chicken biscuit, hash browns, and a medium cup of coffee please."

The cashier mumbled, "That all?"

Rachel kindly responded, "Yes, thank you."

She mumbled again, "That gonna be fi' dollars and fidy-three cent."

Rachel's order arrived on the counter several minutes after.

When the cashier gave Rachel her order, she looked into the cashier's disturbing eyes, and said with all her heart, "Have a blessed day."

As she proceeded to put cream and sugar in her coffee, the cashier watched Rachel and appeared intrigued by Rachel's pleasant attitude despite her unpleasant attitude. By the time Rachel got in the car, her eyes were full and heart heavy. She started praying for the cashier and her family. After praying, she turned on the radio. A song ignited Rachel's spirit. As she listened to the song, Rachel started thinking of the pain in the cashier's eyes. She felt every hurtful feeling the cashier obviously endured and was enduring.

Rachel thought, *"There is an overcomer in everybody, but she has to recognize it and believe it!"*

She passionately cried out, "Lord if she only knew that she is somebody and not beneath anybody. I know the cashier can go further. If she could only see herself as an overcomer, her whole outlook on life would change. She deserves better. Lord, let her know she is loved and I pray for her salvation if she is not saved."

Rachel proceeded to the shelter after she got herself together. As she drove she gave God the utmost Glory.

Rachel arrived at the Atlanta City Shelter. She found her place to serve as usual. As she helped serve the food, Rachel noticed one of the other volunteers staring at her. She tried her best to ignore her because of her negative spirit. Although she noticed the other volunteer staring, this did not stop Rachel from encouraging and praying for everyone silently that came through the line.

Rachel and all the other volunteers were cleaning after breakfast. She noticed the volunteer who was staring earlier, slowly coming towards her.

The volunteer asked, "Why do you come here?"

Rachel replied, "Excuse me."

She asked again, "Why do you come here?"

Rachel offered her hand to the volunteer.

She answered, "My name is Rachel. And what's your name?"

"My name is Dana." The volunteer said with a nasty attitude. Rachel I have seen what kind of cars you drive."

Rachel smiled as she responded, "What do you mean by that?"

Dana looked unhappy and disturbed, "Do you do this to make yourself feel better?"

"Dana, I love helping and encouraging people."

"I've seen your kind. I'll bet all of your friends live in the same neighborhood and drive the same kind of cars." Dana offhandedly responded to Rachel.

"That has nothing to do with the reason why I volunteer. Yes, I know it seems as though I have lots of materialistic things, of course I do. Dana, I am truly blessed not because of the materialistic things that you see, but I am blessed because Jesus is the head of my life."

Dana said hatefully, "He would be ahead of my life as well if I lived like you live. It must be nice."

"Dana, if God can do it for me He can do it for you."

"Rachel, some of us are destined to succeed and some of us are destined to fail, she said with a bitter attitude.

Rachel asked, "Dana, why do you belittle yourself in such a way? That is negative thinking. You should have positive thoughts."

She selfishly replied, "You would say that."

Dana immediately walked away.

Rachel prayed silently, *"God touch her hardened heart. Bless her family. In Jesus's name, Amen."*

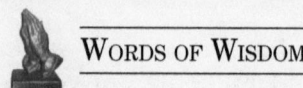

Brothers and Sisters, we have to always keep in mind when people are going through something so painful, dramatic and life changing, their eyes will always tell the story. Stop, look and listen! Give love, Jesus did.

CHAPTER 7

Psalm 38: 4-6 My guilt has overwhelmed me like a burden
too heavy to bear.
I am bowed down and brought very low; all day long I go
about mourning. (N.I.V.)

It was a Friday night in March. Rachel arranged for all the ladies to have dinner at The Shalamar Lounge. At this lounge one could eat a bit of real soul food, relax by the fireplace, and listen to a little gospel and Jazz. They all absolutely loved this place. Rachel especially loved it because they did not sell alcoholic drinks and the atmosphere was heavenly.

When the ladies arrived, they all looked as though they stepped out of a vogue magazine. After everyone greeted one another, they all sat in the luxurious sofas that sat by this beautiful fireplace. Above the fireplace was a scripture that read, *"Whoever loves money never has money enough; whoever loves wealth is never satisfied with his income. This too is meaningless. Ecclesiastes 5:10 (N.I.V.)."*

Rachel asked the ladies, "How has everyone been?"

Sasha answered, "The salon is going great, but I feel there is something that is always getting me down."

When Sasha responded, without saying a word, all of the other ladies including Rachel body languages shifted as though they related to her response.

Joanne anxiously asked, "Sasha, what do you mean?"

Melody suddenly interrupted, "Does it feel like forces are working against you?"

Sasha anxiously and quickly responded, "Yes, exactly Melody."

"It sounds like everyone has been experiencing the same stronghold," Rachel commented.

All of the other ladies agreed with Rachel. Rachel looked around at everyone with that pleasant smile.

She shared, "Yes, I have been going through the same thing."

All of the other ladies gasped and started laughing. Rachel laughed right along with them.

Then she commented, "Ah ladies, I deal with everyday trials as well. You all know this."

Scarlette opened up as usual. "You all know I am the only one here that does not know this man you all call Jesus. If he loves you all so much then why are you all going through the same pain I'm going through?"

When Scarlette made that statement all of the other ladies, except Rachel were confused because they had the same questions as Scarlette.

Rachel explained, "Scarlette just because we are saved does not give us a free ticket to no problems. This is why we as Christians should always pray and stay in the Word."

Tressie tried to justify. "Everyone always say that, but who has time to stay in the Word? And or they in the Word?"

"We must make the time to stay in His Word," Rachel strongly suggested.

Joanne tried to justify as well. "I know I am a housewife, but I am still busy. I always have something on my agenda."

Melody was convicted, but tried to make an excuse, "Yes, and I have a major business and children as well. Now, where do I find the time to stay in the Word?"

Sasha agreed, "Yes, I agree with Melody and I have the same problem. Where do we find the time to stay in the Word?"

Rachel asked boldly. "Who do you all think blessed you abundantly? Surely you all can find the time."

Melody tried to make her situation seem right, yet again. "No disrespect Rachel, but that is easy for you to say. You don't have businesses to run."

"I know I don't have businesses to run, but I keep a tight schedule. We all can find excuses for not staying in the Word, but the truth is the Word is our lifeline," Rachel explained.

Scarlette curiously asked, "What do you mean your lifeline?"

Rachel tried her best to clarify, "What I mean is whenever

we go through trials and tribulations, there are Scriptures that will help us through anything. God speaks to us as we read the Word. He speaks to us in our everyday lives."

Scarlette amazed, "Wow! Do you mean your Jesus will do that for you? Do you really think this being cares that much? He speaks to you in any situation. I'm sorry that just sounds too good to be true."

Rachel answered, "Scarlette, I know you are not interested, but our God is awesome. If only Christians would wake up and realize the power we possess just by being Christians."

Tressie commented, "Everyone always says that it is so easy, but how many other people besides, *she laughed*, the Richardsons really know the power we are supposed to have?"

Joanne was confused as well. "Yes everyone does say that it is easy, but whenever I do try to read a Scripture or two, I just don't feel Him speaking to me. I guess it would help if I understood what I read."

"Whenever you have a one on one relationship with the Father you will know His voice," Rachel added.

Sasha asked, "Rachel, can He really speak to us reading the Word? I want to feel His power."

Rachel answered, "Yes sisters, Pastor Patterson always say the Father speaks to us through His Word. I am a witness, He will speak to you."

Melody as if she suddenly realized, "I feel convicted because deep down in my spirit I know that I should allow time for our Father. I also know that if it wasn't for the Lord, I would not be where I am today."

All of the other ladies looked as though they suddenly received a revelation. Scarlette even looked as if she got a touch of something; not realizing how our Jesus works. After this conversation, all of the women ordered their dinner, enjoyed the fireplace and the rest of their evening.

As the ladies sat and enjoyed the rest of their evening, there were a couple of other women who came to admire the fireplace and the Scripture.

One lady remarked, "That scripture is becoming to some Christians because they allow their money to be their God."

The other woman responded, "I know many people claim Christ is the head of their lives, but their actions says something totally different."

Both women were smiling, but deep down inside examining themselves. In unison both women turn to one another and thought, *"Am I one of those people?"*

When the two women looked at one another with the same thought, Rachel, Sasha, and everyone else suddenly looked up at the same time.

The next morning at Paul and Sasha's estate, Paul and Sasha arrived from the gym. Their personal chef had prepared their breakfast. The thought was still fresh in her mind from the night before. She thought, "*I know, at dinner, we were not talking about the way we treat others, but I can't help but think about that moment at the Shalamar Lounge. The two ladies were standing and admiring the fireplace. Then all at once, all of us received a revelation at the same time.* Sasha observed Paul and noticed Paul's reaction towards the chef like never before.

Sasha quietly asked, "Why do you always act like he isn't here?"

"Sweetheart, I am cordial and I feel that is all I am required to do, baby. He is just our chef. Why all of a sudden you care?"

Sasha became a little upset and said in an angry tone, "I need to speak to you upstairs please!" Paul was shocked because this was the first time Sasha showed any concern. Sasha and Paul immediately went upstairs to their bedroom. Sasha shut the bedroom door firmly.

"Paul, he is just as good as you are."

He desperately asked, "What do you mean? Honey he just cooks our food. What is the problem?"

Sasha asked, "Do you listen to the sermons that Pastor Patterson so passionately deliver each Sunday?"

"Yes, but I am cordial to the chef always."

"It would not hurt you to hold a conversation more than a few seconds. Your attitude reeks of arrogance."

Paul responded, "I always hear what Pastor Patterson speaks on."

Sasha still very irritated, "Paul, there is a difference in hearing and listening! Why do you think when Scriptures are read they almost always end in, "May God add a blessing to the hearers and doers of the Word." Paul, God wants us to be doers of the word. It says it in the Word."

Sasha, do you think everyone really tries to do what is right all the time?" Paul asked in an honest manner.

By this time Sasha is trying to desperately handle the situation in a godly manner. But Sasha conveniently forgot that she was a sinner saved by grace as well.

Sasha explained, "Paul as a Christian you should always try to do what is right. Now would you want someone treating you like you are less than they are? Even worse, what if Chef Joe was your own flesh and blood?"

Paul immediately started thinking of his family because he knew his family didn't have much. He suddenly got a lump in his throat and looked in his precious Sasha's eyes and realized how ungodly he had been to their chef. It was like a light bulb came on for Paul. He then thought of other people that he treated the same way. Sasha silently prayed for Paul.

Chef Joe was finishing up breakfast.

Paul walked over to Chef Joe slowly and awkwardly, "Chef Joe, I would like to apologize to you from the bottom of my heart."

Subconsciously Chef Joe knew what he was apologizing for.

"Forgive me for treating you like you are beneath me."

Chef Joe responded, "Mr. Jones I always come to do my job and do it with the best of my abilities. I knew something was a little off Mr. Jones. But at the same time, I always respect a man and his household."

He really felt bad after Chef Joe's last statement.

"Wow! I am supposed to be the Christian. And here it is you are showing me how to be a true Christian," Paul suddenly realized.

"Mr. Jones I accept your apology," He kindly accepted.

"Chef Joe, call me Paul."

Chef Joe was excited and feeling like a load that he did not realize he had, had been lifted off his shoulders, "Are you sure?"

Paul replied feeling a little bit better. "My wife made me realize you should always treat people with kindness and respect no matter what their statuses are. Chef Joe this is strange because as a Christian this should come to me automatically."

"Paul what matters is you sincerely apologized. Hey man, not too many men are willing to admit that they have been wrong."

Paul suddenly realized he never knew anything about Chef Joe.

He asked, "Do you have a family?

"Yes, I have been married 10 years and I have four children. My wife stays home with the children. We decided this would be best for the children and our financial situation."

Paul sincerely hoped as he thought about his family back at home. "I hope your situation gets better soon."

"I know it will. The only thing that matters is my family is happy. We may not have much, but our house is filled with love," Chef Joe said with much confidence.

Paul agreed, "Yes, I know because I love my family as well and I can't bear the thought of them being unhappy."

Chef Joe was so happy, he felt as though he found a new friend. "One day I will be like you all here in this neighborhood."

Paul curiously asked as if he didn't know. "What do you mean?"

"I would love to get a home like this one day for my family. I believe one day I will. Man, what man wouldn't want the best for his family?"

Paul tried to give great encouragement. "Chef Joe I believe you will."

By the time they were done with their conversation, it was time for Chef Joe to leave. As they talked, Sasha had gone upstairs to get ready for work. By the time she got dressed and came downstairs Paul was walking Chef Joe out. Sasha was filled because she knew her husband made a great change that morning by stepping out of his selfish bondage.

Sasha thought, "*Lord, we are going to have to start loving others on purpose. You know Paul is not the only one who needed to make a change. The strongholds are so obvious at times. Work on me Lord!"*

When Chef Joe and Sasha left, Paul was sitting in the living room amazed at how he was treating Chef Joe without realizing it was totally ungodly.

Paul thought, *"Lord, I thought I was a nice guy. Better yet, I thought I was being a good Christian. Pastor Patterson always says that we are a peculiar people. That's not being peculiar at all. I am supposed to love someone that I have never even met before. Here this man has come in my home on a regular basis for the past couple of years and I could not talk to him. Forgive me Lord."*

 Words of Wisdom

Brothers and Sisters, we have to keep God the focus of our lives. We have to fight flesh daily. As people we can get caught up in the world's view of success. We all know the world's view of success and this is "Money" and more "Money." Yes some of us as Christians, as well seem to think the more money we can achieve the happier we can be. We can say all day long, "Money cannot make us happy." But as Christians, how do we really feel? What scripture will have your picture screaming in the background, but deathly silent to your actions?

CHAPTER 8

Psalm 127: 1-2 Unless the Lord builds the house, its build-ers labor in vain. Unless the Lord watches over the city, the watchmen stand guard in vain. (N.I.V.)

One morning in early April, the Cranes were having a typical breakfast. As they were eating, Meriah seemed very upset. Everyone tried to ignore her because this was her usual attitude. Scarlette was also upset because of Meriah. Ridge tried his best to cut the tense atmosphere.

Ridge pretended to be excited. "Wow! These eggs are great."

Little Cassidy Arnasia agreed, "Yeah, Daddy they good."

Meriah complained as usual. "The pancakes are too sweet. What is so good about these eggs?"

Scarlette immediately commanded, "Meriah, you apologize to Chef Fisher!"

"Why should I apologize for telling the truth?" Meriah made the statement in such disrespectful manner.

Ridge had enough, "Meriah, that is rude! Do what Scarlette says!"

Meriah angrily lashed out. "You are always on her side."

Scarlette responded, "Meriah just apologize."

Little Cassidy Arnasia was unquestionably upset. "It not right in dis house. I don't quite know what goin' on."

Ridge asked with a bit of curiosity, "What do you mean? Everything is fine."

Little Cassidy Arnasia did not know what to do, but what she did know was that feeling she got whenever she was at the Richardsons is all they needed. "Daddy it feel strange aroun' dis here house. Mrs. Rachel house it feel happy."

Scarlette tried to explain. "Sweetheart, it is happy here also. Right now your sister needs to just apologize."

Little Cassidy Arnasia was heavy-hearted, "No Mommy, it feel strange a lot here in dis house. Mommy, our family alway scream."

"Sweetheart, we have to raise you two. Mommy and Daddy cannot let their children walk all over us."

All of a sudden, Chef Fisher walked over and joined the conversation. "I don't mean to be rude, but I think I know what little Cassidy Arnasia is talking about."

Chef Fisher was saved and filled with the Holy Spirit. He felt what little Cassidy Arnasia was trying to explain to her parents.

He asked, "Who is Mrs. Rachel?"

Ridge answered, "Rachel Richardson is our friend. The Richardsons are some of our so-called Christian friends."

Chef Fisher wondered, "What do you mean so-called Christian friends?"

He replied, "Let me ask you this. What do you think Cassidy Arnasia is speaking of when she says it's not right in this house? Every family has his own problems."

Ridge remembered how pleasant the atmosphere is when they are in the presence of the Richardsons. Suddenly Ridge's entire demeanor changed.

Ridge said, "Cassidy is just a four-year-old kid."

Chef Fisher was in a serious state of mind. "Sir, you have to wonder what she means by that statement."

Scarlette looked as curious as Ridge.

Ridge was very anxious by this time. "Chef Fisher, what do you think she means by that?"

Little Cassidy Arnasia suddenly interrupted. "Mommy Daddy, you know what I feel."

Scarlette got up, grabbed Little Cassidy Arnasia and rushed upstairs.

"I didn't mean to upset her." Chef Fisher sincerely apologized.

Ridge told Meriah to go upstairs as well.

She rudely responded, "But I'm not finished eating."

"You will finish your food later."

Meriah stormed upstairs to her room.

Ridge was annoyed, "I don't like my children listening to

these conversations."

Chef Fisher politely replied. "It seems you are a little uncomfortable; we can end the conversation."

He anxiously responded, "No, to be honest, I want to know what you think she was talking about."

"I hope you noticed that I am a Christian as well. I feel strange saying that because no Christian should have to announce they are a Christian."

Ridge replied, "I noticed that you are peculiar."

He started to explain. "Sir, your little daughter feels the spirit of God when she is over Mrs. Rachel's house."

Ridge disturbingly replied, "I refuse to believe that is what my little girl was talking about."

Chef Fisher carefully asked, "Sir, then what do you think she was talking about?"

"I mean no harm, but how do you believe in something or somebody that you cannot see?"

Chef Fisher slowly explained, "Sir, I have known Jesus most of my life. Trust me, if you ever decide to follow Him, you will see and know that He is Jesus. When you get to know Him you will feel and see what I am telling you."

Ridge got more curious as Chef Fisher spoke. Of course, he wouldn't dare appear curious. But Chef Fisher already knew he was.

Ridge genuinely asked, "This man you Christians call Jesus, why does he allow bad things to happen to good people?"

Chef Fisher answered, "There are many things that happen and no one will ever have answers to, but when you know Him for yourself, you know everything is going to be alright whatever happens."

Ridge commented, "Chef Fisher, it sounds like you have no doubt."

Chef Fisher smiled and proclaimed, "Without a shadow of a doubt, I know Jesus is real!"

Ridge tried to sound as assured as Chef Fisher. "Chef Fisher, I know that my family is going to be fine and I don't need anybody name Jesus to reassure me."

It took all that Chef Fisher had to remain calm when Ridge made that comment. This was a tremendous test of humility for Chef Fisher.

He calmly responded. "I know you say you don't believe in God, but I wouldn't survive one second without my Heavenly Father."

Without knowing it, Ridge looked at Chef Fisher in such a respectful manner. "Man, you are convinced."

After their conversation Chef Fisher finished cooking and headed home. For the rest of the day Ridge thought about Chef Fisher and his faith.

 Words of Wisdom

Brothers and Sisters, God speaks through our children all the time. What is your child constantly and repeatedly telling you? How many times are we going to go around the same mountain? We should always be aware of the people whom God place in our lives, and remember God can use anything or anybody to make a transformation in our lives. Be aware of those divine, sweet, silent whispers from our Father.

CHAPTER 9

Psalm 69: 1-3 Save me, O God, for the waters have come up to my neck. I sink in the miry depths, where there is no foothold. I have come into the deep waters; the floods engulf me. I am worn out calling for help; my throat is parched. My eyes fail, looking for my God. (N.I.V.)

Psalm 114: 1-4 When Israel came out of Egypt, the house of Jacob from a people of foreign tongue, Judah became God's sanctuary, Israel his dominion. The sea looked and fled, the Jordan turned back; the mountains skipped like rams, the hills like lambs. (N.I.V.)

It was a Saturday morning in the middle of April at Sasha's salon.

Whenever clients walked in Sasha's salon they thought they were at one of the most elegant salons that they had ever seen. On one wall of the salon there was a mural of a salon with a gospel choir that surrounded a salon. At a distance one thought that the figures were the choir members. But as one got closer to the mural, one could see that the choir members were actually angels. The director of the choir, of course appeared to be a person, but the person was actually *The Arch Angel*. Sasha's husband, Paul painted this mural. It most certainly was a conversation piece for this clientele.

As clients came in for their appointments, they were given the royal treatment. There were girls who served snacks, tea and coffee. Everything was served on the most beautiful, fine china. Sasha ran the salon as professional as anyone possibly could, and the stylists were just as professional. There was always gospel or jazz music playing softly that always created a delightful atmosphere. Every now and then Sasha would have a trying day for whatever reason. But this day was very different than any day before. On this particular day Rachel, Trina,

Tressie, Scarlette, Joanne and Melody had made appointments around the same time.

Tressie, Joanne, Scarlette and Melody arrived at the salon the same time. About 15 minutes later Rachel and her friend Trina arrived. Trina was one of Rachel's friends from the homeless shelter where she volunteered. When Rachel and Trina entered the salon everyone turned around and all eyes were on Trina. She looked different than anyone else in the salon. She was an African American woman whose hair appeared as though she had not relaxed it in about eight months, and clothes looked as though she had worn them for several days. Her shoes were a dusty gray and needed to be washed.

As they walked in, Rachel silently prayed for Trina. *"Father, touch Trina right now Lord. Give her peace like she has never had before. May you use her and her story to open people's eyes to another dimension, in Jesus's name, Amen."*

Trina walked in with a boldness that only comes from God. Everywhere she looked there were designer clothing, designer purses, designer shoes and bling. As Trina looked around, she began to imagine being in a dream. She never imagined having her hair done in such an elegant and sophisticated salon.

As she walked closer and closer to the mural she realized that the choir members were angels. It took all Trina had to hold back tears; at this point she thought she was walking through a dream.

Trina thought, *"Father, you never disappoint. You always give me a sign when I am in unfamiliar territory. Father, I am just as blessed as anyone in here! I thank you."*

As she continued to walk some of the clients stared and some just whispered. All of the people in the salon, not only stared and whispered, but Rachel's so-called Christian friends and Scarlette stared and whispered as well.

Rachel and Trina entered the waiting area where Rachel's so-called Christian friends and Scarlette sat. Rachel introduced Trina to her Sisters in Christ. Tressie acted as if Trina had some sort of disease. Joanne pretended as though Trina was a lost cause. Melody looked at Trina as though she was a lost animal. Scarlette just grabbed her purse.

Sasha was embarrassed because her clients knew Rachel was one of her closest friends. Rachel had this *unpolished lady* with her who did not look up to par, step foot in her salon. She felt as though she would have to explain to her clients how and why this *unpolished lady* was in the salon.

Rachel discerned the spirits that covered her friends, and was so displeased with them. She expected this sort of behavior from the other people in the salon. She knew Trina was a strong child of God, but wanted to be certain that she was fine spiritually and mentally.

Rachel asked Trina, "Honey, are you alright?"

"Rachel, I feel what you feel and I must say I have peace and I know God is here with me and I will get through it."

By this time Rachel was in tears. Trina looked to Rachel and boldly replied. "Rachel this is my mountain let me climb it. I'll be alright."

Trina looked over to the mural and pointed at it. She couldn't say anymore. When Rachel looked at the mural, she knew there was nothing else to say. God had already made His presence known in her heart in this situation.

Rachel smiled while tears flowed and said, "May God continue to keep you as you go through, Trina." Rachel and Trina embraced.

While Rachel talked to Trina on the side, the other ladies were whispering. Tressie and Joanne looked at one another in disgust. Scarlette gave Melody a smirk look. Tressie got all of the other ladies' attention.

Tressie whispered, "Sometimes I just don't know about Rachel. You know she can't save everybody. Why would she bring someone that looks like that in here? Honey, she just doesn't fit."

Joanne agreed, "She looks like someone from that shelter where she volunteers. I know everybody is supposed to be equal, but you have to draw the line somewhere."

Melody commented, "I have seen people that work out at the gym that look more presentable than that. It is very disturbing. How can you come out of the house looking like that?"

Scarlette looked at all the ladies with that smirk smile and asked, "Ladies, what would your Jesus say about this situation?"

At that moment Rachel walked up to the ladies and immediately said, "Scarlette, you are an adult. Whether you believe or not, no one should get treated that way."

She looked to the other ladies in disappointment.

"And for you other ladies, Jesus would not approve of his children treating one another in such an ungodly way." *She smiled just a little.* "Now I am going to pray for you ladies because this is not of God."

All of the ladies immediately felt convicted.

Joanne was discontented. "Rachel, I just don't understand you sometimes. Your heart obviously goes on forever."

Rachel quickly responded, "Honey, it is not me it is Jesus that lives in my heart."

Joanne shamefully got herself together.

Tressie tried to give advice. "Rachel sometimes it is not worth it."

She responded, "Tressie, when Jesus lives in your heart it is worth it every time."

Tressie dropped her head in embarrassment.

Melody asked, "Rachel where do you draw the line?"

Rachel explained, "Melody, Jesus didn't draw the line anywhere so who am I to draw the line on any situation or anybody?"

Melody slowly looked away, Trina walked up. Tressie, Joanne, Melody, and even Scarlette could barely look Trina in her face. Although in Trina's spirit she knew the ladies were saying things that were not of God, she endured the harsh treatment from everyone, but through it all she stood tall with Jesus leading her.

All of the ladies were in the process of getting their hair

done. Thankfully Trina's hairstylist was a strong woman of God and she was also a member of Faith Deliverance Church of Atlanta. All around the salon, all of the customers were still watching Trina as she got her hair done. They made sure they did not get close to her. When Trina got out of the dryer chair or shampoo chair, the hairstylists made certain that everything was sanitized.

Rachel's spirit felt uneasy. All of a sudden Rachel went over to Sasha to talk to her about what was weighing on her precious heart. Sasha was styling her client's hair. As Rachel approached Sasha, she noticed Rachel seemed a little upset.

Sasha thought, *"This is not like Rachel."*

Rachel humbly asked, "Sasha, may I speak with you in the back?"

They went into Sasha's office.

Rachel said as calmly as she knew how, "Sasha, this is not how anyone should be treated. I don't care how much money they have or how little they have."

Sasha felt this strong conviction.

"Rachel, I cannot help the way the clients are in the salon. You know the type of clientele I have."

Sasha suddenly thought, *"How can I think this way? I am acting the same way Paul acted towards Chef Fisher. But, I have to protect the reputation of my salon."*

She realized she was being a hypocrite yet again.

"Sasha, we as Christians should strive to do what is Godly at all times. Yes, we have to struggle with the flesh daily. The way Trina is being treated is distasteful; Joanne, Tressie, Melody, and Scarlette were acting the same way towards her. Scarlette is fitting right along with the Christians. What is setting them apart from Scarlette who is an atheist? Sasha, Trina may not have the lifestyle that everyone else has in here, but she has a personal relationship with the Lord. You know that is worth more than any two or three million dollar homes or those Benz's and Beemers that are parked outside."

Sasha hesitated, "Rachel, I understand what you're saying.

But try and understand why they are reacting the way they are. Come on Rachel, you see her appearance."

Rachel's heart broke for Trina. She looked at Sasha with tears in her eyes.

"Sasha, Pastor Patterson preached on this subject just last Sunday. How can you allow this type of behavior to go on in your salon? Honey, this is your salon; you are allowed to run it the way you choose."

Sasha loved her high profile lifestyle. She knew that having this type of clientele supported her lifestyle.

She responded as truthful as she knew how. "Rachel you know I love you, but to be frank I am embarrassed because everyone in here knows that you and I are close friends. When you bring someone in here that looks the way your friend Trina does...I'm sorry, but they will automatically assume that I befriend people in the same category."

Rachel humbly replied, "Sasha, I am going to bring you the sermon from Sunday and honey please listen to it. I love you and I hope that you truly open your heart and ears while listening to it. My heart goes out for you."

Sasha stated, "Rachel I will watch it and I love you too sister. I hope you understand. You know I have to protect the salon's reputation at the end of the day."

Rachel and Sasha were walking out of the backroom. The radio personality introduced a song that would turn the salon's atmosphere into a God enhanced atmosphere. As the song played, it seemed as though the entire salon got totally silent. Everyone in the salon that was a Christian got truly convicted and the ones that did not profess to be a Christian all of a sudden felt guilty. Trina's unwanted appearance immediately started awakening client's spirits. This so-called raggedy and dirty appearance turned into a revelation.

As the song continued, the words of the song were leaping on hearts like this salon had not seen before. Some clients' heads dropped when they began praying silently. Others appeared to have let their guards down. Good seeds were planted in the clients' who didn't understand the change in the atmosphere.

Tressie, Joanne, Sasha, and Melody's conviction sent them right to Trina. They apologized for treating her like she was nobody. Even Scarlette felt guilty about the way Trina was treated.

Scarlette walked up to Rachel and wondered aloud, "Rachel, what kind of song was that? I have never experienced this feeling in a song. I mean, I have songs that I love, but this song was totally different. It was like an energy I have never felt before. Rachel was that your Jesus?"

Rachel with a peaceful spirit responded, "Yes, that is His spirit."

Scarlette said the only thing that she could say, "Wow, that's your Jesus!"

Rachel looked at Scarlette and smiled. She knew in her heart that it would be a matter of time before Scarlette would come around.

 WORDS OF WISDOM

Brothers and Sisters, how do we react when we encounter someone who in our eyes and mindsets is not riding in the same boat as we are? Or have we ever been ostracized for whatever reason? We should always remember how we felt when we fell into this position. As a Christian, do we welcome that individual into our hearts or ignore their presence? We all are going to experience discomfort sometimes in our lives and this is the time your light should really shine!

CHAPTER 10

Proverbs 19: 6-7 Many curry favor with a ruler, and everyone is the friend of a man who gives gifts. A poor man is shunned by all his relatives- how much more do his friends avoid him! Though he pursues them with pleading, they are nowhere to be found. (N.I.V.)

A week after the incident at Sasha's salon, the church was having their yearly spring barbecue. The church activity area was beautifully landscaped and manicured. There were gazebos with scriptures and inspirational words throughout the church activity area. In the middle of the activity area was a huge play area, so that parents and children could both enjoy themselves when the church had fellowship events. Sitting areas were scattered throughout the activity area and each sitting area was covered with awnings colored burgundy, gold, silver, and cream.

It was around 11:30 am on Saturday. The parking lot and the activity area were filled with security guards and policemen. The security guards were directing traffic and checking bags, because the event was always open to the public, just the same as the church doors. Cars were coming from everywhere. Sadly, some people were unruly, disrespectful, and ungodly.

At the moment, everyone is in place and ready for Pastor Patterson to give his sermon. Rachel and John, Tressie and Ronald, Melody and Reese, Joanne and Howard, and Sasha and Paul sat together in an area close to the podium.

Nanny Nellie was in the play area with Stacey. On the other side of the playground Nanny Nora tended to Howard and Joanne's children: Ashley, Ashton, and Amira. Somewhere in the middle of the play area Nanny Abby played with Reese and Melody's children: Nia, Samone, and Tremaine. Nanny May walked little Sehara around, Paul and Sasha's daughter. Melinda and Steward were helping with the barbecue. Charlotte and Charles socialized with some friends.

Pastor Patterson always wanted to give a word anytime the church had a gathering. He gave a mini sermon before the church barbecue. The title of this particular sermon was "Accepting Everyone." As Pastor Patterson preached the message, people quietly discussed it among themselves.

A lady at one table quietly said to her friend, "Sometimes it's just not good to invite everyone in."

The lady's friend replied, "Yeah, tell me about it. I'm sorry, but I am just not there yet."

Over in another part of the fellowship area, other couples sat together.

One of the ladies whispered to the other couples, "Do you think he really accepts everyone?"

Another lady answered with authority, "Jesus did it."

She looked around to all the couples. "We should try our best to immolate Jesus."

Over on the other side at another table, one gentleman whispered to the gentleman sitting next to him, "There he go with the unity and community message again. *He smiled.* Brother, you just can't trust everybody. Man, I need to tell Brother Pastor that it is easier said than done."

The other gentleman responded, "Yeah, but is that a cop out? I feel ashamed and guilty right now."

Over where Rachel was sitting, all the other ladies felt guilty all over again about the incident that happened at Sasha's salon. Tressie, Sasha, Joanne, and Melody got this overwhelming chill over their bodies during Pastor Patterson's sermon.

Rachel looked at all of them, gave them a smile and humbly whispered, "God knows your heart."

All of the ladies were sitting next to their husbands, but Rachel's presence was that of an angel. They all locked eyes with Rachel as she reassured them. Somehow, she was always with the ladies when they needed her. They could not help themselves, they all cried. All of them put themselves in Trina's shoes on that unforgettable Saturday morning. Of course, none of them told their husbands about what happened in Sasha's salon. Their husbands were consoling them while wondering why they were crying, but on the other hand, their husbands knew that if Rachel was in the picture, Jesus was always the head of the pack. The ladies had not realized they needed to ask God for forgiveness. Rachel got up, went around the table and had all of the ladies stand to ask God for forgiveness. Pastor Patterson noticed them standing and went over to the table where they were. There were many other women and men who were touched by Pastor Patterson's message. These members and friends who got up and joined them were people who were, no doubt, blessed with material things. On the opposite end, there were members who despised people who were, in their eyes, well off which ate at their spirits with negative thoughts and negative energy. The members who despised others with material things were members who could not make ends meet.

The associate Ministers, Deacons, ushers, and Mothers of the church came together and began to pray for everyone who surrounded their table. The spirit was so strong throughout the fellowship area, the children that were playing with their nannies and their parents all of a sudden got calm and content. Some children peacefully hugged each other, the swings stopped, and some children held hands in a circle. Some family and friends that were not saved silently sat in their seats. There were people praying for their families and their financial stability, some were praying because they felt convicted of treating other people like they were *nobodies*. There were quite a few people who were praying for their children and grandchildren.

While this is going on First Lady Naomi found herself where the others were. She was also convicted of being so unlike our All Mighty God. Pastor Patterson looked up and there his wife stood near him; he immediately started praying for her as well. Everyone started singing Thank You Lord Jesus. Women and men started shouting. When people fell out, the nurses and ushers were there to assist them. The spirit of God came through the fellowship area like lightning, but still as calm as the day after the storm. For thirty minutes everyone was united.

Several hours after Pastor Patterson's message there were still people coming to enjoy the barbecue. On the other side of the fellowship area there was an incident that needed security. Some people rushed over to see what was going on and others watched from afar. When security arrived, there was a couple cursing and shouting at one another. The woman's eyes looked as though she had been crying for days, her hair was in disarray, and evidently she had just thrown on whatever clothes she could find. The man looked liked a human bulldog because of the evil tormented look that settled on his face. He appeared as though he had not rested for days and reeked of alcohol. Their young children were screaming and holding on to their ears for dear life; terrified. Their older children just stood in embarrassment. When security finally managed to settle the couple down, the couple had a chance to tell their story.

The man had been laid off of his job of ten years for several months. In the meantime he had no choice, but to humble himself in order to work at Burger World as a cook. He worked every day for long hours. All this and it still wasn't enough to take care of his large family. They had no choice, except to rely on assistance from social services. This young man had always taken care of his family without assistance. His current situation led him to drink and become angry. The woman stayed home because they had three smaller children. The three were under five years of age and two older teenagers.

Pastor Patterson rushed over with concern as soon as he knew.

He walked over to the husband and desperately asked, "What is the problem, son?"

The young man burst out in tears before he could say anything, letting go of every last bit of his ego. There was a pause that lasted about two minutes. The young man had to get himself together due to the embarrassment of everything that happened and the situation that he and his family had to endure.

The young man said, "Pastor, it is rough not being able to provide for my family. Pastor, I had a good job, maybe not making what a lot of the other members make, but it was enough. I got laid off and now I work at that…"

He had to catch himself. He'd gotten so use to saying any and everything out of his mouth.

Pastor Patterson kindly asked, "Son, first tell me what your name is."

"Raymond Bell, Sir."

"Mr. Bell how can the church help you and your family?"

Mr. Bell was defiant. "I don't like taking handouts."

Pastor advised, "Son, sometimes as a man we have to do what is going to be the best for our family and not our egos."

Mr. Bell obnoxiously replied, "Yeah, easy for you to say."

Pastor compassionately offered, "Mr. Bell, why don't you and your wife come with me and my staff so we can get you all some help."

Mr. Bell paused for a few minutes. Then he shook Pastor Patterson's hands.

Meanwhile, some of the Deaconesses comforted the wife and some of the nurses of the church took the smaller children. The youth group leaders took the two teenagers to their conference room in the church. Deaconess Mrs. Barbra West felt like she needed more information about everything. Her face always looked as though she was sipping on a piece of lemon.

She walked over to Mr. Bell's wife and boldly commented, "You know you don't act that a way in public, besides you got yo' chil'ren too."

The young woman was humiliated, "Ma'am, I don't mean to be disrespectful or anything, but I do have a name and it is Natalie Bell. By the way what is your name?"

Rachel knew the type of personality this particular Deaconess possessed. She never said too much to Rachel and would always give Rachel these mean looks and walk the other way. As soon as she saw Deaconess Barbra West supposedly comforting Natalie Bell, Rachel decided to try and help the situation. When Natalie saw Rachel, she of course recognized her friendly face from church, but she also recognized her from one of the shelters in downtown Atlanta. She was so relieved. Her spirit connected with Rachel's. Natalie started crying and broke down. Rachel called for a couple of Deaconesses. They escorted her inside the church.

As they escorted Natalie in, there were people looking as though she committed a crime, some people chose to ignore the situation, others appeared to show some sort of concern. A few carried on a conversation about the incident, only looking on the outside, passing judgment. There were some *Seasoned Saints* at one table who were praying their hearts out. Some folks seem to conveniently forget that they have had problems at some point. On the other side of the fellowship area, there were people foolishly making fun of the incident.

Pastor Patterson, Deaconess Ruby Fry, Deaconess Cheryl Coleman, Mother Mary Stevens, Rachel, Raymond and Natalie Bell gathered in one of the conference rooms. In the room there was a spirit of love. Everyone who gathered in the conference room was very concerned about Mr. and Mrs. Bell and their family. Without saying a word, everyone came into agreement by naturally holding hands to allow Pastor Patterson to pray.

While Pastor Patterson prayed, everyone that was in the circle in some way put themselves in Mr. and Mrs. Bell's position. The expressions on everyone's faces emulated everything the couple had gone through and is going through. Afterwards, there wasn't a dry eye in the room. Everyone from Pastor Patterson to Rachel embraced the couple and gave them words of encouragement. Pastor thanked everyone and then excused them afterwards.

As Pastor excused everyone, Natalie told the Pastor she wanted Rachel to stay.

Rachel asked, "Honey, are you sure?"

Raymond looked at Natalie as though he did not agree. But Natalie knew in her heart that God sent Rachel for such a time as this. Pastor Patterson called Rachel out of the room.

Pastor Patterson showed his appreciation. "Sister Richardson, you are a beautiful light. God is well pleased. Your spirit is welcoming. I am grateful to God for saints like you. Sister Richardson, a light such as yours is hard to find. God bless you."

Before Pastor Patterson could finish, Rachel was in tears.

After Rachel got herself together, she shook Pastor's hand thankfully, "To God be the glory."

They went back to the room. When they got there, Mr. and Mrs. Bell were embracing.

Pastor Patterson's heart rejoiced. "God is good and prayer changes things."

He arranged several things for this broken family: counseling for the couple and their children, promised Mr. Bell he would be able to find him a job that better suited his family, set up a women's day out with Mrs. Bell and First Lady Naomi. Last but not least, he organized a date night for the couple.

 WORDS OF WISDOM

Brothers and sisters, there is a time to joke and a time not to joke. Yes, laughter is good for the soul, but we must be careful that it doesn't make someone else's trials and tribulations just a little bit more unbearable. We must realize our motives. The enemy can be so crafty when we allow it. There are times that we have hidden motives without recognizing it ourselves.

CHAPTER 11

1 Timothy 4:12 Don't let anyone look down on you because you are young, but set an example for the believers in speech, in life, in love, in faith and in purity. (N.I.V.)

It was late April, Howard and Joanne invited one of Howard's employees and her family over for dinner. Nanny Nora could not work because of a family emergency. Therefore, Howard and Joanne were in the position to try and use some type of parenting skills for this particular night.

Chef Meg was a perfectionist at all times. The meal and table setting were fit for royalty. Howard and Joanne's dining room was gorgeous. The cathedral ceiling was hand-painted of The Last Supper by Sasha's husband Paul Jones. The windows were oversized with custom draperies. There were golden sculptured figurines and sculptured lamps. The table was a beautiful walnut set imported from Germany.

Howard and the kids came downstairs. The children sounded like a herd of elephants trampling downstairs. Joanne was sitting at the table looking as calm as she possibly could, along with Howard's employee Carol, her two daughters, Kerry, Chelsey and husband Jim. It took about twenty minutes to settle Ashley, Ashton, and Amira down just a little.

Everyone was introduced. Joanne nervously started to say grace. As soon as she started to say grace, Amira started screaming for no reason.

Joanne stressfully tried to smooth things over. "Nanny Nora isn't here tonight because of a family emergency. Please forgive us."

Joanne and Howard smiled nervously.

Howard immediately said, "Please excuse her, she does that sometimes."

Joanne was interrupted as she attempted to pray again by their thirteen-year- old daughter, Ashley. Ashley was griping at her nine-year-old brother, Ashton. Ashton irritated Ashley continuously by teasing her about her weight.

Joanne and Howard looked away in embarrassment.

Jim and Carol glanced at each other. Their hearts went out for Howard and Joanne as parents.

Out of the blue thirteen-year-old Chelsey went over to where the other children were sitting. With firm authority, she said, "Look at your Mom!" *The children surprisingly looked to their parents.* "They are asking you all to behave."

Immediately Ashley, Ashton and Amira voices diminished and the three of them sat in their chairs properly.

Chelsey looked over to Joanne and Howard. She asked, "Mr. and Mrs. Stone, Do you mind if I blessed the food?"

Joanne with a straight face thought, *"Oh God, can it get any worse? The children are miraculously behaving."*

Chelsey began to bless the food and pray for the family. Joanne and Howard were stunned at how this thirteen-year-old child stood the ground that they should have stood long before this moment. They secretly glanced at each other with a look of guilt and shame while Chelsey prayed.

Joanne thought, *"My God, What will they think of me as a Mother? Will they tell anyone?"*

Howard thought, *"Gee, Nanny Nora picked the perfect time and day to have a family emergency. God, I feel like such an idiot!"*

At this point, Howard and Joanne knew as parents they needed to step up to the plate.

When Chelsey began to pray, Little Amira held her head down. She looked from side to side watching everyone. She would not move. Ashley held her head down making sure that she doesn't look her brother's way. Ashton politely bowed his head.

Chelsey prayed slowly and cautiously. *"Father God, thank you for our health. Thank you for the food that was prepared for the nourishment of our bodies. Touch every child that is present here, even me Father. Father, help us as children to respect our parents and help us to realize how blessed we are to have our parents. Put a loving feeling in our hearts when we feel the need to disrespect our parents. Keep all of us in your loving arms. Continue to show us how to love; and thank you for allowing our parents to love us and put up with us every day of our lives. Last, but not least Father, always remind us to respect our parents and keep our parents in an authoritative position. In Jesus's name, Amen."*

By the time the prayer was over, everyone was in tears. Howard looked over to Chelsey and firmly said, "Young lady you are going to grow into a mighty woman of God someday."

He then turned to her parents with tears flowing down his face and commented, "You all are truly blessed."

"*Out of the mouth of babes,*" Joanne was moved.

She looked at Chelsey admiringly, "I need you around here all the time."

The tears in Joanne's eyes were flowing down her cheeks like that of a rainforest. She kindly smiled.

Chelsey's Mother Carol was also crying uncontrollably. She was so overwhelmed by her thirteen-year-old daughter. When a Mother witnesses her child standing up for something that is so righteous and at the right moment, it is truly a great blessing to a Mother's dear heart.

While she wiped her tears, Carol explained, "We don't have much, but God is blessing us in a mighty way. You know Joanne and Howard I always wondered. What does success really mean? I believe success is defined in a different way, with each individual."

Joanne added, "I believe we are successful because of the lives that we live. God knows we have lots of materialistic things that we so admire, but when a child does something that adults should have done a long time ago, I have to at least wonder whether it is really success."

Howard with great pride disagreed, "Joanne honey, of course that is success."

Joanne looked over at her three children - all straight haired brunettes.

She thought, *"Lord, help me parent my children. Help me be a better Mother."*

As she held her head down, she continued thinking, *"Lord, why did the light bulb have to be in the form of a thirteen-year-old little girl? How embarrassing!"*

Everyone then began to eat their dinner.

Amira asked, "Chelsey, you go to our church?"

She answered, "No, Amira, we go to a small church outside the city. The name of my church is Way of the Word Baptist Church."

"You not scared to pray? Cause my Mommy and Daddy, they scared to pray. They always argue about who is gonna pray."

All of a sudden Howard felt the need to chastise. "Amira, that is enough!"

Ashton rudely joined the conversation, "Yeah, Amira always runs her mouth."

Amira replied, "Daddy, you know I always talk. Be quiet, Ashton!"

She looked at her Daddy and smiled. Ashton started laughing; initiating drama from Amira.

Instantly Howard stepped in and corrected. "Son, don't start anything with your sister. Now is not the time for senseless fighting."

Ashley commented, "Yeah, we have been behaving nicely a while. So, yeah don't start."

Little Amira looked at Chelsey with the cutest little smile. "You pray lack the people at church."

Chelsey responded, "Amira, you are so funny."

Everyone finished their dinner. At this point Joanne was very concerned about her children. After Chelsey stood up and prayed, this bothersome feeling of emotion in Joanne just could not rest. The light bulb that came on for Joanne brightened.

Joanne thought, *"Now, it is time for change."*

Howard saw the look in Joanne's eyes that he had never seen before.

He thought, *"Lord, I have never seen Joanne look so serious. This is a sign that we need to buckle up fast."*

Howard gets this overwhelming feeling like he has never felt before then he started crying uncontrollably. Joanne suddenly felt the same overwhelming feeling and she was also crying uncontrollably. In a split second, they were as one. Carol and her husband, Jim was also in tears. They got up and instantly started praying for them because they knew what was taking place. All of the children started crying as well. Ashley, Ashton, and Amira went over to their parents to embrace them.

After they prayed, Amira felt the need, "Mommy, Daddy, I love you. What's wrong?" Joanne gave Amira a kiss. Then she said with great confidence, "Amira, honey everything is going to be fine."

Howard shook his head in agreement with Joanne. Ashton looked at his Dad with great concern. "Dad, what is going on?"

"Just like your Mom said everything is going to be alright, son."

Chef Meg began to clear the dinner table. While she was clearing the dinner table everyone moved to the living room to continue the conversation.

Chef Meg went in the living room. She asked out of curiosity, "Mr. and Mrs. Stone, is everything alright? I could not help but hear what was going on. I don't go to church, but I felt those powerful prayers that Carol and her family prayed."

Carol and Jim responded, "We give God all the Glory. Thank you."

"Chef Meg, why don't you go to church? Carol asked."

When Carol asked that question, Joanne thought, *"Why haven't I had that conversation with her?"*

Chef Meg answered, "Well, to tell you the truth most people that I know who go to church act no different than I do. I always thought why should I waste my time? There isn't anything that is special about them."

Jim quickly jumped in the conversation. "You are right. There are Christians that blend right along with others who aren't. Everyone who goes to church is not saved. When you are a true Christian, the church is in you."

Chef Meg asked, "What do you mean by that?"

"There are people that go to church every Sunday who are not Christians."

She responded, "Jim you put a different light on my thoughts when it comes to Christians. I know I should be going to somebody's church."

Jim shared with Godly love, "Let me give you a little advice that will last for eternity…Give your life to Christ."

Chef Meg inquisitively looked at Jim. She asked, "Do you mean get saved?"

Jim got excited, "Absolutely!"

By that time, their conversation had gotten everyone's attention. Chef Meg seemed to have gotten a little nervous when she noticed everyone's interest in their conversation.

Chef Meg apprehensively said, "Yeah, we'll see Jim."

Meg weaseled her way out of that conversation quickly. She went back to clearing the table. As she was clearing the table, she was reminded of the conversation she just had with Jim.

She thought, *"I need to get back in church, but when?"*

She glanced in the living room where everyone was sitting. She remembered Carol's daughter praying.

Even though she was reluctant and fearful she thought to herself, *"I have to get back in church. I need to be saved."*

When Carol and her family were leaving Howard and Joanne's home, Jim was curious. "Carol, how would you like to live that type of lifestyle?"

Carol smiled, "Honey, this neighborhood is everything any woman would want, but do you think they are really happy? You know, I think most of them are Christians and they go to church from the way Howard talks at work."

"Carol honey, you know I don't mean any harm, but what took place on tonight tells me that having lots of materialistic things does not mean you have it all together and that you're happy."

Carol agreed, "It is always awesome when God uses us in a powerful way."

She then looked in the back seat at Chelsey. She said, "That was a powerful stand you made at the right time Chelsey. I'm sure God is very pleased."

Chelsey replied, "Mommy, before we left home, I asked God to help me be a blessing to someone else. I noticed at school there are lots of students and teachers that are just not happy, Mommy. I feel someone needs to step up, why not me?"

Carol reached back and patted Chelsey on her leg. "I know you have been here before; you are not a normal thirteen-year-old. Chelsey honey, there is an anointing on your life."

Little sister Kerry, who doesn't say very much proudly agreed, "Big sister Chelsey, you cool. I wanna be just like you; you a cool big sister."

Jim, Carol, and Chelsey chuckled.

The family arrived home after twenty-five minutes. Their home was a two bedroom house with a dining and living room that was connected. Their house was on a cul-de-sac and it was the only house on the cul-de-sac that was well looked after. The yard was beautifully kept. The inside was immaculate.

As everyone walked in, Jim looked at the bills that were in a box, tucked away neatly. He looked at his precious wife. "Carol, I know God is still in charge."

Carol was assured, "Honey, if he can do it for them, he can do it for us. The bills will be all paid off soon. We just need to continue working hard and saving every dime that we can, then one day we will be debt free."

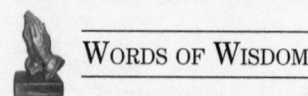

Brothers and Sisters, we should never underestimate our children. We should always remember, children are full of wisdom from God. It always seems to happen just in a nick of time. Remember, we should not ignore, but explore. Brothers and Sisters, when we are visiting someone and it seems they have everything we may desire to have, we should never develop the negative energy of jealousy and envy. As soon as we feel those ungodly emotions speak these words out of your mouth, "No weapon formed against me shall prosper." As anyone could see in this part of the story Jim and Carol were not jealous or envious. God planted them in the right place just in a nick of time for Howard and Joanne's growth in their walks with Christ. If we are not where we want to be in life, we should not look right or left, but we should always look up to the Father!

CHAPTER 12

Proverbs 1:20-21 Wisdom calls aloud in the street, she raises her voice in the public squares; at the head of the noisy streets she cries out, in the gateways of the city she makes her speech: How long will you simple ones love your simple ways? How long will mockers delight in mockery and fools hate knowledge? (N.I.V.)

Reese and Melody Ford threw their *April Party Bash* for their employees.

Nanny Abby arrived to pick the kids up to go take them to The Unity Gazebo Courtyard. This was a beautiful, elegant, spacious place located in the middle of all of these "Million Dollars" estates. The outside was shaped just like a huge gazebo. It was used for gatherings such as: bible study, get together for neighbors and of course for the children's nannies to hang out with them just because.

The children were a little unsettled when Nanny Abby arrived. Little Nia was screaming because she could not have chocolate chip cookies considering she had them throughout the day. Samone was arguing with her Father because he did not go out to get more CDs to add to her collection. Tremaine was moaning because he wanted to go to the movies earlier, but Reese and Melody did not have time to take him due to prior engagements.

Nia had a bit of chocolate on her cheek.

As Nanny Abby wiped her cheek she said, "Nia, too many chocolate chip cookies are not good for you; I am not going to give you another one. Suck it up and dry those tears."

Nanny Abby grabbed little Nia as if she was a football.

She went to Tremaine's room. "Now, you are the oldest and should be setting an example for your sisters."

Little Nia interrupted to annoy her brother, as she pointed. "Yeah, you da ol'est."

Nanny Abby said with a quickness, "Baby girl, zip it now!"

Little Nia smiled then covered her mouth.

"Nanny Abby, I just want to spend time with my Mom, Dad and believe or not, my little sisters too." Tremaine poured his heart out.

Nanny Abby knew this young soul was right.

"Son, I told you before when you get weary always call on the name of *Jesus* and He will give you peace."

Tremaine poured out his heart even more, "Nanny Abby, I get so mad sometimes. Nanny Abby, are you my Jesus?"

Nanny Abby smiled. At the same time her heart went out to Tremaine. *Nanny Abby tried with all her might to fight away her tears.* "Tremaine, you tickle me with the things you say son. Come on let's go. The party will be starting soon."

Tremaine followed Nanny Abby and Little Nia into Samone's room. As they entered the room, Samone was slinging her old CD's all over the floor.

Nanny Abby asked with an authoritative tone, "Samone, now who are you hurting?"

Samone angrily replied, "Daddy and Mommy should have walked through the door."

"Don't be silly. Samone pick up all of those CD's now," Nanny Abby said with her authoritative tone.

With no hesitations, Samone picked up the CD's. As they headed out of Samone's room, Nanny Abby grabbed Samone pulling her closer.

As they headed out, they ran into Reese and Melody.

Little Nia asked, "Mommy, we got time to go to da park Sat'rday?"

Melody was all dolled up and ready for the party bash. She started to feel a strong guilt, but tried her best to ignore. She could barely look her daughter in her eyes. When she finally got herself together, *trying her best to be convincing*, she answered, "Nia honey, Mommy will try her best to make time for the park next week."

"Mommy, you say it all da time. Mommy next week

neba come."

Melody looked at Little Nia and gently smiled it off. Reese reached over and kissed Little Nia on the cheek. Samone looked at her parents then quickly dashed out to the car with Tremaine behind.

Nanny Abby was putting the key in the ignition, she tried to remember how to start the engine. Tremaine reminded her that she only had to push one button. Of course Nanny Abby still proudly drives her orange1978 Monte Carlo. She looked around in this beautiful Mercedez Benz with all the bells and whistles; it was everything anyone could ever want. Then her heart admired these precious children who were sitting and waiting for her love for the next several hours. As she continued to look around in the back seat, Little Nia blew her a kiss. When she looked at Samone, *who was still angry with her parents*, Samone somehow found it in her disappointed little heart to tell Nanny Abby, "Thank you Nanny Abby."

Nanny Abby, with a most gentle tone responded, "You are so welcome, my child."

She turned to Tremaine.

Tremaine asked, "Nanny Abby, I often wonder how we would be kept without you around."

She reached over and patted him on the shoulder. She assured him, "I'm here for a reason son."

As they headed to the Unity Gazebo Courtyard, she thought, *"Father, I would choose these babies and my '78 Carlo any day."*

She felt a warm, gentle touch from God. Nanny Abby's heart was full.

As soon as Nanny Abby and the kids left, both Reese and Melody felt guilty about not having enough time to spend with their children.

Melody said, "Reese honey, I feel so horrible."

Reese pretended he didn't know why Melody was feeling so horrible. He wrapped his muscular arms around his Barbie Doll of a wife, which he so adored. "Baby, you know the kids are always upset about something or another. We give them too much and that is the problem."

Melody responded, "We give them too many things and not enough time."

Reese reminded her. "Honey, you know we have businesses to run and besides, we have an awesome lifestyle anyone would want."

Melody was always sweetened by Reese's so-called comforting words.

She calmed down, "Honey, you always make me feel so much better."

Reese smiled, ran his fingers through his hair.

He admiringly looked at Melody from head to toe. "Baby, how beautiful can a woman get? Yeah baby you look hot tonight as usual. Now, are you ready to have a party?"

Melody was excited by this point. They gave each other a high-five while they laughed with excitement.

The chef and bartender arrived at Reese and Melody's estate. The bartender, *Trek*, overheard Reese, Melody and the chef having a conversation about their church services.

Before Trek thought about what he was doing or saying, he went over to where they were, while he intuitively smiled. "Yo, I don't usually bartend for church folk. I couldn't help, but hear your conversation with the chef."

The entire time he was speaking to Reese and Melody he was checking Melody out. When he made that statement, an overwhelming feeling of guilt came over Reese and Melody again. They paused immediately; Melody was almost in tears. As macho as Reese usually was, this statement caught him off guard as well.

Trying his best not to show it, Reese said, "Church folk, why? Man, do you think church folk aren't supposed to have fun?"

Trek responded quickly. "Oh, I didn't say that."

Melody told him. "Yes Trek, Christians are allowed to have fun as well as anyone else. So Trek, are we the only Christians you've ever seen that had an alcohol bar?"

Trek admiringly looked at Melody. He asked, "Do you really want to know the truth?"

"Of course, that's why I asked."

Trek answered not realizing what he was saying at the moment. "No, but there are so-called Christians who go to church every Sunday and there are your Christians who try their best to be like Jesus."

By that time, Melody and Reese are feeling less and less of a Christian.

Melody inquired, "Trek, are you a Christian?"

No, I'm not saved, but when that day comes I know I am going to have to ditch this job."

Reese and Melody asked at the same time, "Why?"

Trek nervously answered, "Mr. and Mrs. Ford, I am sorry if I have made you a little upset."

Reese responded, "Bro, it is cool. Let's just end this conversation. It will be easier on everyone."

Trek was in an uncomfortable place. He immediately responded. "That's cool with me."

As Trek walked away to set up for the party he thought about what just happened and how the conversation just didn't add up.

Everyone was arriving at the party, dressed to the nines; and very excited about the time that they were going to have. They were having their pictures done when they entered the party. As everyone walked through, they admired the scenery.

There were live cut flowers inside vases that were hand made in Italy. All of the curio cabinets were sparkling like they were freshly cleaned. The fine china was breath taking. The 14 karat gold around the tips of the china grabbed everyone's attention. The living room was a huge, round room filled with furniture that was a mixture of walnut and mahogany custom made. The den was just as beautiful with walnut furniture throughout. There dining room were all set for a formal dinner although they were having a party bash. Reese and Melody had the furniture set up for a party. The bathroom was similar to a women and men's dressing room. On the men side, there was cologne for men, manly lotions, men ties, handkerchiefs and Cuff links. On the women side, there was a huge, luxurious dressing area. Perfumes, lotions, nail polishes, shawls, earrings, fancy fans, and everything else that a woman may need at any moment. The entire bathroom was a cream color and twenty- two karat gold framing the mirrors and the dressing chairs. Whenever someone walked in, it took one's breath away.

John and Rachel, Tressie and Ronald, Sasha and Paul, Joanne and Howard, and Ridge and Scarlette all had arrived, they all were mingling. Ridge and Scarlette had their Long Island Ice Teas. Joanne had a screwdriver and Howard had a light beer. Sasha and Paul had strawberry daiquiris. Tressie had a Long Island Iced Tea and Ronald had sweet tea. John and Rachel had their usual sweet, ice tea.

As they mingled, a young lady that was a little tipsy came over to them. She asked, "Hey, aren't you guys the Fords' rich, church folk friends?"

Everyone looked at one another not knowing how to respond.

Scarlette laughed and sarcastically proclaimed, "Well, my husband and I are the rich friends, but not the church folk friends."

The young lady kept pulling her skirt down with her drink in her hand. The high heels she wore were so high she looked as though she was wearing stilts.

The young lady asked Scarlette. "What do you mean?"

Rachel jumped in before the conversation got heated.

"Sweetheart, now what does it matter whether we are rich or church folk?"

The young lady responded, "Church folk don't party."

Joanne and Tressie said at the same time, "Why not?"

The young lady answered loudly, "Yeah, seasoned saints!"

All of the men looked at one another and secretly smiled.

Tressie and Joanne began to get more annoyed. Rachel immediately jumped back in the conversation. When she got back in the conversation Reese and Melody came over to see what the problem was. When the young lady realized Reese and Melody was there, she knew this was not good for her, although she was a little tipsy.

Reese and Melody automatically turned to Rachel and asked, "What is the problem?"

Rachel felt for the young lady and kindly explained. "Oh, the young lady is just being a little silly; it is nothing that we adults can't handle. Everything is fine."

Reese ran his fingers through his hair. Then he let go of Melody's hand. "Eve, *referring to the young lady*, you are lucky we invited you to come. You are always causing trouble at the gym!"

Eve was tipsy but alert, "Big Boss, I'm feeling good right now. I didn't mean any harm."

Instead of ignoring the young lady, Joanne blurted out. "Reese, yeah she meant no harm, but she called Tressie and I Seasoned Saints."

Tressie was feeling a little tipsy as well as Joanne. Tressie asked, "Now, Reese do we look like seasoned saints?"

Rachel longed to keep peace, "Ladies, this young lady is young enough to be your daughter. Please, can you ladies find it in your hearts to forgive her? You don't know what this young lady is going through."

By this time, Eve was feeling acceptance and love like she had never felt before. Eve thought, *"Someone actually care about me and she is a stranger."* She quickly looked up to heaven.

Sasha, Scarlette, Joanne, Melody and Tressie were having a conversation with Rachel. John was standing with the other men having a conversation, but carefully watching to see if Rachel needed him.

Sasha wondered, "Rachel, how do you always seem to make things better in the moment of chaos? Eve was clearly wrong. I don't care how young she is. She is old enough to know what an insult is."

Rachel explained, "Sasha, you have to remember she is young. If you think about the things we use to say and do at that age. It would be easier to ignore some of the problems we run into."

Scarlette laughed then commented, "Never mind the young lady Eve; let's take a look at these *Seasoned Saints*.

Joanne and Tressie tried their best to look away. They knew what Scarlette was trying to say. Of course, Scarlette did not care.

Sasha ignorantly asked, "Rachel, is it always appropriate to include God at parties? People are clearly sinning including me. I know I have had more than enough alcohol."

Rachel was as calm as a cucumber. "Sasha, you know that you should always include God in everything that you do."

Sasha quickly defended herself and the others. "Christians are allowed to have fun as well. I don't know anyone that is always operating in the spirit. People expect to let their hair down at parties."

Rachel explained, "Christians are allowed to have fun, but there is a name that you as a believer have to uphold and that is the name of Jesus. Remember Sasha, we are to be in this world not of this world. No one is perfect, but God also gave us common sense and I firmly believe we should use it at all times."

Sasha responded arrogantly, "Rachel, I don't mean any harm, but everyone is not as perfect as you. If I could have a pinch of your walk with Christ…"

Tressie jumped in the conversation. "Rachel, I feel I am in lock down when you are around. I feel so guilty."

Rachel, having that bold spirit for the Lord turned to her. "Maybe you need to pay attention to how you live instead of how I live. Sister, you know I love you. And I will do anything for you, but I'm not the reason you feel that way."

Joanne jumped in agreeing with Tressie. "Yes, I agree with Tressie; I feel like I am in chains when you are around. I just feel like I can do nothing wrong in your presence."

Rachel explained, "See, that's the problem; I am not the one you should be worried about. Ladies, I don't have a heaven or hell to put you in."

Melody related to the other girls. "This is ironic because Reese and I had a similar conversation earlier with the bartender. Christians should be allowed to have fun just as well as anyone else."

Rachel explained even more. "Of course Christians are allowed to have fun, but if whatever you are doing doesn't line of with the word of God, it is not godly, therefore it is not right point blank."

Scarlette looked from one lady to the next jokingly commented. "Now now ladies, what would your Jesus do at this party? I don't believe in God or Jesus. But would your Jesus or your God be drinking until drunkard? As a matter of fact would he even associate himself with other people who are not in the same boat as him?"

Rachel commented, "Scarlette, I know that you have been drinking, but you make a good argument. Scarlette, my Jesus, as you would put it loved everyone. Like I said before, you should always strive to live according to God's commands and God's commands only. Scarlette, but I must say this. Jesus mingled with people, others would not associate with."

Scarlette asked sarcastically, "Rachel, I don't know, but do the other women know that?"

Although the other ladies were drinking continuously, they still somehow felt a knot in the pit of their stomachs as soon as Scarlette made that comment. They started questioning themselves again. Rachel knew after that comment and those questions that it would affect the ladies. Not long after Scarlette made those comments, the ladies and their husbands prepared to go home.

When they were preparing to leave, all of Melody and Reese's employees were mesmerized with their presence because of their status in the community. While they walked through the party, to the employees they were shadows of movie stars. There were employees scattered all over Reese and Melody's home. Many of them were drinking and dancing. There were employees that actually weren't drinking. They just mingled. In the den, there were a few couples that were sitting together.

One of the young men said, "That must be what being a celebrity is all about; man those people have a certain aura around them."

The other young man laughed. He commented, "No man that is all that money that you feel. Man, I was checking those women out. Every one of those women had on designer dresses, shoes and purses."

One of the young ladies commented. "Yes with all that they have I wonder if they are happy?"

The other young lady, with a childish tone, responded, "How can a lady not be happy driving what they drive, wearing what they wear and for the most part living where they live. Besides, who would not want to live in the Ridgeland Towers of Atlanta? You know all around town everyone has this saying, *"You haven't made it until you are at the top of the towers."*

Another young lady commented, "Yes, that's all you here. It just makes you wonder -will I ever get a touch of the hem of His garment?"

The young lady's husband replied. "Honey, if He can do it for one person, He can do it for the next person. The question is- do you have faith?"

The other young man asked, "Are they really Christians? Man they were drinking just as much as anyone else."

Another young man commented, "Yeah man, there are lots of people who wear that name. The question is…do they wear it well? Or do they wear it just because it sounds good when they speak?"

Sasha and Paul, Scarlette and Ridge, and Joanne and Howard all walked home to their estates. Tressie and Ronald, of course, arranged for their limo to take them home. There was no reason for them to have their limo waiting, but Ronald would do anything to please his wife.

Several minutes later, Rachel and John went to say good-bye to Reese and Melody. They felt in their spirits that Reese and Melody desperately wanted to talk.

Reese wondered, "John man, I have been wondering, what did you think of the party?"

"Reese, you know our parties usually end up being a prayer meeting. Every time you and Melody have your parties, man I support it because you are our friends. To be honest, sometimes we struggle with the decision to come."

Reese ran his fingers through his hair with a sudden lump in his throat. Deep down inside he knew what John was thinking.

"Man, you know I have these businesses and we have our reputation to uphold. I'm the boss and I should stand out."

John was a little annoyed. "Reese you have to know your employees and anyone else of that matter don't have a heaven or hell to put you in. I don't worry about pleasing man, I worry about pleasing God. You have to change your way of thinking. It is powerful when you have a renewed mind."

Melody commented desperately wanting sympathy. "John, I just feel like we have gotten beat up the entire night because we want to have a little fun."

John responded with a most gentle tone. "Look Melody, I did not come to judge. Reese simply asked a question and I gave him an honest answer. You should know us by now. Now, if I told you what you wanted to hear, then I would not be my brother's keeper. Melody, you know we love your family and we will never do anything to hurt you. We are here only to help you."

Rachel smiled. "Melody honey, we need to do what is in the word."

Melody was really frustrated.

She commented to Rachel. "Everyone acts like it is a crime to have fun."

John strongly suggested, "Look, why don't the two of you talk to one of the associate Ministers or one of the Deacons at church. It seems to me you all know deep down in your hearts that you have to change for the good of the family."

Reese ran his fingers through his hair. He raised his voice slightly and of course he was frustrated at this point. "Forget it man, I don't want to discuss my personal business with anyone else."

Rachel tried to bring a little comfort. "Reese, sometimes counseling is all a family needs."

John and Rachel glanced at one another and decided it was time to depart.

John said, "Brother, I can imagine how you feel. You and Melody should discuss it because this is concerning your walk with Christ. You have to remember, it's not about us, it's about Jesus."

Rachel and John said their goodbyes, gave their friends a hug and went home.

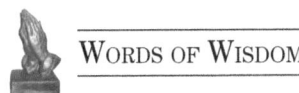
*Brothers and Sisters, how many times do we have to go
around the same mountain before we learn our lesson? Will
it take a life time to grasp what God is telling us? Time is
too precious to waste on strongholds! Remember God speaks
through our children all the time. Sometimes, we take
the backseat of being the adult and at the same time not
recognizing our children are in the drivers' seat. When are
we going to wake up and realize we need to give children
more credit? What does it take to change one person's
life? A simple word or phrase can change the course of
someone's life. We must always be cautious of what comes
out of our mouths at all times. We should always remember
what the word says, "What goes into someone's mouth does
not defile them, but what comes out of their mouth, that
is what defiles them." Matthew 15:11 (N.I.V). We must
remember man in this case is referring to a woman or
man. Are we speaking life or death with our tongues?*

CHAPTER 13

1 Peter 4:12-13 Dear friends, do not be surprised at the painful trial you are suffering, as though something strange were happening to you. But rejoice that you participate in the sufferings of Christ, so that you may be overjoyed when his glory is revealed. (N.I.V.)

It was early May.

John, Rachel, and the kids traveled to Rachel's hometown in South Carolina.

It was bitter, sweet while they were packing for the trip.

Charlotte asked, "Mommy is it going to be better this time?"

Rachel answered, "Sweetheart, I just hope and pray that it will be a blessing this time."

Charles commented, "Mom, I would rather stay home where there is peace and quiet. There is always a showdown in South Carolina. They don't appreciate you and Daddy, Mom. Do they hate us?"

"Kids we really have to trust God and believe one day it will get better." Rachel kindly tried to uplift the children's spirits.

Charles and Charlotte all at once said, "Mom that's what you always say."

Rachel replied, "Our time is not God's time."

John said with a smile, "Rachel that's what you always say."

To lighten the mood a little, John laughed. Sweetheart, we have to add some humor in it."

Rachel looked at John. She smiled, but was frustrated at the same time.

"John it breaks my heart to see my family live the way they do. We all grew up in church. John they know who Jesus is."

By this time Rachel was in tears. John wrapped his arms around her.

"Leave it in God's hands sweetheart."

"I know you are supposed to leave it in God's hands, but it is so much easier said than done, especially, when it comes to my family because they need miracles right now. Truly, John you know that I know got work miracles every day. You have to put some sort of effort forward."

They were half the way to South Carolina. John was flipping through the stations and suddenly he heard a song that always reminded him and Rachel of their childhood and the elderly back in their hometowns. He turned the volume up because both he and Rachel absolutely adored this song. As soon as he turned the volume up, everyone woke up. Rachel turned to John. Tears were flowing as she thought about the many folk in South Carolina who played a big part in the woman that she had become. John took her hand.

As she took in the words of this song, Rachel started thinking about her childhood. She thought about the church Deacons and the lovely old Mothers of her church back at home. They would always give her guidance and tough love whether she wanted or not. When Rachel became old enough to realize God placed these very people in her life just for her, she loved and respected them even more.

She held her head down because of the overwhelming love and compassion she had for everyone.

Then Rachel tried as she did numerous times before to make sense of it all. She thought, *"Yes, they are elderly, but there has to be a reason why they are in those situations. There are young folk who are doing worse than the elderly; that's even sadder. Everyone knows Jesus back at home. Is He really the head of their lives? Surely, God does not want his people to struggle. They struggle so... nearly everyone. This makes my spirit cringe because I know things could be so much easier if they truly put God ahead of their lives."*

Charlotte commented, "Mommy does that song make you think of people back at home? Mommy, I like that country song. It's pleasant in my ears."

"Yeah Momma, this song makes you think of older people and how they are really doing. It really makes you think about them." Charles felt the need to give his opinion as well.

John explained, "Yes, we should never take anything for granted and we should always look after our elders even if it's just a prayer from our hearts. Children we have to consider all of the elderly, not just our family, strangers as well."

As the song came to a close, John and Rachel wiped their tears away.

All of Rachel's family members were still living in South Carolina. Rachel was the only one that moved away. John, Rachel, and the children stayed with her parents. It just so happened, Rachel's parents had enough room this time. Rachel's parents' home was a place of refuge for the entire family. If someone would get laid off or any of the family members wanted to save money, they would stay at Mama Lula and Papa Ray's until they got on their feet.

This home is the home that John and Rachel so graciously purchased for them. For years they helped practically everyone that they could until they came to a conclusion. It did not feel right in their spirits to continue the support. They felt as though they were hindering instead of helping. The situation frustrated them to no end.

When they came home, it was like they were movie stars. Everyone was waiting, as usual, for them over at Rachel's parents' house. Momma Lula and Poppa Ray were waiting at the door with open arms. As they walked through, her three brothers-Byron, Raymond, Sammie and their children were there. Her three sisters: Sharon, Terri, Patricia and their children were there waiting as well. There were church members, other family members and friends who stood waiting patiently also. No one would miss their arrival.

They always made sure they did not forget anyone because their hearts were so beautiful. They genuinely loved everyone. The nieces and nephews absolutely loved John, Rachel and the kids. As they made their way through the house, one of

Rachel's cousins gave her a hug.

Afterwards, she looked Rachel in the eyes and sarcastically asked, "Cuz, you forgot way I live? What, you too good to come see me. Yeah, my house not a castle lack yours, the leas' you kin do is come and at leas' stay a few minutes."

"Vanessa honey, I can't make it to everyone's house, but thank you for coming today and it's nice seeing you."

Vanessa looked at Rachel with evil eyes. In turn Rachel gave her a smile and a big hug again, as always. Rachel went to the next set of relatives which was her ten-year-old niece Nicole, and her twelve-year-old niece Nija. These precious little children felt John and Rachel's beautiful spirits that oozed Jesus Christ's attributes. As they talked to the nieces, all the other children found themselves gathering around.

Nicole was very excited. "Hey Aunt Rachel yall; we couldn't wait 'til yall came home. You know Aunt Rachel, we love yall. I don't know why our fam'ly act lack that. I wanna be lack you when I grow up. Yall that light the preacher always talkin' 'bout. Auntie that's hard to spot 'round this ol' small town."

Nija agreed, "Yeah Auntie Rachel, yall movie stars."

John kindly flipped the subject. "Sweetheart, we are not movie stars. Did you know you can be anything you want to be?"

"Uncle, I wanna have a lotta money lack yall."

He looked down at little Nija. He explained, "Baby, you have got to know Jesus Christ. Anyone can have lots of money, but when you have Jesus you have everything."

Nija said, "I know Jesus, Uncle."

Charlotte said with great excitement, "Nija, I know Jesus too!"

Charles jumped on board, "Yeah, some people don't believe in Jesus."

Rachel felt the need to expound. "Yes of course, Charles, there are lots of people who don't know Jesus. Listen! *She looked at each child one by one.* This goes for each of you.

Always pray that others will also know Jesus as well as yourselves. There is nothing to hard for God!"

As John and Rachel made their way through the entire house showing love in the same way that Jesus did, they came across some relatives and friends that were not godly towards them. They felt uneasy as they continued walking through, but still spread their love throughout. Meanwhile, the little children were being blessed because of the seeds that the two planted just by showing love for others who did not appreciate what they had to offer.

Everyone gathered for dinner where ever they could find a place to eat, whether it be standing, sitting at the table or sitting on the floor.

John said the grace. *"Father, bless this food and the hands that prepared it. Father, teach us how to love each other with your love. Bless each household that is represented in this house on today and the ones that weren't able to make it. Help us to realize how important family is and to cherish every moment that we have with each other. Father, last but not least add a special blessing over Mama Lula and Papa Ray."*

As he was saying the grace, practically every child's head was bowed. Many adults bowed their heads as well, but then there were other adults that just refused to bow their heads. Some were talking to one another, being totally disrespectful. One of Rachel's little cousins jerked her mother's hands to let her know John was saying the grace. One of Rachel's nieces took it upon herself to let the adults that were gathered around her know that Uncle John was saying the grace. With convictions and embarrassment, these adults bowed their heads, adhering and listening to the children who took a bold stand. The adults who chose to fall by the waste side talked the entire time John said the grace. These adults carried misery, distress, trouble, bitterness, and sadness all over their faces.

Everyone was eating. Papa Ray and Mama Lula were talking to Rachel and John. They were asking Rachel and John about their church, their friends, and their social life. Everyone got quiet when they were having a conversation. John and Rachel's lifestyle always fascinated everyone. But oh no, many would never admit it. All they wanted to do was make John and Rachel feel guilty of being blessed.

Across the table where Rachel and John were sitting, one of Rachel's cousins, with a mouth full of food and his elbows stretched out on the table asked, "Hey Cuz you think if I move to Atlanta I kin fin' me a good job?"

John kindly answered, "I don't know, Cousin BJ, but we can certainly pray about it."

Cousin BJ burped. All the kids giggled. Cousin BJ commented, "Man, you pray about everything."

"We are supposed to pray about everything."

Cousin BJ laughed loudly and obnoxiously. He commented, "Yo, so that's how yall always rollin' in them Beemers and Benzes."

Everyone at the table laughed. Rachel's sister, Patricia, looked over at another cousin and gave a negative and disgusting look. Another cousin nudged the other and gave Rachel and John the creepiest look. There were some teenaged cousins that were in one of the bedrooms and they all were laughing and joking about the comment Cousin BJ made. Mama Lula had enough.

She chastised, "Now yall know that ain't right in God's eyes. Yall should know better, this fam'ly. Did yall hear sweet son-in-law prayer? God not pleased!"

Papa Ray agreed, "Why yall act that a way to'ard fam'ly? Now this time yall not gonna treat 'em all kinda ways. It ove' now, if yall ain't gonna treat'em right, leave!"

Everyone got themselves together; because they knew when Mama Lula and Papa Ray spoke in an authoritative voice, it was time to switch gears and quick.

Mama Lula and Papa Ray would always have a little gospel music playing softly whenever the family sat down to eat a meal.

Soon after Papa Ray's comment, a song came on the radio

that everyone related to. On Sundays, growing up everyone would gather at someone's house. They would play this gospel song and the whole time it was on all the children would just sit, listen and sing. The adults would sing, cry and praise God the whole time.

This was a beautiful, touching family song. The song reminded everyone of how valuable our time is with our family. One of the guys in the background had a very deep voice. Throughout the song he sang, *"Tomorrow is not promised to us, therefore family is not promised to us tomorrow!"* The background singers hummed the entire song. The background singers *humming* were contagious to all listeners. The leader of the song ministered, *"What would you do if you suddenly lost a loved one? Let go of the small stuff! Let go of the past! Tomorrow is not promised to anyone!* At the end of the song the leader powerfully ministered, *"Our Mother, our Father, our sister, our brother is not promised to us tomorrow! Love your family today!"* As the song played, Rachel, her sisters, brothers and cousins instantly felt the bond that they once shared with one another when they were children. John realized instantly that this song was very powerful. He heard the song before, but not this version of it. This song's anointing ripped through Mama Lula and Papa Ray's house like a silent twister. There were about fifty family members and friends in Mama Lula and Papa Ray's house. When the song was on, there was family unity that they haven't had in years. There were some family members who started praying. Others started opening up about their walk with Christ. Some who wasn't going to church started thinking about going back. Others asked about salvation. When the song was over, the few that had not heard it before asked, "What group sings that song?" The family started putting forth their best effort to be on their best behavior. The rest of the afternoon was truly a blessing for Rachel's family.

John, Rachel, and kids went to church with Mama Lula and Papa Ray. Rachel grew up in this very church. It was called

Pleasant Valley Baptist Church. A lot of the Deacons and Seasoned Saints were still there. Every time Rachel came home, the church had a packed house. Folks wanted to know anything was possible when it came to our Almighty Father. In a silent cry, folks wanted to be encouraged just by being in church sitting near the Richardson family.

The Pastor asked for the visitors to stand. John, Rachel, and the kids stood up and there were several other couples who stood up. Rachel and John always felt an overwhelming presence of God when it was time to speak, because they knew that it was nobody, but our Almighty Father who was the reason why they were so blessed. When Rachel and John stood up to speak, there were whispering all over the church, as always. Some were pleasant comments and some were not so pleasant.

One person obnoxiously asked, "Why they cryin'? They got ever'thing in the world. Shoot, we the ones need to be cryin'."

Everyone turned around and could not believe that anyone would comment so loudly.

Immediately afterwards, John and Rachel automatically looked in the direction that the comment came from and before they knew it, at the same time both gave their blessing. "God bless you."

John said respectfully, "To the pastor, the first lady, officers, members and friends, it is great to be able to visit our family and to visit my wife's church one more time. You know, my wife and I always pray for you all and hopefully you are praying for us as well. I thank God because he paused... *John started rocking back and forth.* I don't know where I'd be if it wasn't for the Lord on our side. *Tears streamed while he looked around to catch every eye he could possibly catch.* Now, I want you all to know that we love you and if there is anything that we can possibly do for you, we will."

As they sat down, John and Rachel's heart was full, Charlotte slowly wiped away her tears and Charles' eyes and heart took everything in while observing his family.

In the middle of the service, the adult choir started singing one of Rachel's favorite songs. Mama Lula and Papa Ray's eyes watered up because they knew this was one of Rachel's favorite songs. When Rachel was a child, she only knew she loved this song, but not knowing exactly why. The words were so simple, but powerful in a mighty way.

As soon as Rachel heard this song, she started thinking of the times at church when she was a youngster. She also thought about lost souls in her family and any other souls that were lost. As the words of the song ministered to Rachel, the presence of God trickled on everyone in the congregation. John, Mama Lula and Papa Ray were up on their feet shouting and praising the Lord. If anyone was there that did not feel the power of God they didn't have anything in them. As the choir sang, Rachel went into a daze while she praised. She went to another place imagining everybody actually taking the Lord with them everywhere they go. Rachel imagined them taking the Lord in the streets, in the crowd, in their homes, and even when they were all alone. As the choir continued singing, she pictured everybody taking the Lord on the highways and bi-ways.

Rachel's cup runneth over, saturating everyone else who surrounded her.

After the benediction, Rachel and John were bombarded with people wanting to talk, searching for advice. The eldest mother in church went up to them. Rachel immediately embraced her because, as always, seeing Mother Steverson brought back childhood memories. Ever since Rachel could remember, she knew her. Mother Steverson always encouraged young children to always strive for the best and settle for nothing else. She always gave treats to all the children in the church. If she didn't have enough for every child, she would not give at all.

As Rachel embraced Mother Steverson, she slowly spoke with a very low tone, "God is sho blessin you baby. Yo—yo babies have precious spirits. Yo—yo man is sho hand---some."

Rachel and John smiled.

Rachel gave Mother Steverson a kiss. "Thank you Mother, you look beautiful. I see you are still taking care of yourself and you are still giving encouraging words of wisdom."

As they were having a conversation, Cousin Roy and his wife Rosa went over to Rachel, John and the kids, and hugged each of them.

"Cuz, we didn't make it to Mama Lula and Papa Ray house. I heard yall got 'motional. You know Cuz that was our song on Sundays. We need to bring them days back. I still love you Cuz; I don't know what wrong with fam'ly. Yeah, that song came at the right time."

John said with great confidence, "Cousin Roy, we pray for everyone even when we are being attacked for no reason. We do hurt when people, especially family, intentionally hurt us. Yes Brother, it is hard sometimes turning the other cheek."

Cousin Roy gave his opinion, "Man, if that was me I would'a knock somebody on the cheek. We in chuch now, but I would'a laid'm out in some… if you know what I mean Cuz, colorful words."

Rosa agreed, "We proud of yall. They should be happy yall doing good. That is bad when yo own fam'ly can't be happy fo' ya."

John and Rachel glanced at one another then looked at Rosa and gave her a kind smile.

Later that day after church, Rachel ran into one of her cousins that she had not seen in years. This cousin had a child who had autism. Several years prior Rachel tried to get in contact with her, but for whatever reason was not successful.

John, Rachel and the kids were getting some groceries for Mama Lula and Papa Ray's. Rachel noticed Michelle before Michelle noticed her. She quickly ran over to her as she got closer, she noticed the stress in Michelle's face. When their eyes met, Rachel quickly felt the intense trouble and heartbreak that almost brought her to her knees.

When Rachel felt this intensity, she quickly prayed to herself, *"Father, you know what Michelle needs, please Father give me whatever I need to help me be a blessing to my cousin. In Jesus's name, Amen."*

When Rachel got herself together, she and Michelle embraced like they were not going to see each other, ever again.

"Michelle, I'm sorry I didn't get in contact with you."

Michelle softly replied, "Rachel, I didn't want to be contacted. When I found out my youngest son had autism my whole world came tumbling down. I felt like before the autism I was almost a carbon copy of you and your life. As you know, my husband had a great job making lots of money. I was in college, aspiring to be a counselor. We had a beautiful home."

"You can still have those dreams. Michelle, I know you know who Jesus is. Jesus can turn any situation around. Honey, you have lost your passion for Jesus."

By this point, John, Charles, and Charlotte were waiting in the car.

"Rachel, I lost my passion for everything when autism tapped me on my shoulder without any warning. I have been on Prozac for a while now and my son, Brock, is on Ritalin. I never thought I would ever have a child with special needs. It has been several years since we found out and I still don't know how to handle the situation in a positive way; and getting a divorce sure doesn't help."

Rachel looked at Michelle with great concern. She asked, "Michelle, where are you living now?"

"The kids and I are living with Mom in her single-wide trailer. Yeah, Rachel the story gets better."

Rachel heart bled even more. "Honey, I am going to wait in the car and then follow you home. I feel the need to sit and talk with you for a while. I'm sorry, do you mind?"

After Michelle got finished shopping, she came out with her groceries and got in the car. Her car was a couple cars down from John and Rachel's. Rachel watched Michelle as she got in her car and realized how deep her valley must have been. As Michelle cranked her car up, Rachel and John noticed her car seemed like it did not want to start. John immediately jumped out of the car to help. As soon as he got to the car, Michelle's car started.

John dropped Rachel off at Michelle's Mother's house. As Rachel and Michelle walked in the house Rachel spoke to her Aunt Minnie.

"Hi Aunt Minnie, I haven't seen you in a long time. How are you doing?"

Aunt Minnie answered with an uplifted spirit, "I'm gonna make it child. As long as I got Jesus, yeah child I keep on keepin' on. That's what I tell my baby Michelle all the time."

Michelle jumped in the conversation. She obnoxiously said, "Momma, not everyone is as strong as you. It is just too much for me to handle. I am at the lowest point in my life. I never thought I'd have to go back to where I came from."

Aunt Minnie said, "Baby sometimes God let us go thu things so he can get yo 'tention."

Michelle is even more annoyed by this point. Rachel felt the need to interrupt the conversation.

Rachel said, "Michelle, Aunt Minnie has a point. Honey, do you blame God for the situation?"

As soon as Rachel made that statement Little Brock came in and abruptly jumped on his Mother Michelle. He was making noises continuously sounding much like the human beat box. Michelle hated when Little Brock made those noises. Rachel desperately tried her best to smooth things over for a moment.

Michelle with great hurt and pain looked Rachel dead in the eyes and said, "Now, how would you like this lifestyle? Rachel, your lifestyle is spectacular. Look at your house and what you drive. Yes, of course God has blessed you. You have it easy."

Rachel explained, "Honey, I know that I am blessed. I feel like I am abundantly blessed because of my relationship with God. The materialistic things are just a bonus. If I lose all of it today or tomorrow, I will still have enough because I will still have Jesus. Do you think it is easy when the people I love continue to struggle? It is hard, even, watching a total stranger struggle."

Michelle remembered, "Rachel, there was always something about you growing up. You were always the one who actually loved going to church and you really loved it when we would have quartet groups come to the church. I didn't realize it until just a second ago. My God, you are still praising Him."

Rachel agreed, "Yes, I didn't realize it then, but now that I know who Jesus really is, I know now that our Lord God Almighty was working back then. Michelle, God is working even when you think He isn't. You hold on because before you know it change will come."

Michelle's whole demeanor changed at that moment. Her face lit up like a Christmas tree and Little Brock's noises were slowly disappearing. Her eyes became filled with tears and the love that she once felt for Jesus Christ was there in an instant. She felt God's touch and automatically went to her knees.

Michelle screamed, "Momma! Rachel! I am going to be alright."

At that point, Rachel and Aunt Minnie's tears were running like an over flowing river, but this river was over flowing with joy.

Aunt Minnie said, "Baby, you goin' back to chuch?"

Rachel reassured Aunt Minnie. "I know you are Michelle; I can feel Jesus all over you."

Michelle was still holding Brock. She looked to Aunt Minnie then to Rachel, "It is going to be different from now on. I realize how I love Jesus and how I can trust Him. I don't understand the sudden change of heart, but God knows I receive it."

She dropped her head slowly and with a very low tone, "Father, how could I forget you? You were right here with me all the time."

Aunt Minnie looked at Rachel. "Baby, she los' huh husban' and huh nice home and cars, but baby it don't cost a thang for our Jesus."

John and the kids came back. Rachel opened the door. As

soon as they came in they felt the presence of the Lord.

Aunt Minnie admired Rachel's family, "Baby, you have a fine fam'ly. My child, how them chil'len grown. Young man, *referring to John*, you 'memba me yo' Aunt Minnie?"

"Yes, Ma'am I do. How have you been Aunt Minnie?"

"Son, I'm go be alright 'cause I got Jesus by my side."

Charles and Charlotte went outside where the other kids were.

John said to Michelle, "I don't know what was trying to disrupt and invade your mind, but we can do all things through Christ who strengthens us."

"Rachel, you and John are such an inspiration for the entire family. You have beautiful children, a beautiful home, and beautiful cars. What really stands out is the relationship you have with Christ. May God keep you guys and continue blessing you. I know it is going to take some time, but I am going to get back on my feet and every day is not going to be Sunday."

Rachel wiped her eyes. "Michelle, I am so touched because your whole outlook is different from within an hour ago. God works in ways that even the most intellectual speaker or person can't explain."

Aunt Minnie was very excited. "Baby, ain't Jesus good? I know my baby and grandbabies go be alright."

Rachel said, "Michelle and Aunt Minnie, if John and I can be of any assistance, please let us know. I am going to leave our information with you all and we will be also calling from time to time."

Rachel and John, without realizing it, went over to little Brock. Little Brock looked up to Rachel then to John. Rachel knelt down then John knelt as well. She grabbed his hand. Little Brock started to sound like the human beat box again. John and Rachel glanced at one another.

Rachel silently prayed. *"Father, you have the power to continually keep little Brock calm and you have the power to heal. Father let your will be done. In Jesus's name, Amen."*

Right afterwards little Brock smiled. He gave them a hug.

As they walked out of the door, Michelle quickly ran up to them and whispered, "He never looks anyone in the eyes or touches anyone other than myself or Mama. I thank God for you both."

The next day at Mama Lula and Papa Ray's, there was a house full for breakfast. There was a spread throughout the dining room table. The food included: pancakes, eggs, sausage, turkey bacon, country grits, bagels, homemade biscuits with gravy, rice pudding, tomatoes, orange juice, apple juice, and southern sweet, sweet tea. All of Rachel's siblings, children and husbands or wives were there for breakfast. The adults ate at one table and the children ate at another table or anywhere they could find a comfortable seat.

The adults were eating in the dining room while the children ate in the big, great room fit for children. There were fun dinosaur high chairs, elephant toddler chairs, leopard print sofas; a great big beautiful inside outdoor table just for the teen agers. Place around the big table were tiger print smaller tables. All of the centerpieces were equipped with scriptures and surrounding the scriptures were photos of all the children from the time they were born until most recent.

The atmosphere was always thick and a little uneasy for everyone. Rachel broke the ice as usual and asked her siblings whether or not they were coming to Atlanta to visit anytime soon.

Rachel's eldest sister Sharon commented, "You know you always say that when you come home."

"I mean it because I love all of you. You know this big Sis."

Rachel's sister, Terri, spitefully asked, "Who wanna come to yo' house to feel lack we nobodys?"

John immediately got into the conversation. "Terri, Rachel and I love all of you. It breaks my heart to hear you say that, especially to your sister."

Rachel's other sister, Patricia, felt the need to share. "Yeah, Nija and Nicole think yall some kind of king and queen."

Rachel commented, "I love my nieces and nephews and I want all of them to be successful in whatever God calls for them to do."

Patricia asked, "Oh, so we don' want the bes' fo' our chil'len?"

Her oldest brother Byron protectively jumped in the conversation. "Wait a minute! The only thing Li'l sis ever done was help us. How can yall sit here and say dat. Man her and John even help me out. The thing is I was so stupid 'cause I did wrong things wit' the money."

Papa Ray was overwhelmed. "Yeah, baby girl help all us out. They had dis here house build from the ground up fo' me and yo' Momma."

As soon as Papa Ray said those words, Patricia rudely commented. "Daddy I'm so sick of you sayin' dat. Are we ever gonna live dat one down?"

Rachel's brother, Raymond, rudely agreed. "Yeah Daddy, why we always gotta hear dat. Everybody not rich lack them."

Mama Lula was frustrated. "Son, the only thing yo Daddy is saying is baby girl and sweet son-in-law bless us and still is."

Raymond commented, "Yeah, everybody round town know it to Mama."

Rachel was as cool as a cucumber. "Now I want you all to listen to me and listen well. When John and I blessed Mama and Papa or anyone else it is because Jesus lives in our hearts. Besides, we are supposed to take care of our parents. Now, if you all have a problem with it, take it up with Jesus. John and I will do anything for anyone whether he or she is family or anybody else for that matter."

At this point Rachel was tearing up because those conversations were what she and John always dreaded.

"I love all of you."

Before everyone realized it, their eyes were full.

Youngest brother Sammie finally gave his input firmly and strongly. "Why don't yall give credit way credit is due? I wish I lived for Jesus. That make a big difference."

Mama Lula and Papa Ray were weeping at this moment. Rachel and John got out of their chairs to contain themselves, then came back after a few minutes.

Sammie said, "See that's why they so blessed. Yall wrong, if yall get yallself t'gether then maybe yall will see why they so blessed. I know I need to git myself t'gether."

Terri begrudgingly made a statement. "If I had me a man, I would have it t'gether."

Mama Lula responded, "Terri baby, it don't take a man to git yo life t'gether. Jesus can reach way down baby. He git you way you at."

Patricia with a great resentment commented, "Wait a minute, I'm married wit' chil'len, now 'plain dat."

Mama Lula said, "Patricia, baby, you know who Jesus is. You go to chuch all the time. Course it take more than jus' goin' to chuch."

"That's the problem it's a whole lot of people go to church Sunday after Sunday that jus' can't git it together because they don't put Jesus first. Mama, it's hard to put Jesus first. Oh, it would help if my husban' would at least go to church, at least, once a year."

Mama Lula replied, "Baby, ain't not'ing hard about that, just do it."

Rachel tried again to encourage, "Yes, it doesn't take much to commit your lives to Christ. I wouldn't have it any other way."

John, of course, agreed with his wife. "Yes, Christ is all we know and our children as well. I will say this… we would not be where we are today if it wasn't for the Lord. You do have to humble yourselves and be obedient. Every good thing comes from God. We acknowledge that fact whole heartedly."

Rachel said with all of her heart, "If you are not saved, please get saved. That is the only way you will make it into heaven. My prayer is to see all of my family members in heaven. You know tomorrow is not promised to any of us."

All of Rachel's siblings' demeanors changed in a split second.

Sammie was thankful. "Sis, you and John always make me wanna live my life better. I love yall."

Rachel's brother Raymond recognized, "Yeah, I need to git myself t'gether too. Man maybe one day. It's easy with yall lifestyle; yall rolling in the doe."

Byron said, "Lil Sis, I hope one day I can be lack yall and that is at peace."

He laughed.

He continued, "Oh and the cash would be a blessed bonus."

Mama Lula gave a little wisdom. "Baby girl and Son-in-law, yall listen and listen good. Don't yall let nobody change the way yall livin'. God is well please wit' yall."

Papa Ray whole-heartedly agreed, "Yeah, keep lettin' yo light so shine. Baby girl, *he pointed to his heart*, it good for my old trouble heart."

 WORDS OF WISDOM

Brothers and Sisters, will you be the light for your lost loved ones? We all have family members who need our undivided attention, for at least a moment of our lives. Sometimes our family members need our love, but sometimes our family members are so spiritually dead until they are immune to the enemy's tactics. This situation is detrimental to anyone's walk with Christ. Can you imagine a person who doesn't know Jesus? Take the time out and pray for the souls in our families!

CHAPTER 14

Proverbs 2:1-5 My son, if you accept my words and store up my commands within you, turning your ear to wisdom and applying your heart to understanding, and if you call out for insight and cry aloud for understanding, and if you look for it as for silver and search for it as for hidden treasure, then you will understand the fear of the Lord and find the knowledge of God. (N.I.V.)

R achel called Melody after the South Carolina trip.
Rachel asked, "Are you two going to get counseling?"
"Reese and I talked. We just don't think it is necessary. We are high-class business owners who have to upkeep our image."

"I don't mean any harm, but when you are living for Jesus, you have to uphold his image and his image alone."

"Rachel, it just seems so easy for you and John."

Melody hesitated.

Melody wondered, "I often wonder whether it is as easy as it seems from my perspective."

"Melody, John and I are human and no it is not as easy as it seems sometimes. We have disagreements like anyone else. The main ingredient that makes us as one and that is Jesus. We are trying our best to immolate Him. Now we will never be perfect."

"I know there's no perfect marriage, but if there was one close that would be you and John's."

"Praise God for that compliment because without God it would be impossible to do anything. Melody honey, you should never compare yourself to others because it only frustrates you and your situation."

Melody changed the subject. "How was your trip to South Carolina?"

Rachel paused then explained, "There were some moments that were beautiful and other moments that just weren't necessary. There are many family members that still do not care too much for us for whatever reason and there are some that appreciate us. But, you know Melody I feel in my heart that things are really looking up for my family."

"That is great I hope everything works out for the best for you. You know Rachel you are such a joy to have in anyone's life."

"To God be the glory. Oh, how are the kids doing?"

Melody said, "I don't know what I would do without Nanny Abby."

"Your children are going to be fine; you all are just going to have to put your foot down."

"I know Rachel; it is so easy to buy them anything they want and that way you don't have to hear them scream or cry."

Rachel pleasantly explained, "Honey, you know that is the problem. I know you all have the Fitness Centers, but you all should spend quality time with the children because you are gone a lot. When you and Reese adhere to what God whispers to you, before you know it, the children's attitudes and school work will change for the best."

"Rachel that is easier said than done. By the way, how are Charles and Charlotte?"

"They are doing great, but they are kids."

Rachel and Melody laughed.

"Well Melody, I have to go. I'll see you all at church on Sunday."

Melody commented with a sigh. "Yes, we will be there with the kids and of course Nanny Abby. Thank God for Nannies."

It was mid June- the night before Stacey's dance recital. Everyone was having dinner at the Ivy Estate.

Ronald asked Stacey, "Are you ready for the recital, sweetheart?"

Stacey got so excited. "Yes, Thaddy yes. Everybod' Thaddy go be there."

Steward encouraged his little sister. "Stacey you are going to be great. You practiced everywhere, at home and at the dance studio."

Big sister Melinda climbed on board. "Stacey you are going to knock them dead."

Nanny Nellie, with a great big smile, reassured Stacey. "Sweetheart, Nanny Nellie is so proud of you."

Ronald hyped Stacey up even more. "Sweetheart you have to make sure we have your leotards, dance shoes and everything else that goes with your dance attire."

As fake as she could probably ever be along with a great, big smile Tressie said, "Yes honey, you are going to be great!"

Everyone at the table felt the atmosphere change in the room.

Stacey asked, "Mommy, you go thu be there? I know my Nan' Nell' go thu be there."

"Of course honey, Mommy's going to be there. You are being silly."

Before Steward realized it, he commented, "No, she's not Mom."

Everyone glanced at Steward, but did not say anything.

Ronald tried to smooth everything over. "Of course your Mommy is going to be there sweetheart."

Not long after, Nanny Nellie took Stacey upstairs to help her get ready for bed, while everyone else was downstairs in the den.

Melinda curiously asked, "Mom, did you invite Mrs. Rachel, Mrs. Sasha and your other friends to come to the recital?"

Steward was curious as well. "Yes Mom, Stacey is going to be excited to see her friends at the recital."

Ronald commented, "Yes, that would be great for our Little Stacey to see all of her friends. I know some of my colleagues from work are going to come and support her."

Tressie's body immediately shifted to one side; it was so obvious.

Melinda asked again, "Well Mom, did you invite some friends?"

She slowly answered, "I invited people, but everyone had prior engagements."

Melinda was very annoyed.

She looked at her Mom with suspicious eyes and asked, "Everyone Mom?"

Tressie responded, "I know, I hate when I wait until the last minute to inform people of events that are going to take place."

Steward commented authoritatively, "This is not just an event. It is a huge milestone for Stacey. To other people this may be an ordinary everyday thing, but for Stacey this is like moving a mountain."

Melinda agreed, "Steward, I could not have said it better myself. That little girl up there deserves a lot more credit than what people give her. Special children add special blessings to our lives when we accept them the way our God Almighty accepts them."

Tressie with a guilty conscience responded, "Of course our Stacey is a very special blessing. I know it. You know it; and everyone else knows it."

Steward just could not help himself. "Um, Mom I'm not sure how to accept that comment."

Ronald saved the day for Tressie one more time by shifting the subject.

"Honey it will be a blessing tomorrow to see strides that our Little Stacey has made."

Ronald kissed Tressie on the forehead. Steward and Melinda kindly went upstairs. They just could not bear to see their father pull their mother out of the dirt one more time.

Melinda went to Steward's room to talk to him.

Steward with eyes full of tears asked, "Melinda, how can she still behave this way about Stacey?"

Melinda could not hold back her tears anymore. Barely getting the words out of her mouth, "Steward, Stacey deserves all the attention like any other little girl. How can she call herself a Mother? She is just a woman who gave birth to a child."

Steward held Melinda as she shed her tears, he could not hold his tears back any longer.

When they got themselves together, Steward poured his heart out, "We are going to have to continue playing the role of Stacey's Mother. I love our Father, but he is not helping when he tries to make everything alright when he knows good and well everything is not alright. I'm sorry Melinda, but Dad needs to get a backbone and I so want to say something else instead."

"Steward, Dad adores Mom; he only wants to see her happy and comfortable. To be honest with you, if he didn't try he would be miserable because Mom will not have it any other way."

"Melinda let's pray for our family."

She replied, "Great, we need God to move quickly in this family."

Steward said, "Melinda, this is going to seem crazy, but let's leave enough imaginary room for Mom and Dad. I feel like we are standing in the gap for them at this moment."

Steward prayed, *"Father, please hear our prayer. Strengthen our Mother and Father right now Lord. They need your strength to raise our little sister Stacey. As you know she has special needs. God reach down and pick our parents up when they are at their lowest. We thank you for using us to help raise our little sister. We know now that sometimes the roles are reversed because you trust us. Lord, give our parents the insight to realize when something is wrong. Continue to bless our little sister Stacey and thank you for her beautiful spirit. Without her we would not be the people we are today. Father, hold us when we are in need and keep giving us the Love that we need in order to hold this family together. In Jesus's name, Amen."*

Melinda embraced her brother then went back to her room.

Tressie forced herself to Stacey's room. She was feeling so guilty because she knew she did not want anyone to come to Stacey's dance recital.

When Stacey saw Tressie she got so excited, "Mommy the 'cidel is t'morro. You gonna be dar Mommy?"

"You know I will be there. I told you, honey, when we were at the dinner table."

"Mommy, I know Nan' Nell' gonna be dar. She always dar Mommy. Sometime I git mad Mommy."

Tressie of course, pretended she didn't know what Stacey was talking about.

"Honey, what are you mad about?"

Tressie then sat on the bed next to Stacey.

Stacey looked up at her Mother desperately wanting to know. "You happy Mommy, fo' me? I know Nan' Nell' happy fo' me Mommy. I feel happy when she be wit' me, Mommy. I feel lack someting wrong, Mommy when you round."

Tressie felt like someone socked her in her stomach with a baseball bat. It took her a couple of minutes to get herself together to respond to Stacey.

Tressie, with a trembling in her voice responded. "Baby, why will there be anything wrong if I am around? I am your Mother, sweetheart."

Stacey said, "Lack now Mommy, I feel lack somet'ing goin' on."

"Sweetheart, Mommy loves you and always will love you."

By that moment, Stacey was mentally and physically tired and ready to go to bed. Tressie gave Stacey a kiss and Stacey fell asleep soon after.

Everyone had gone to bed at the Ivy's estate. Tressie paced the hall way because her lie was eating her alive. After pacing for thirty minutes, she went down stairs in the living room to pray. As soon as she started praying, she began to weep.

"Father, please hear my cry and please forgive me because I have sinned again. It is about my little Stacey who I truly love with all my heart, but for the life of me I do not know how to handle her disability. Father, you are the only one that I can really come clean with and Father to be frank, I don't care to handle it in anyway. I want to tiptoe around the situation hoping that one day the problem will just go away. I know I always ask this question- Why me? The way I feel inside is like someone took my heart and forgot about me. You said you will never leave me nor forsake me. Please God, for the recital tomorrow give me a Mother's heart that I need at least for the recital. Continue to work on me as a Mother and please open my eyes to obstacles that I cannot see. In Jesus's name, amen."

The next day at the recital, as they walked in the Atlanta Concert Hall where the recital was going to take place, Stacey got really excited because she knew the time was near. When Stacey got excited, Tressie pulled her hat down and adjusted her shades. Tressie adjusted and pulled until she almost bumped into someone.

Nanny Nellie respectfully asked, "Mrs. Ivy, did you want to join us while we help Stacey prepare for the recital?"

Tressie responded as quickly as possible. "Oh, the both of you can take care of it."

Little Stacey commented, "Nan' Nel' yall fix me up." *She waved her hand to Tressie,* "By Mommy."

Melinda didn't say anything. She reached down and gave her little sister a kiss. She then grabbed her other hand while Nanny Nellie had the other. As Nanny Nellie and Melinda walked Stacey to the back of the Concert Hall to prepare for the recital, Stacey spoke to everyone. Everyone loved her because her spirit was contagious and everyone without realizing wanted a part of her existence. While Melinda and Nanny Nellie were helping Stacey in the back, Tressie, Ronald, and Steward sat in their seats. Ronald got up when he noticed a couple of his colleagues that he invited had arrived. As Ronald talked to his colleagues, they looked over to Tressie and she gave them a quick wave.

Everyone was coming in who Ronald, Nanny Nellie, Steward and Melinda invited. Of course Ronald, Nanny Nellie, Steward and Melinda greeted everyone to tell them how much they appreciate their presence and support. Meanwhile, Tressie was going back and forth to the ladies room to dodge whoever she possibly could. She did not want to talk to anyone; she just wanted the night to be over.

The recital finally started. When it started you could hear children shouting Stacey's name. As a familiar voice shouted "Stacey", Tressie looked over to her left a few rows away from them and there was Melody and her two daughters, Nia and Samone.

As soon as she saw Melody and her girls, she immediately whispered to Ronald, "I have to go to the ladies room. My nose can't seem to stop running."

On her way to the ladies room, she spotted Joanne and her two daughters, Ashley and Amira. Tressie felt like she was in a nightmare that would not end. She went in the bathroom to get some tissue to use for another security blanket. When Tressie came back out, she spotted a seat she thought was perfect for that moment. That seat was in the very back of the Concert Hall. As the recital went on, she heard many parents admiring their children as they danced.

Tressie thought, *"Lord, this is why I cannot be happy. You have Susie homemaker wanna be's all over this Concert Hall and their little girls are just perfect. Now, you tell me, how I'm supposed to feel about my daughter who has disabilities. Is this fair?"*

The recital continued. The couple that Tressie sat next to noticed Stacey. The lady commented, "That is the little girl who has a disability. Bless her little heart; she is certainly trying her best to keep up with the other little girls. She is such a beautiful child and she's always speaking to everyone."

Tressie pulled her hat down even more and adjusted her shades. Tressie thought the couple that she sat next to each smoked a pack of cigarettes before they came to the recital. Between the smell from the couple that she was sitting next to and the dance recital, she didn't know whether she was coming or going. Tressie could hardly breathe because of the smell coming from the couple.

Tressie thought, *"Lord, is this my punishment for lying? Oh my, the smell is unbearable."*

Meanwhile everyone was wondering what happened to Tressie.

Melinda wondered, "Dad, where did Mom go? It shouldn't take her that long to use the ladies room."

Ronald tried his best to relieve Melinda, "Melinda, you know your Mother is very particular about how she looks at all times."

"Dad, I hope that is all it is."

Ronald acted as though he had no clue to what Melinda was insinuating, "Melinda what else would it be?"

Steward interrupted, "Why would she go to the ladies room unless it is an emergency. It is little Stacey's dance recital!"

Ronald hoped and prayed. "Son, I'm sure your mother will be back soon."

All of a sudden, something happened on stage. Everyone wondered what was going on. Ronald, with his motherly instinct and Nanny Nellie immediately got closer to the stage to see what the problem was, and sure enough little Stacey was having a fit. Stacey would have these fits, periodically, when she got very upset and frustrated. They rushed on stage to assist with Stacey. As soon as the dance instructors saw them, they immediately backed away. Ronald and Nanny Nellie was the only people that could actually calm her down. They took Stacey in the back.

Ronald instantly started caressing Stacey's hair and said as lovingly as any Father could in this situation. "Honey what happened out there? I thought you wanted to dance. You were so excited yesterday."

Stacey, with puppy dog tears running down her face said, "Thaddy, somet'ing wrong. Thaddy, somet'ing wrong. I don' know. Somet'ing wrong Thaddy. Why I feel, Thaddy?"

Nanny Nellie comforted Stacey as well. "It's alright sweetheart, we're here."

Ronald and Nanny Nellie looked at one another with tears in their eyes, and then looked away without saying a word to one another because they knew why Little Stacey was frustrated and brokenhearted.

Meanwhile, Tressie was sitting in the back of the Concert Hall. She saw people whispering and wondering whose child was having a fit.

A lady several seats down from Tressie commented to her friend. "How dreadful! That's not how young ladies are supposed to behave. Her Mother must be sitting under her seat by now."

Her friend responded, "Honey you know our girls are just perfect when it is time for their dance recital. Those two just would not think of making a mistake much less make a scene.

"The lady that was sitting next to Tressie said to her husband with such sympathy, "You know that was the little girl with the disability. Oh, I feel for her parents, they have got to be embarrassed."

Her husband replied with heartfelt sympathy, "That's got to be hard on the parents."

Tressie could not take any more comments. She rushed to the bathroom again and this time she really needed lots of tissue. She got in one of the bathroom stalls, took off her hat and shades. She began to weep like there was no tomorrow; she could not hold up the cape any longer. Suddenly someone entered the ladies room and called her name. It sounded so soft and light, she thought there was no way this could be anyone human, but the voice sounded all so familiar.

This angelic voice called her name again, "Tressie, are you in here?"

Tressie was afraid to answer. Then she caught the person's voice and it was no other than Rachel.

She answered, "Yes Rachel."

Rachel felt Tressie's hurt so deep as if it were her own. "I thought that were you that dashed by me wearing that hat and those shades. Tressie honey, why do you have that big hat on your head?"

Tressie opened the bathroom door.

Rachel was even more concerned, "Sister, I feel your hurt. It hurts me to see you this way."

Tressie could not wait anymore.

"Rachel, I can't take it. I don't know how to handle it. Rachel, *disability* is a word that cuts deeper than any hurt you have ever felt."

"Tressie honey, I can't say that I know exactly how you feel, but I do know that I am hurting for you right now. I can tell your pain lies deep." Melinda and Nanny Nellie came looking for Tressie. When they came in the ladies room, of course Tressie and Rachel were crying. Without anyone saying anything, Melinda and Nanny Nellie started to cry as well. Rachel kindly consoled Melinda and Nanny Nellie as well.

Rachel asked, "Tressie, have you thought about getting counseling? Honey, I feel for you deeply. We are going to have to get you some counseling. I'm sorry honey, I know you need counseling."

Rachel looked to Melinda in this desperate moment and asked, "Will you please go get your Father?"

Tressie was determined. "Rachel, I don't want Ronald to see me this way."

Rachel firmly suggested, "I'm sorry honey, Ronald needs to know how badly you have been hurting. Besides you need his support to get you to and from counseling."

Melinda agreed, "Yes Mom, Mrs. Rachel is right. You need Dad and everyone else in the family."

Melinda ran out to get her Father. As Melinda went to get Ronald, there was a sea of people standing in the hallway from the ladies restroom all the way out into the Concert Hall. Some people knew what was going on and others didn't know and wanted to find out. Everyone, including the men, was lined up to go to the ladies restroom. When Melinda made it backstage, Ronald had managed to calm Stacey down. Melinda was very frustrated because she didn't know what to feel. She was afraid, embarrassed and angry.

As soon as Ronald saw her face, "Sweetheart, what is wrong? Is it your Mother? Is she alright?"

At that moment, Melinda burst out in tears. "Dad yes, it is Mom! She's in the bathroom! Everyone is watching and they are all in a line just to see what is going on!"

Ronald did not ask any questions. He grabbed Stacey by her hand and headed to the ladies room, Steward followed. As they walked through, everyone looked and whispered.

One person said, "Oh, that's the little girl with the disability and her Father. Um, I guess that girl is her sister."

Another person commented, "Yeah, poor thing she fell out on stage in the performance."

Another person unpleasantly said, "I guess that's what happens when you try to mix *disability* with *ability*.

Someone else asked, "Who is in the ladies room?"

Before they entered the ladies room, Melinda and Steward took Little Stacey to the side so she would not become upset again. Melody and Joanne somehow made their way through the crowd once they found out Tressie was going through one of the most difficult times of her life. By the time Ronald got to Tressie, her hair was in disarray. Her eyes looked as though she was first cousins to a raccoon. She wept so much until her top looked as though she just ran a marathon.

Rachel said, "Ronald, she needs counseling right away. There are lots of things that she has to let out."

"Rachel, I don't know that she will go? If she doesn't what will happen then?"

Melody suggested, "Ronald, she needs counseling like yesterday."

Joanne sympathized, "Ronald I feel her. I am a Mother. I can't help, but put myself in her place right now."

Rachel was as honest as she knew how. "Brother, you know I love you. Now is the time to put your foot down. It is time to open your eyes to what is really going on with Tressie. I admire you to want to be her knight and shining armor, but there comes a time when you are going to have to face what is really going on with your wife."

"Rachel he was just trying to protect me and make me feel as comfortable as I know how with our daughter's disability."

At that time all of the dance instructors and staff were in the bathroom to find out what was going on.

The head dance instructor asked, "What is going on? You all frightened me. The way folks were sobbing all through the Concert Hall, you would think someone died."

Tressie answered, "Yes, I am Stacey's Mother and I did not want to be here at this dance recital and I did not invite any of my friends, but somehow they are here anyway. I lied to my family. What kind of Mother does that make me?"

The head dance instructor answered, "Mrs. Ivy, I am so sorry you feel that way. Stacey always does her best in class and she has never fallen out before."

Rachel looked at all of the dance instructors and staff. She proceeded to walk down the hall where everyone stood. She then turned around and walked back to the head dance instructor. "I'm Rachel and I am a close family friend with the Ivy's. This may seem a little strange, but I would love to pray for my friends. Now, I don't know who you believe in, but we believe in God, Jesus and the Holy Spirit."

Everyone that was in line and in the ladies room was feeling everything Tressie's heart was screaming silently. Tressie's pain that was as deep as a valley; had no end and flowed into every person that was in the Atlanta Concert Hall. As soon as everyone found out why Tressie was weeping, every Mother in the Atlanta Concert Hall naturally put themselves in Tressie's shoes for that moment. The Fathers automatically thought about themselves and their wives. Everyone held hands before the prayer.

Rachel prayed, *"Father, we come to you as humble as we know how. Touch the Ivy's right now. They are in need of your grace and mercy. Bless little Stacey, and Lord, God whatever your will is for her life, I ask that it be done in the name of Jesus. Teach my Sister Tressie how to love her child with Godly love. Show her that whatever we go through in life is for us and for us to grow in you Lord. Father, if we did not go through storms, we would not appreciate you in the fullest. You did not promise us that this road would be easy, but you did say that you will never leave us or forsake us. Father, we are standing on your word and your word alone. Lift this Mother and Father's spirits right now, Lord. Only you know how much pain that they have endured. Give them the peace that they need to get through this difficult time in their lives. Show them that they are not alone and they do have brothers and sisters that are around them who love, care and are willing to pray with them and for them. Father, those of us who are around when these trials arrive in others lives speak to us so we will not be ignorant to others needs. In Jesus's name, amen.*

After the prayer, the dance instructors, staff and other parents and family members went to Ronald and Tressie to give them their love and support. There were people giving the Ivy's their number and email addresses. Tressie was just so overwhelmed. She never thought in a million years people would give this much love to her family concerning her beautiful daughter who just happen to have a disability. They then went up to Rachel with their insight and revelations.

One of the Mothers, Mrs. Cummings, went up to Rachel. "That was beautiful. I have a different outlook on anyone that has a disability. I am a school teacher and will make it my business to enlighten my students' knowledge on disability and the many different kinds that we come in contact with, but just don't know it. I'm sorry, I stand corrected. First, I will enlighten myself with information on disability and the many kinds. Then I can share with my students. I have students who are gifted. My students are very intellectual, but what good is it when you cannot help your fellow student who lacks in your ability. When all of us stood together holding hands, being strangers at the same time struck a chord in me. We are all in this together. I need you and you need me."

Rachel's heart was full and all she could do was cry tears of joy. Rachel had to immediately hug Mrs. Cummings because she knew this was how God operated. Rachel thought she was just praying for Ronald and Tressie, but God was doing a work in each and every parent and family member that was present. She had such peace because she followed God's commands at the very moment.

Rachel was grateful. "Thank you for blessing my friend and by coming and sharing with us what you thought. And you are right I need you and you need me. If everyone came to that realization, this would be a magnificent world. God bless you for allowing God to speak to your heart."

Another Mother, Mrs. Page, came up to Rachel. "I felt your love for the Ivy's and I also felt your pain as well. My Pastor always tells the congregation, "When you hurt, I should hurt." God really touched my heart. I know as a Mom, I feel Mrs. Ivy's pain, but for me it went way beyond that level. Sister, there is power in prayer and unity."

Rachel was still full from the other comments. "To God be the Glory. Your Pastor is absolutely right. We should hurt when others hurt. If you don't mind, share that insight with someone else as well."

Mrs. Page replied, "Of course I will."

Rachel gave Mrs. Page a hug.

After everything died down Rachel asked, "Ronald, do you need some assistance with getting some counseling?"

"No thank you, Rachel. I will make the necessary calls tomorrow. I have a few colleagues that I can talk to get everything set up for Tressie. The entire family could benefit from counseling."

Ronald slowly held his head down, fighting back the urge to cry again.

"Praise God, Ronald you guys are going to be just fine. You are such a great man of God. If you need anything just give me a call."

"Thank you so much. I know we can call on you and John anytime."

 Words of Wisdom

Brothers and Sisters, pay attention to your surroundings when you are attending an event or just out shopping. You never know what someone maybe going through. Don't get fooled by wealth because with or without it, there will be trials and tribulations. Remember, when one of your Brothers and Sisters are going through you should be there, even if your shoulder is all you have to give. When we stand in unity, powerful happenings transpire. Recognize your surroundings when you are just a bystander. Trust and believe there is something significant you are supposed to grasp out of someone else's mountain. By the way our mountain is waiting for us, but remember our father tells us he will never leave us or forsake us.

CHAPTER 15

Proverbs 20:27 *The lamp of the Lord searches the spirit of a man; it searches out his inmost being. (N.I.V.)*

Proverbs 22:22-23 *Do not exploit the poor because they are poor and do not crush the needy in court, for the Lord will take up their case and will plunder those who plunder them. (N.I.V.)*

It was the middle of May.

In the exquisite neighborhood, *Ridgeland Towers of Atlanta*, there was an enjoyable place out in the middle of all these gorgeous estates. Residents had a place to mingle together outside if they so desired.

Everyone mingled after work on this day. On this particular day the garbage was being picked up late. When the garbage truck came, Rachel happened to be nearby. One of the men jumped out of the truck to make sure trash was not spilled. Rachel naturally spoke.

The garbage man said, "Ma'am, these houses nice. He immediately corrected himself. I mean, these houses are nice."

"Thank you, it is a nice neighborhood and we are blessed," Rachel replied with the friendliest smile.

The garbage man cleared his throat. He slowly said, "Ma'am, this is the neighborhood everybody wives want to live."

"You keep working hard like you are now and this is possible. Remember there is nothing too hard for God."

The garbage man felt inadequate, "I understand that, but I still say it's out of my league. This is a dream for most folks, ma'am. You know especially for black folk."

Rachel looked at the garbage man with encouragement centered deep in her heart. "Life and death is in the power of the tongue. Young man, do you know what I'm saying when I say that?"

"You a nice lady, but you don't know my background."

"Yes, but you don't know this man name Jesus, because if you truly knew him, you would know that anything is possible when it comes to Jesus the Christ."

"Ma'am, I do need to get back in church because I was raised in church."

Rachel explained, "It would be great to go back to church, but the most powerful gift you can do for yourself is to be saved."

He agreed, "Yeah, my Moms tell me that all the time. Ma'am, we have to finish our route. Thank you for taking out the time to talk to me because in this neighborhood and ones that are like this one, you know, people rarely notice we exist."

As the garbage truck continued to the next house, Rachel waved to them goodbye. She bowed her head as she walked back. She prayed, *"Father, show those young men the way to salvation. Let them know, it is not about the neighborhood. It is truly about you and only you! In Jesus's name, Amen."*

The children were playing and the adults were just having conversation. The ladies were at one table and the men were at another. Sasha, Melody, Joanne, Tressie, Scarlette were at the table waiting for her.

As soon as Rachel sat down, Melody sarcastically asked, "So Rachel, what did the garbage man have to talk about?"

She ignored the sarcasm that was all over Melody.

"He was saying this was a nice neighborhood and all of the wives want to live in this neighborhood."

Tressie jokingly blurted out, "I'll be willing to bet you told him he has a chance."

Sasha commented, "Rachel, you are such an angel, even angels can't make everything happen."

Rachel smiled as she looked at all the women at the table, including Scarlette, "Anything is possible when it comes to Jesus Christ."

"Yes, I know that is written in the Bible, but do you really believe a garbage man could ever own one of these houses?"

Joanne asked with total denial.

"Yes, of course Joanne. You must remember this as well. God can give and he can also take away."

Joanne did not know what to think after the statement from Rachel. Joanne calmly settled down.

Scarlette was sitting there with that smirk look stirring the pot, "Rachel it seems to me what these ladies are saying is a garbage man doesn't have a chance to live in our neighborhood. Now you ladies let me know if I am wrong or not when I say this, that doesn't sound like the Jesus that Rachel talks about. That Jesus has a better reputation than that. Doesn't He?"

Rachel responded, "Scarlette honey, when anyone professes to be a Christian, you have to be a living example of Christ."

Meanwhile, the men were having their own conversation.

Howard nosily asked, "John, I wonder what Rachel was talking to the garbage man about."

"Brother, knowing my wife she was probably talking to him about getting saved and asking him what church he attends. You know that's what we live and breathe."

Ronald had gratefulness in his heart. "John, your wife is like an angel on earth."

He began to tear up.

"I am not sure how she was there at the right time. She was a blessing to our family and the other families who was there that night. I knew Tressie did not invite anyone for whatever reason. John you should have been there, it was beautiful when Rachel stood in the gap for us when we needed her the most. You know Tressie is having a time accepting our little princess Stacey."

John replied, "She is such a beautiful child. God would not have given you two your little princess Stacey if He did not think you could handle the situation."

Paul was discouraged and annoyed, "Evidently God thinks Sasha and I are as strong as they come. We have been trying to have another child since Sehara was two years old. Sasha gets so angry. Sometimes when we are out and she sees a Mom that looks like she might be single, she literally goes off and sometimes it is beyond my control."

John reassured Paul, "Brother that is when we grow. When we are going through that valley are climbing that mountain, we should count it all joy."

Reese ran his fingers through his hair. "Since you guys are laying it out on the table. My kids just seem like they respect the nanny more than they respect us. You know what I mean."

Reese whispered.

"As a man, it hurts when they don't listen to me or respect me. That's why we give them whatever they want and whenever they want it. Man, we have these businesses to run and it is hard trying to juggle the kids and the businesses."

"Brother, I thought you two were going to try counseling."

"John, I have to make sure my businesses are running properly. You should know how that feels when you have to play that part of the top dog?"

"Reese you know money isn't everything."

He blew the idea of getting help off yet again.

"Man, I have to keep it running and I have to keep my prestige."

Then Ridge released, "I would be alright if my outside daughter could get along with my wife. They put me in an awkward position every time because my daughter Meriah absolutely hates Scarlette because she is not her natural Mother. Scarlette doesn't like the idea of Meriah existing. She believes it spoils the picture perfect family."

"Brother, you have to acknowledge that she is a child. And some time or another Scarlette is going to have to accept your child." *John's heart went out for Meriah.* "She's a part of you."

Paul commented, "John, you and Rachel always seem like everything is just perfect. I don't mean to take anything from my beautiful wife Sasha, but Rachel has it all together. Hey man, all jokes aside, I know and everyone else as well knows no one is perfect, but Rachel and Rachel alone is the only woman that would come close. There is something about Rachel and it goes beyond physical beauty."

Paul and Ronald's eyes were full.

Paul continued, "John you are truly blessed."

John felt the need to share. "Everyone thinks Rachel and I have no problems, but we do have disagreements time and again. Thank you for your kind words towards Rachel. Of course I believe she is the best because she is my wife and I love her like Christ loves the Church. Trust me, Rachel and I have come a long way. It wasn't always as smooth as it is now. We had to live and learn one another for years."

Howard asked, "So John, what is the secret ingredient?"

John gave them all a beautiful wide smile and answered, "First and before all our Lord Jesus Christ, staying in love, respect and truly being as one."

All the guys laughed and teased John.

Everyone was scattered about doing whatever.

Stacey ran to her Father, she began to talk loudly. Tressie cringed because she did not want all the attention on Stacey. Little Stacey started having a conversation with Sehara, Amira, Ashley and Meriah. All the children loved having conversations with Stacey. Tressie tried with all that she had to do the right thing, but still ultimately chose to walk the other way. As soon as Tressie started walking the other way, Ronald went after her.

Ashton had an attitude towards everyone. His parents, Joanne and Howard, were trying their best to put their feet down when it came to disciplining their children. Ultimately, they still struggled. Rachel was talking to Charlotte, Charles, and Cassidy Arnasia. Nia, Samone , and Tremaine were with their nanny.

Little Cassidy Arnasia was talking to Rachel.

Little Cassidy Arnasia asked, "Mrs. Rachel, when I comin' to stay wit' you?"

"You can come whenever your Mommy and Daddy allow

you sweetheart."

Scarlette was near while Rachel and Little Cassidy talked. Out of the blue, Little Cassidy started looking at everyone else except her family. Then she pointed at everyone, one by one.

She said, "She go to chuch. He go to chuch. Her go to chuch, you Mrs. Rachel you go to chuch. But my fam'ly don't go to chuch."

Scarlette and Ridge stopped Little Cassidy before she could say anything else. Scarlette then took Little Cassidy on the side to talk to her. A couple of minutes later, Scarlette took Rachel to the side to talk with her about her conversation with Cassidy.

"Rachel, you know I love you as a friend. Ridge and I respect your religion, but please do not try and push it on my family."

She kindly explained, "Scarlette, I didn't say anything about church. Little Cassidy Arnasia mentioned it."

"I don't know what is wrong with her Rachel. Sometimes she gets very intuitive about that church thing."

Rachel responded standing on the Word of God. "I'm sorry if I offended you in any kind of a way, but know this...I don't apologize for being a Christian."

As soon as Meriah saw that Scarlette was a little upset about Rachel and Cassidy's conversation, she headed over to talk to Rachel. As she walked over to Rachel, Ridge stopped her knowing she was going to have the same conversation with Rachel as Little Cassidy Arnasia, just out of spite.

As everyone was leaving to go back to their estates, Rachel stood back taking in everyone's trials and tribulations. Rachel observed each family as they proceeded to their estates.

Sasha walked next to Paul while holding Sehara's hand. Paul walked next to Sasha and Sehara, but yet so far away thinking of a solution to his problem.

Ronald, Tressie, Stacey, Steward and Nanny Nellie head back to their estate. Ronald held Tressie's hand as if he has that strong wife he had been waiting for, for years. Nanny Nellie held Stacey's hand. Stacey looked up at Nanny Nellie with helpless eyes. Steward thought about how his family could be. Melinda was walking directly behind Nanny Nellie and Stacey as if to say *I've got your back*. Melinda observed her little sister Stacey. As Melinda was watching her, Nanny Nellie looked and caught her eye. She grabbed Melinda's hand.

Joanne and Howard were distance a part as they walked back. Ashley pushed Ashton searching for attention. Little Amira ran to her Mom and gently held her hand as though she felt her Mother and Fathers' desperate need for each other.

Little Cassidy Arnasia and her big sister Meriah was walking in the middle of Ridge and Scarlette. Ridge looked up as though he was desperately searching for an answer, but from whom? Scarlette looked over to Meriah with a look of resentment; then looked over to her precious Little Cassidy Arnasia with eyes full of love. Ridge looked over to Meriah. His heart was filled with love and great pity. Meriah caught Ridge's eyes. Immediately her eyes filled with water as if she knew exactly what her Father was thinking at that very moment.

Reese and Melody were holding hands, both looking around as though they had no idea where they were going. Little Nia slowly walked behind her Mother and Father. Nanny Abby held Samone and Tremaine's hands as though she was giving them their attention for the last time that day until she saw them again the next day to do the same thing yet again. As she held Samone and Tremaine's hands, she gave Little Nia a quick glance; then with loving and prayerful eyes, she looked up to the sky.

John, Charlotte and Charles walked apart, but their facial expressions were content and united their hearts. Rachel could barely wait until she got into her prayer closet to pray for everyone. Rachel felt the unspoken crying in the midnight hour, the dysfunctions in marriages and the struggle of strongholds that tarnished every aspect of their minds.

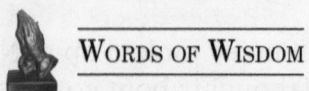

Brothers and Sisters, are we praying for our friends? Whether we know it or not, our friends need our prayers more than anything. The enemy will come from every direction, even if your house is in order. And on the other hand, if our houses aren't in order, the enemy work effortlessly. Remember, when we truly put God first, everything else will fall into place. Start today, by reading "The Word" which is and always will be on the best sellers list!

CHAPTER 16

Daniel 2:21-22 He changes times and seasons; he sets up kings and deposes them. He gives wisdom to the wise and knowledge to the discerning. He reveals deep and hidden things; he knows what lies in darkness, and light dwells with him. (N.I.V)

It was early June.

After church on Sunday, Joanne was giving out invitations to a party just for women. As she was giving these invitations out, this one woman who was associated with the other ladies that she had given invitations to, had an expression like that of a kid at a playground who no one wanted to associate with, because she just didn't look the part. She obviously and desperately wanted to be invited, but of course she wouldn't breathe a word to anyone. Rachel was nearby and caught the woman's facial expression. Rachel simply touched her and gave her a smile. The woman gently touched Rachel in return, signifying her appreciation. Afterwards, the lady gathered her children then went home.

Joanne did not feel confident in herself to conduct the party. She asked Rachel to conduct the party. Rachel gladly hosted the party for her. The decorators had live cut Roses everywhere and beautiful burgundy and red candles everywhere. The scenery was like walking in a Valentine's Day dream for ladies, but it wasn't Valentine's Day it was just a night for ladies. They were arriving in their Bentleys, Mercedes and Jaguars.

The ladies entered Joanne's home. All of them admired the home's décor. In Joanne's dining room, the painting of *The Last Supper* was always a conversation piece. Although Sasha, Tressie, Melody, Rachel, and Scarlette had seen the painting numerous times before, it still took their breaths away when they walked in Joanne's home. Everyone got their nonalcoholic drinks, nibbled on D'oeuvres and socialized for about half an hour.

Although Scarlette was an atheist, she always respected everyone when it was time for prayer. Rachel opened up with a prayer. One of the other ladies who always were in church every Sunday said with an undertone, "Must we always pray before every little event?"

Rachel heard the rude comment and kindly continued praying.

After the prayer Rachel nicely smiled then she said, "I don't know who made that childish comment, but I for one pray about and before everything, big or small, might I add may God bless you and your thought process. I would like to thank everyone for coming out tonight to support Joanne's *Ladies Night Out* party. And to Joanne thank you for opening up your home so we can be blessed tonight. I believe with all my heart, we can be blessed anytime and anywhere. I hope that everyone can open their hearts so that you can receive a blessing that God has waiting for you. I would like for everyone to state their name and something about themselves. If you feel led to give a testimony so that others could be blessed, please feel free to do so. Another question would be… If you lost everything you had today or tomorrow, will your walk with Christ change?"

A lady name *Corrine Bay* was the first who stood up to introduce herself. As she stood up everyone was drawn to her overwhelming self confidence. Corrine was dressed in all black. Her jewelry was that beautiful twenty-two karat gold that made her black outfit pop. As she stood up, her jewelry glimmered. She sported a beautiful swinging bob haircut that was freshly done. She was a powerful, award winning business owner who thrived on competitiveness.

Corrine said with a great, conceded attitude, "I actually love myself and my lifestyle. I feel if I lost everything tomorrow, to be quite honest, I would be nothing. Look ladies it's heaven to me when I am out shopping and the only thing I have to worry about is the size of my clothing. You ladies should know what I am trying to portray here."

She looked around at all the ladies with a great big smile. "This is a beautiful life. Who wouldn't want to live it?"

When she got done, some of the ladies felt some of what Corrine just spoke about herself. They saw themselves in Corrine. Therefore, her attitude was displeasing to them. In other words, they were in the mirror, but afraid to look into the mirror. Corrine smiled as she sat down. She felt some of the ladies spirits connect with hers and at the same time somehow there was a disconnection.

As soon as Corrine was done, *Lois Ferguson*, who worshipped the ground Corrine stood on, stood up next. She so admired Corrine's lifestyle. If she could she would gladly trade places with her. Lois looked as though she was a carbon copy of Corrine. She was dressed similar and wore the same haircut.

Lois was excited as a little kid would be simply because she was hanging out with Corrine Bay. "If I could change anything about myself, it would be my skin color. I would love for it to be exactly like Corrine's skin because she has a lighter skin complexion. Society prefers the lighter skin black females. That's why Corrine is so successful. If I lost everything today or tomorrow, I feel like Corrine feels. I would be nothing. I mean, where would I be without my designer clothes, shoes and purses? I really would not be anything because I am living paycheck to paycheck already. Having nice things makes me feel fantastic. I love going shopping with Corrine. She always makes me feel great because she is my friend. She inspires me. Ladies, I aspire to have my own business one day and Corrine always tells me that she will help me with my business. It is such a blessing having her as a friend. She always tells me that I deserve the best no matter the cost."

As she sat back down, Rachel immediately came back with a positive and encouraging comment due to the immaturity Lois possessed.

Rachel gave insight, "Sister, I noticed you are a young lady and the only one you should worship and His name is Jesus Christ."

Corrine immediately looked as though someone burst her bubble.

The next person to introduce herself was a lovely lady name *Maranda Hickory*. She absolutely loved being a housewife; her husband was a construction worker. They treated one another with the utmost respect. Maranda didn't live in one of those fancy neighborhoods and did not shop very much. They were always on a budget. This was normalcy for Maranda and her family. She made it a habit of shopping at thrift stores. She was a very stylish woman who could make a T-shirt look fantastic and was always very well dressed and blessed.

Maranda was excited and led by the Lord, "I want to give an awesome testimony. God has blessed me to be married for twenty years and I have two beautiful children, ages sixteen and fourteen. My husband truly leads my household and we are as one. God has blessed me to be able to stay home and concentrate on being there for him and the children."

As Maranda gave her testimony, Corrine face dropped. She seemed to be a little disappointed because she always noticed that Maranda was always full of joy.

She continued, "The advice I would give any married young lady is, well most women that I know hate this word, but be *submissive* to your husbands. I must add, your husband has to be led by God. If not you are not obligated to do so. May God bless all of you women and I only wish that God continue to bless you all and continue guiding you."

All of the women started smiling and making comments on being submissive to their husbands. When Maranda sat down, they thought about her testimony. There was no question about her happiness and joy yet she didn't live like most of the women who was there. Maranda's spirit was gentle and free.

Another woman by the name of *Alice Truman* stood up. Alice was also a well-to-do business owner who had been married for about thirty years. Her husband had not work for years and just let himself go. Alice was a cougar; she looked just as good as her twenty-five-year-old daughter. Over the years she had fallen out of love with her husband. She was very sharp wearing a beautiful red wrap dress that hit every curb she had. Her stunning pair of red six inch heels matched her dress and personality perfectly. To top everything off, she wore a sharp short haircut that looked as though it was just done.

Alice was eager to share. "Hi everyone, and for those who don't know me, although I don't see why not, my name is Alice Truman. I have a very successful business that has always been on the top. I know this is going to sound a little conceited, but I absolutely love my life oh yes and my body. I always get lots of compliments where ever I go. If I lost everything tomorrow, my relationship with Christ would deflate. I know we should put Christ before anything, but I would be worth nothing without my attachments. Trust me, I give God his time. The only time I miss church is when I am on business. My advice to everyone would be to always eat right and exercise, no matter how old you are. The only thing that I would change is my husband. That's a terrible thing to say. Yes and I said it. Pray for me."

As she sat down, she felt all the tension in the room. All of the women sort of looked around not knowing how to respond. The women felt embarrassed for her. What is so disturbing is that some of the women could relate to Alice.

To make her feel a little at ease, Rachel smoothed things over. "Alice, it can't be that bad. You know you think your husband is the worst until you hear someone else's testimony. Mrs. Truman, when that happens; you will know it because it will be just like a light bulb that lights up in your head."

Alice thanked Rachel with a quick fake smile.

The next woman who stood up looked like she just stepped out of a vogue magazine. Her name was *Deborah Niles*. She was married to a big time lawyer and she always had problems with other women wanting to take her place. She chose to ignore the fact that he had countless affairs because she absolutely loved living the lifestyle.

"If I lost everything tomorrow, I would feel like I lost a

part of me. Just like several other women admitted. Whether we like to admit it or not we start thinking we are who we are because of the things that we acquire in life. But I do know Jesus is the one we should put our trust in and nothing else. Therefore, my walk with Christ would be crushed."

The spirit that was in the room was tainted. Everyone looked around at each other as though they were examining themselves. Tressie could not stand it anymore.

She quickly stood on her feet. She paused for a few seconds to get herself together.

"If I were to lose everything today, would it change my walk with Christ?"

Tressie looked at Rachel with troubled eyes.

"I'm afraid it would, because I don't have that one on one relationship with Christ."

She was affected by what most of the other ladies talked about. She instantly saw herself in the other ladies. They permitted themselves to submerge in such ignorance.

"I have a one on one relationship with materialistic things. I only call on Him when I need Him to make me feel better. For those of you that share the same feelings as I do, we are going to have to change. We have to know that it isn't right."

She looked around to all of the women with great concern.

"How many times are we going to go around the same mountain?"

By the time she finished, all was in tears. A lot of the ladies could not grasp what Tressie was saying, but they swallowed her words of wisdom not knowing one day it will blossom in their lives later and her life as well.

Joanne got up in a shy manner.

"I'm sure everyone knows me here, of course, this is my party. I would, *she paused*, like to give a testimony. This is the first time I have shared this testimony.

She paused again to get herself together.

Not long ago, Howard and I invited one of his employees and her family over. Now ladies, I usually have my nanny over to take care of my three children. She is the only one that can really control my children. My children were fighting with one another at the dining table. My husband and I were so embarrassed sitting there in front of our dinner guest not being able to discipline our children at the dinner table. Ladies this was one of the most amazing and embarrassing moments that happened in my life. Just out of the blue my guests' thirteen-year-old daughter handled my children with a touch of God's hands. She started saying the grace and she said a little prayer. For my husband and I, this was truly a revelation. It was also a bitter, sweet moment for me because I had to face my incompetence as a Mother. On the other hand, this moment was a part of my life that needed to be changed. Ladies, prayer is powerful, if you don't already know it."

She choked up remembering that moment. As she sat down, some women smiled and others cried.

Sasha stood up next. She was touched and bothered by everyone's testimony throughout the night, along with her mountain that she was climbing. She took a minute to get herself together. She held back every tear, "I hate when I choose to let it all out."

She paused; finally let it all out.

"My husband and I have been trying to have another baby for about five years. We have tried everything. Nothing has worked. I find it very disturbing when I see a young woman and she is single, but she has this beautiful baby and probably many more at home. I always say to myself, *"Lord, God my husband and I are married and have been trying for years to conceive and here we have some ware fare chick over here that has as many as she wants. Paul and I cannot be blessed with our second child."* Ladies! If I hear *it's all in God's timing* again, I think I'll just scream. I feel as though I am being punished. I have always heard people say money cannot by you happiness, I am living proof. Ladies, I pray that God gives me the perseverance that it takes to make it through this awful and grueling period in my life." Sasha was choked up as she sat down.

Joanne and Tressie ran over to Sasha to comfort her. Sasha started weeping. As Tressie and Joanne held Sasha, they felt her pain. It was infectious to the other ladies that were there. Everyone got up and huddled over Sasha. While Rachel prayed, Scarlette wept in the corner.

When the ladies got themselves together, Melody stood up while wrestling in her mind about the conversation she had with a young bartender, Trek. She decided to tell everyone about the conversation she had with Trek.

"Only a few people know what I have been struggling against."

She looked over to Rachel with a smile.

"Like many of you, my husband and I have several prosperous businesses. We have parties throughout the year and when we have the parties we normally have a bartender. We used a different bartender for our last party. This particular bartender asked us before the party whether we were Christians or not. If you haven't figured out, he asked the question because we claimed to be Christians. My husband and I justified it by saying Christians are allowed to have fun as well. We even talked to Rachel and her husband."

She smiled at Rachel again.

She continued, "Rachel and John always give their advice. They don't agree with the alcohol at parties because they don't drink. My husband and I feel we need to keep up our reputation because we are CEO's. We have to keep up with our competition. This habit that my husband and I have haunts me to no end. Sooner or later, we are going to have to make that wise decision. We have to pray continuously about our strongholds that we let creep into our lives."

Tressie stood up again.

She thought, *"Oh God, do the other ladies know what happened at the Concert Hall?"*

She looked upon Rachel for immediate support.

Rachel realized Tressie needed support, therefore she

responded quickly, "Sometimes in our lives we need that support from a true friend who truly wants the best for us. Ladies, as some of you know Tressie has had this immense mountain that she has been trying to climb all by herself. There are times when you need someone who truly loves you to actually pray on your behalf. We are so wounded and don't know what to do. Ladies, never try to go through anything alone. We should always look to our Lord, Jesus Christ for guidance. Many of times an individual's walk isn't strong enough so, therefore he or she needs a human to stand in for the immaturity in their walk. If you don't have friends whom you trust, make an appointment with the Pastor. If he's not available, I'm sure one of the associate Ministers will be happy to counsel you."

Tressie spoke again. "Rachel has been truly a blessing to me and my family. Everyone needs a friend like Rachel. Although some of the things that she does for people sometimes, I just don't understand. I know she is an angel here on earth."

All of the other ladies shook their heads in agreement.

Rachel made her closing remarks.

When she was done, all of the ladies stood up, clapped and gave a standing ovation. As everyone was standing, Scarlette out of nowhere walked to the front where Rachel was standing. Of course Sasha, Joanne, Tressie, and Melody wondered what she had to say and Rachel smiled.

Rachel remarked, "Scarlette it seems to me you have something that you want to say."

The room was silent at this point. It was as though everyone knew what she was going to say was for them. Scarlette quietly glanced around the whole room at all the ladies. She then looked up at the ceiling at that beautiful painting of the last supper.

Scarlette was shaking in her boots. "To those of you that don't know me, my name is Scarlette Crane."

She started to speak slowly as her voice cracked.

"You may be shocked to hear this, but I am an atheist.

I always ask my friends: Rachel, Sasha, Tressie, Joanne and Melody, How can you believe in and worship something or someone you cannot see?"

As Scarlette spoke, some of the women that did not know her could not believe she was in their presence and confessed she was an atheist. They started to judge her. They totally forgot about the thorns in their sides.

She continued, "As I listened to all of you get up and share, my heart truly went out to you. Eventhough I don't believe in yall's Jesus, the words that you have spoken tonight I can relate to as well. I don't mean to step on anyone's toes, but what is the difference between you and me?

Many of the ladies felt this overwhelming feeling in their spirits. Corrine Bay dropped her head in unspoken shame. Deborah Niles looked as though she was in a trance. Lois Ferguson glanced at Corrine with embarrassing eyes. Sasha, Tressie, Joanne and Melody, as always, looked to Rachel for encouraging words. Rachel was not lead to say anything. Maranda Hickory held her head high because she knew deep in her heart that Jesus truly was the head of her life. Alice Truman turned her head the other way as though she could care less. Scarlette looked in every woman's face, desperately searching for what was so different about these so-called church going women who claim Jesus as their savior.

Scarlette was nervous. "I'm confused ladies because I really don't know why I chose to speak to you at this moment."

Rachel immediately and effortlessly walked over next to Scarlette. She gently grasped Scarlette's hand. Scarlette's nervousness disappeared as Rachel took over. The atmosphere was very tense.

"Ladies, I know you may feel a little thrown off or uncomfortable right now, but you all should know this is how God operates. What you feel in your hearts right now is what you ought to feel. God loves us and He surely wants us to be the best that we can possibly be. He doesn't want us to depend on anything or anyone to define who we are. We are the children of the most high and we should live our lives accordingly."

As soon as Rachel finished speaking, the ladies mingled. Soon thereafter a gospel song came on the gospel radio station. This song was an old song, sung by a quartet group. Rachel, Melody, Sasha, Joanne and Tressie began to smile because this song was one of their favorite songs.

Scarlette went over to them and sarcastically asked, "Girls, isn't that one of those Jesus songs you all like listening to?"

They ignored her and continued listening to the song. Everyone got quiet. Corrine Bay was having feelings that she could not explain.

Corrine went over to Rachel inquisitively said, "Sister that song is moving me like I have not known before."

Lois Ferguson walked over to share. As she spoke her voice cracked. "Ladies this song brings back fond memories of my childhood. They just don't make songs like that anymore."

Rachel, Melody, Sasha, Joanne and Tressie teared up. Maranda, Alice and Deborah joined the other ladies. Before everyone knew it, they all were in a circle holding hands as though they were a continuous connecting chain for Christ. As the song played the music captured every lady's spirit.

Every lady including Scarlette was in tears. They were clinging to one another like everyone had known each other for years. This unity and connection was what every woman needed. When the song ended, the ladies all wanted to start the party all over again. Corrine Bay, Tressie, Alice Truman, and Deborah Niles were cuddled up in a group looking up at the painting of *The Last Supper* in the ceiling of Joanne's dining room. It was like they were in a dream and in the dream they were all looking at Jesus sitting at the table of the last supper. Joanne, Sasha, Melody were all in a group silently praying for each other looking towards the painting of the last supper. Scarlette somehow ended up in the middle of the room where the ladies were. Scarlette just stood there with her eyes closed and wondering why she was such an emotional wreck. All the while she thought about what happened at Sasha's salon and the song that just went off of the radio. Rachel and Maranda Hickory were looking towards the painting praying for every woman that was present. God allowed them to feel exactly what the other ladies were feeling. Jesus made himself known through this song, obviously a song that was God sent. Hard hearts were softened and revelations came like the wind that came out of nowhere.

WORDS OF WISDOM

My Sisters in Christ, we have to take our sisters who seem to be on the outskirts of our so-called reality into consideration. We shouldn't get blindsided by the lifestyle that God has so graciously provided for us. Remember, God bless us to be a blessing to others. My Sisters in Christ, acknowledge the woman that everyone seem to bypass. I promise you she will be one of the biggest blessings in your life. Brothers and Sisters, especially my sisters, have compassion for others. You never know what the next person is going through. Consult God in all that you do. We should always think of how we felt when we were intentionally isolated. Better yet, we should think of our children and how they would feel if that was to happen to them.

CHAPTER 17

*Proverbs 18: 1-4 An unfriendly man pursues selfish ends;
he defies all sound judgement. A fool finds no pleasure in
understanding but delights in airing his own opinions.
When wickedness comes, so does contempt, and with shame
comes disgrace. The words of a man's mouth are deep
waters, but the fountain of wisdom is a bubbling brook.
(N.I.V.)*

It was the middle of June.
Scarlette and Ridge's friends were having a party. Their friends lived a couple hours away from Atlanta. As they pulled up in the driveway they drove up on bags of trash that should have been thrown out weeks ago. Scarlette and Ridge got out of the car first. When Scarlette opened the back door, their Little Cassidy Arnasia was shaking her head from side to side signaling *no*. Meriah connected with Cassidy and shook her head from side to side as well. After a couple of minutes, Meriah and Cassidy finally got out of the car.

As they walked in the house, everyone stared because the Cranes carried themselves differently. Although these people that were at the party were all atheists, somehow they share totally different worlds. Some people were in the corner playing cards, others were in another corner cracking jokes on one another, not to mention, beer bottles and wrappers scattered throughout everywhere they stepped. There were teenagers in one room listening to music and dancing appearing to be having the time of their lives. In another room there were adults listening to *oldies but goodies*. As they walked through the house Kyle, Ridge's childhood friend, realized they were there. He was so glad to see them. Kyle always admired Scarlette just a little too much. He always said Scarlette looked like a living Barbie doll.

"Oh if it ain't my good old Pal Ridge and his beautiful fam'ly."

Kyle looked at Scarlette from head to toe.

He continued, "So, man how life been treatin' ya? Man, I tell everybody about yo' rags to riches story. I wish I kin git a break lack that. I'd be set man. My fam'ly would be beautiful lack yo's."

Kyle and his wife laughed hysterically.

Kyle's wife, Mindy, grabbed some chairs for them. She had to take a rag to wash them down due to the filth. As they sat down in the chairs they couldn't help, but wonder whether they were clean.

Little Cassidy Arnasia had an intuitive moment, "Daddy, somethin' not right."

Meriah agreed, "Yeah Dad, something isn't right."

Scarlette had a look of approval on her face.

Ridge pretended he had no clue. "Don't be silly girls."

Knowing how Cassidy gets when something's on her mind, Scarlette tried to lighten the mood, "Honey, we're going to have a great time."

"Mommy, I feel somethin' around me. It not good, Mommy. It not good."

Mindy came over smiling, showing that great big gap in the very front of her mouth. "Sweetheart, kin I git you some skittles? I know you lack skittles; I love 'em."

"No, I don't want skittles."

Little Cassidy looked at Scarlette scared for dear life.

"Mommy, somethin' feel funny."

Scarlette was on her best behavior; she was as kind as she knew how to be. "Mindy, let me take her somewhere and talk to her. I just don't know what's wrong with her today."

They went into a corner for a little privacy.

Scarlette whispered, "Honey, not now. Will you wait until we get home?"

"Mommy, I wanna go home. Somethin' wrong Mommy."

"Honey, we are not going to be here long."

Mommy, I wanna go see Mrs. Rachel."

"Of course, we will go see Mrs. Rachel."

Little Cassidy Arnasia finally calmed down. When they got back to their seats, there was a crowd formed all around. Everyone wanted to ask them questions about their lifestyle. Obviously Kyle told all of their business.

One guy name Bill asked, "So Kyle, What's it lack living high on the hog?"

Ridge answered, "What are you talking about?"

"Yall look lack movie stars. Yall look lack money man. Yall, even, smell lack money."

Everyone started giggling hysterically. Ridge knew they would not be there for very long.

As Kyle laughed he said, "Ridge he joking old Buddy."

Mindy was smiling as usual. "They know he was just joking."

She turned to Little Cassidy Arnasia as her smile got even bigger. "Ain't that right baby?"

By this time, Scarlette was on the edge of her seat.

Little Cassidy said, "Mommy, I don't lack what they laughin' 'bout. Mommy, why are they laughing lack that?"

Ridge said, "Honey, they are just having fun."

Meriah could not hold her peace any longer. "Just having fun, Dad how we live is nobody's business. Maybe they need to start their own business."

All of their heads turned to Meriah. They started laughing uncontrollably again.

Kyle tried to cheer her up. "Meriah, baby we don't mean no harm. This here how we have fun."

Ridge felt the need to explain. "Kyle, my girls are getting upset. So if you and your friends could back off, it would be greatly appreciated."

"Ridge, man you know we jus' messin' wit' ya."

"No Kyle, that is quite enough for one day."

"So sensitive old buddy."

All of Kyle's friends backed off.

All of the women were eating in one place and all of the men were eating in another place in the house. The women were in the packed dining room with a spread of food that included: rice, potato salad, hotdogs, hamburgers, fried green tomatoes, fried chicken, homemade French fries, lemon pie, coconut cream pie, red velvet cake, pineapple cheesecake and several pound cakes. The beverages included: soda, beer, hard liquor, wine coolers, and mixed drinks. The table looked as though a five-year old prepared the food and placed the food on the table. Everything was uncovered, flies were everywhere. There were children coming in from the outside fixing their food without washing their hands. Obviously the adults thought it was quite alright.

Scarlette looked around, touching, and testing everything. One young lady was eating like there was no tomorrow, ignoring the fact that she was at least three hundred pounds. There were two other women standing over in the corner cursing and fussing about their *no-good husbands*. Both ladies were smoking like a chimney; a cigarette in one hand and a bottle of gin in the other. There were two other women sitting directly across from Scarlette and Little Cassidy Arnasia. They whispered and talked amongst one another mumbling. Every now and then they would look over to Scarlette and sip on their beer.

Mindy was a little tipsy. "Scarlette, yall still hanging 'round them people who love somebody or somethin' that they can't see."

Scarlette was uncomfortable, and not only because of her current surroundings.

She thought, *"Why am I so uncomfortable? I am always saying Your Jesus. Why am I irritated with this question?"*

Mindy thought Scarlette was daydreaming. She clapped her hands to get Scarlette's attention.

Scarlette explained, "Oh yes we are, but it does not matter what they believe in. We know where we stand."

The other ladies looked intuitive.

One of them, whose name was *Margie* bluntly blurted out. "Ain't that straddling the fence?"

"No, that's not at all straddling the fence. Plain and

simple, we enjoy their company. Besides, Little Cassidy here loves being in their company as well. "

Margie responded, "How in the world can you call yourself an atheist?"

"I am a grown woman and quite frankly, I befriend whomever I please. Who are you?"

Little Cassidy Arnasia looked up towards her Mom. "Mommy, I feel strong now."

Margie smiled as she covered her mouth. "Barbie boo upset and her li'le angel."

Mindy interrupted, "Margie, that's enough."

There were many deceitful and devious chuckles all around the table.

Meanwhile, Ridge was sitting with the men in the living room. The living room was filled with men who were smoking and drinking. This house smelled like old cigarette butts that had been sitting for months and winos that had not showered for months. Every other word consists of a curse word. Ridge blended in well once he desperately psyched himself up.

All the men were a little tipsy or drunk at this point.

Kyle's friend Bo tried to pry. "So pretty boy Ridge, that's a sharp Benz sittin' outside. Um, how many mo' you got in yo' carport?"

"Man, how many do you have in your garage?"

"Wait, wait a minute pretty boy Ridge. Can't a man ax a quest'on? We jus' havin' a li'le fun; that's all."

All the other men burst out laughing. Some coughed like they were going to cough up a lung at anytime. Meanwhile there was a vulgar smell that took up the living room. Ridge laughed along with them just to keep the atmosphere somewhat bearable.

Ridge cracked a smile and finally answered. "Of course you can ask a question."

Ridge smiled again.

Ridge continued, "But, don't call me *Pretty Boy.*"

Bo cracked a joke. "Yeah you right, I sho want want you

to call me *Pretty Boy.* I be dog gon it, I don't quite fit that name anyway."

All the other men laughed hysterically. Ridge laughed as he looked around. Most of the men covered their mouths while holding a can of beer in the other hand. Other men had no care in the world to show the couple of teeth that was left.

Ridge thought, *"I share a common bond with these men. Why am I here? These men are nothing like I would want to be in a million years. I love our friends who are Christians, but I don't believe."*

Another man name *Van* asked, "I got a question for ya. How is it havin' a woman that look good lack that?"

Ridge acted as though he had the faintest idea what he was talking about.

"What do you mean by that?

"Yo wife is drop dead gogous, man. Man if I had a wife lack that, I would keep her lock up. My wife tell me all the time I'm jealous. I know you jealous wit' a woman lack that."

"No, I'm not jealous. We trust one another. Besides, we are compatible."

Van slowly said, "com-pa-ti-ble, what you mean?" As soon as the other men heard Van trying to pronounce the word *compatible*, they all started laughing hysterically.

He explained, "It means we are a great match."

"Yeah, yall do fit t'gether. I guess me and my old lady is com-pa-ti-ble."

All the men laughed hysterically again.

Ridge tried to encourage him. "I'm sure you two make a great couple."

Kyle anxiously interrupted. "Old buddy, you reckon I kin fin' me a old lady lack yo's?"

"Don't say that, because it is disrespectful to your wife."

Van said, "Yeah, but the trut' is the trut'. Ain't no way 'round that."

One of the women heard what they were talking about; she instantly cursed her husband out and immediately went and told the other ladies. Before long, some of the wives were very upset and ready to go home. The couples who did stay were not speaking to one another.

Ridge suddenly appeared. He noticed Scarlette was upset along with Little Cassidy Arnasia. Little Cassidy still had that intuitive look.

Ridge asked Scarlette, "Honey, are you ready to go?"

"Yes, get Meriah and let's get out of here."

They went in the back to get Meriah. Then he went to Kyle to say his goodbyes, "Thank you for inviting us. I think it is about time for us to head back to Atlanta.

Kyle apologized, "Look ol' buddy, sorry 'bout all the hiccups. It ain't yo' fault.

He looked at Scarlette from head to toe, smiling, with a bottle of beer in one hand.

Scarlette immediately turned her head away and dropped her head.

"Don't worry, we are fine," Ridge quickly responded.

Mindy rushed over to Ridge, Scarlette and the girls. Mindy observe all of them from Ridge down to Little Cassidy Arnasia.

She smiled with that open space in the middle of her mouth. She apologized. "Sorry 'bout all our friends. When they start to drinking they always start acting lack they ain't got no home trainin'. Yall want some beer fo' the road?"

Scarlette anxiously looked away.

Ridge and the girls had already left.

Kyle was a little confused.

He commented to his friends, "Somethin' goin' on wit' my ol' pal."

Van laughed then commented. "Maybe it's all that money."

All the others laughed as well, but Kyle thought, *"I can't put my finga on it. He not the same pal."*

On the way home, there was total silence until Little Cassidy Arnasia broke the ice.

"Mommy Daddy, it was not right at that house?"

Ridge answered, "I hate to admit it sweetheart. I think you

were right this time."

"That house was cloudin' my head. Oh Daddy, I always feel like I right. Daddy, you know I get that feelin' and I jus' know it right, Daddy."

Scarlette asked, "Sweet heart, what do you mean by clouding your head?"

"Mommy you know like they faces and some of the teet'. Mommy, what happen to some of the teet'? They not right, Mommy."

Scarlette replied, "Yes Sweetheart, I know what you are talking about trust me.

Meriah commented, "Daddy, that house should be off limits to adults much less children. Those children were acting like they were high. Why do you make friends with people like that?"

"We have a great deal in common, honey. You know we have been friends a long time."

"Yes Dad, I remember Kyle and Mindy ever since I was a little girl."

Scarlette interrupted, "Meriah did you forget Mr. and Mrs? We have taught you a little better than that."

"I have a question, when adults behave like children, do you still have to show respect?"

Scarlette had to admit, "I can't believe this, but that is a great question.

Scarlette paused.

Ridge replied, "I believe no matter what, always show respect."

"It's hard to respect old people who drink and smoke for entertainment."

Scarlette asked, "Well, what do you think when your Dad and I drink?"

"I guess people do what they want to do when they don't have anything they believe in."

Ridge conveniently jumped in the conversation, "Meriah, what exactly do you mean by that statement?"

"I think everybody needs something or someone to answer to."

"Now this wouldn't have anything to do with our Christian friends?"

"Yes Daddy, I don't understand why we haven't chosen to believe."

"Honey, there isn't anything to choose from. We have always been atheists and we will always be atheists."

"Daddy, do you think that is a wise decision?"

Ridge felt guilty and did not know why. "Honey, we made the decision years ago and that settles it."

Later on while flipping through stations on the radio, Ridge stumbled upon a country, gospel song which was a story. The story was told by the lead singer. This story was about the family next door. *The family next door was always going through hard times. Once the Mother fought cancer, God was right there. Twice the Father got laid off, God was right there. Three times the children got taken away because of the parents' inability to provide, even though they tried with every bit of their being to provide, God was still there. Four times other relatives stayed with them because they had nowhere else to lay their heads. God was right there. Oh, but the fifth time the Lord sent a million dollars to their doorstep because of their perseverance and faith. The family who watched all the trials and tribulations over the years was UNBELIEVERS!*

As the song played the car got silent. It was as if everything was in slow motion. Ridge stared straight ahead. Scarlette gazed out of the window. Little Cassidy Arnasia did not say one word; she just looked at her Daddy and Mommy back and forth. Meriah stared out of the window with a slight smile on her face.

They felt chills all over.

Scarlette looked to Ridge. "Do you feel some sort of power or maybe even strange?"

"Honey yes, but we will talk after the song is gone off.

Strangely enough, I want to listen to the rest of the song."

Scarlette whispered quickly, "Oh yes, I do too."

They listened to the rest of the song. Both Ridge and Scarlette was puzzled with what they had experienced.

As the song went off the radio, Little Cassidy Arnasia burst out and said, "Mommy Mommy, I got that feeling when I'm round Mrs. Rachel."

Scarlette and Ridge was silent. Both of them had tears running down their faces. Both had to wipe their tears. As quickly as the tears came, there were more on the way. Meriah knew her Stepmom and Dad were crying; she tried to smooth everything over by saying something.

"Cassidy, we feel it. Give them a minute."

Even as Scarlette cried, she had to smile a little when Meriah actually was acting like a great big sister and great step-daughter.

When they finally got themselves together, Scarlette said, "Cassidy, you're right it felt like Mrs. Rachel was in the car with us."

Little Cassidy Arnasia was very excited, "Mommy, that's a good feelin'. Was that their Jesus?"

Scarlette let go just a little bit more, "It may have very well been."

She thought, *I know that was their Jesus; that feeling felt just like that day that song came on at Sasha's salon and Joanne's party.*

Ridge asked, "Cassidy, did you get that feeling when you were at Mr. Kyle's house?"

Little Cassidy Arnasia explained with eyes full of tears, "Daddy, I don't like the feelin' at Mr. Kyle and Mrs. Mindy house. Daddy, not nothin' good 'bout that house."

Scarlette remarked, "I totally agree sweetheart; it's just not a good way to live."

Ridge whispered to Scarlette. "In the song, the family next door went through some difficult times. At the end of all of it they received a million dollars. They were believers, sweetheart."

Scarlette commented, "The people who watched everything were unbelievers."

Both teared up again then quickly looked away.

Little Cassidy Arnasia smiled and looked over to her big sister Meriah.

She asked, "Meriah, that song, did it feel good to yo' heart?"

"Yeah, it would be nice to feel like that all the time."

Ridge looked out of the window. Scarlette's head dropped.

 WORDS OF WISDOM

Brothers and Sisters, we all have people in our lives that do not believe there is a God. God is continuously working even when we think He's not. We should live our lives as a reflection of Christ. In return, God will do and is doing the rest. I Believe!

CHAPTER 18

Mark 8:34-36 Then he called the crowd to him along with his disciples and said: "If anyone would come after me, he must deny himself and take up his cross and follow me. For whoever wants to save his life will lose it, but whoever loses his life for me and for the gospel will save it. What good is it for a man to gain the whole world, yet forfeit his soul?"
(N.I.V.)

It was early August.

The phone rang; it was cousin BJ on the other line.

Rachel answered, "Hi cousin BJ, how have you been?"

Cousin BJ replied loudly. "Cuz, you sound like you a doctor a somethin' girl. I'm jus' kidin'. Way yo big shot husband? I bet he out makin' dat money."

Rachel knew Cousin BJ's personality. She of course, loved him anyway.

"Cousin BJ, how is your family?"

"They doin' good. Them kids bad as the devil."

"You shouldn't say that about your children. There is power in your tongue."

"Powa in yo' tongue. Cuz, you got me kinda 'fused. What you mean by dat?"

"If you say that about your children they are going to be what you say they are. You have to watch the words that you speak. If you speak negative, you are going to get negativity. If you speak positive, you are going to get positivity."

"Oh, yeah I need to quit dat. Ok cuz we wanna come see yall. Yeah me, my wife, and my kids."

Rachel excited, but deep down inside she knew that she had to prepare herself spiritually and mentally, "Cousin BJ that would be a blessing, but you have to promise me that you and your family will come to church with us."

"Yeah we gonna go cause I know dealin' wit' yall, we ain't got no choice."

Rachel and Cousin BJ laughed.

"You know we love the Lord, Cousin BJ."

"Yeah, Yo ever'body know dat."

"Let me talk to John to see when he will be free to take a couple of days off."

"Cuz, you kinda got me.

He laughed.

"Shoot, I thought you was gonna say we can't come."

Rachel smiled. "Cousin BJ, why would I say no? We love you all."

"Yeah, yall good people."

"I'll call you back later today when I talk to John. You all take care and may God bless you."

"Ok, call me back now."

A couple of weeks later, cousin BJ and his family visited the Richardsons.

Rachel and John had to make sure they alert the gate guards of Cousin BJ's arrival. Charlotte and Charles were outside in the yard. As soon as Charlotte heard a loud noise coming down the street she figured it was her Cousin BJ arriving. Charlotte ran in the house to tell her parents that Cousin BJ was on the way. Rachel came outside so that she could greet Cousin BJ and the family. As she walked out, the only thing Rachel could hear was something that sounded like an automobile that was in need of a set of mufflers. Cousin BJ came around the corner with his 1986 purple custom van with hydraulics. The van looked as though he added every accessory that he could find to fit on his van. The chrome on the rims shined as though he had just got finished cleaning them. The glitter in the paint sparkled just as bright as the rims. The interior was custom done with purple suede all the way through. Inside was clean as a whistle.

When Cousin BJ and his family got out of the car, everyone was there to greet them. John naturally gravitated towards Cousin BJ. Rachel headed towards his wife Memphis. Charlotte and Charles greeted the children.

John was excited, "How are you all doing Cousin BJ?"

"Yo, we fine. Man, this a mansion. Yo, yall livin' it up in Atlanta.

He looked around.

Yeah, I know yall rollin' in the doe."

John and Cousin BJ laughed while they walked over to where Rachel and Memphis were.

"Memphis, did you all have a great trip?" John kindly asked.

"Yeah, Tennessee and Barry Joe Jr. was sleep da whole time. Cuz, yall got a mansion wow!"

John and Rachel admirably thanked them.

Rachel asked, "May we help you all with your bags?"

"Yo Cuz, me and John go handle these bags.

He looked at John.

"Right Cuz?"

"Of course I don't mind helping. John, Rachel and the kids walked Cousin BJ Memphis and their kids to the guess house.

Before their family arrived, Rachel and John always went in the guest house to pray throughout the rooms. To Rachel this gave her assurance that all guests would be blessed. The guest house was absolutely beautiful and peaceful. There were scriptures throughout the house, family pictures, and pictures of the different places that they had gone. The house had three bed rooms, two bathrooms, a huge grate room, laundry room and exercise room. Rachel sat a bible, the daily bread, herbal tea and chocolates out on the coffee table. There was gospel, inspirational and encouraging music that would automatically play for their guests. As their guests entered the guest house they would feel a heavenly flow throughout the house.

Everyone entered the guest house.

As they walked in Cousin BJ commented, "Yo this jest lack one of them suites at one of them 'pensive hotels them stars stay in.

"Cousin BJ, we certainly try our best to be a blessing to anyone that set foot in this sanctuary that God has bestowed upon us," John kindly remarked.

Memphis joked around, "Cuz, when kin we move in?"

Everyone laughed.

Rachel replied, "Memphis it is yours while you visit."

Cousin BJ was excited, "Yo, I ain't gonna wanna leave here."

Barry Joe Jr. and Tennessee came out of their rooms very excited.

Barry Joe Jr. was thrilled and ready to have fun with his cousins, "Daddy, I got my own room."

"Boy, what you talkin' 'bout? You got yo own room at da house," Cousin BJ asked.

"Daddy, I sleep on a futon. I got a king size bed here. This house feel lack I'm in church."

"Yeah the music is kinda peaceful. Yo Cuz, I bet yall did a prayer."

"Cousin BJ, we are always led by the Holy Spirit," John said in a peaceful manner.

Memphis was still very excited. "Yall bless, I can't wait to tell my fam'ly how nice yall place is. Oh, kin we take pictures?"

Rachel and John said, *"yes"* all at once.

"Uncle John, kin yall adop' me?" Tennessee was thrilled.

"You wouldn't want to leave your parents."

Tennessee with a smile as wide as the Joker remarked, "I betcha one hundred dolla's."

When they were finished putting the luggage away, everyone gathered in the great room. Rachel got everyone snacks. Music was peacefully playing while everyone sat around having conversation.

Cousin BJ intuitively, "Cuz, so way yo' office at?"

"Cousin BJ, I work in the heart of Atlanta at my law firm called *Richardson Law Firm and Associates*. It is truly a blessing when you are obedient to what God has called you to do."

"Cuz, you call the shots! That's why you livin' lack a king."

Rachel shared, "Cousin BJ, none of this would be possible without the hand of God."

Cousin BJ was a little choked up as he commented, "I know yall believe in God and ever'thing. Yeah, yall know I been in church all my life, but why would God do all this fo' yall and not do it fo' a broke brothe' lack me?"

John felt where Cousin BJ was coming from. "Please don't get offended by this when I say this, but it is not about going to church. It is about being the church. The church is in you."

"What you mean by dat?"

"The church is a building where people go to worship God together. Sometimes, people go for other reasons. But I want get into that right now. Cousin BJ, are you a Christian?"

"Yeah, Yo I got baptize when I was a kid."

"Being baptized doesn't make you a Christian. You have to confess with your mouth that Jesus is Lord."

John grabbed the Bible off of the coffee table.

He turned to Romans 10: 8-10, then he began to read. *"The word is near you; it is in your mouth and in your heart" that is, the word of faith we are proclaiming: That if you confess with your mouth, "Jesus is Lord, "and believe in your heart that God raised him from the dead, you will be saved. For it is with your heart that you believe and are justified, and it is with your mouth that you confess and are saved. (N.I.V)*

Cousin BJ laughed hysterically afterwards. "Yo, you jokin' right, Cuz you got me in the gut wit' dat."

He paused and the longer he sat, the longer he thought about what John showed him in the Bible and the more disheartening the situation became. All of a sudden everyone got quiet.

John asked out of concern. "Cousin BJ is everything ok? It is my job to make sure you have the right understanding about salvation.

"Cuz, I go to church sometimes, but dat ain't working Yo."

Memphis anxiously jumped into the conversation. "You mean, we really not save, cause I got baptize at twelve too. I thought we was save too."

Rachel explained, "Honey, God works in mysterious ways. This was in God's divine plan for you all to come here on this day to hear that specific scripture. It says in the Word, "My people perish from lack of knowledge." Sometimes it takes someone being out of their usual routine to gain insight."

Cousin BJ and Memphis was stunned.

To ease the atmosphere John explained, "You all have nothing to be embarrassed or upset about. Listen, no one has it all together. I have issues; Rachel has issues. No one is perfect. Cousin BJ, yes I am a lawyer and a successful one at that, but that doesn't make me any better than anyone else."

"Cuz, you good people yo. Yall not lack them other people dat live lack yall do. Yo, how yall git so low key."

"Cousin BJ, we know who is the head of our lives and we

know through Him anything is possible."

Meanwhile the children were sitting in their own area, but in the same room.

Charlotte asked, "How do you like school?"

Tennessee answered, "I don't lack school, 'cause ever'body always fight."

"What do you mean?" Charles inquired."

Barry Joe Jr. explained, "Man they fight on the bus. If they not fightin' on the bus, they fightin' in class. Man, I hate my school."

"I bet yall go to school wit' a bunch of rich folk," Tennessee wondered while cheesing.

Charles shared, "Yes, we do and I don't say this too often. I recognize that our school is pretty cool and not because there are many rich students there."

"Man, I need to come and live wit' yall," Barry Joe Jr. was excited.

Charlotte smiled and said, "I'm sure you would miss your parents."

"Um, I be alright."

Tennessee said, "I know I lack it here. Yall always goin' to church. Yall rich and ain't nothing wrong wit' dat."

Charlotte softly explained, "Mommy and Daddy always tells us to never brag and always be thankful and humble for the things that God has given us."

Barry Joe Jr. said, "Man, if I had a house lack this and cars lack yall got," *while he looked directly at Charles*, "I would have ever'body flockin' to me."

Charles humbly replied, "Our parents would flip if we were to act like that towards other people."

"All the girls at my school would wanna be jest lack me," Tennessee fantasized while watching Charlotte and Charles.

Barry Joe Jr. asked, "Man, do yall really go to church all the time?"

"Yes, we love going to church," Charles said with great confidence.

Tennessee let go. "We go to church every blue moon. I wish we go more."

"Yeah, I do like church," Charles quickly added.

Soon after, John, Rachel and the kids went back to the main house until it was time for dinner.

After they left, Cousin BJ, Memphis and the kids had a conversation.

Cousin BJ started thinking out loud. "Yo Memphis, this a nice house, ain't it?"

Memphis did not answer fast enough.

Barry Joe Jr. was sincerely puzzled. He asked, "Daddy, why some people kin live lack this and some people can't?"

"What you mean Bro? I bet you think we ain't go never be able to have somethin' lack this," Cousin BJ asked.

Barry Joe Jr. answered, "Daddy, be fo' real. We want ever be able to git not'in lack this."

Memphis agreed, "Yeah, this place is nice, ever'body want a house lack this. Come on, this gues' house is way bigger then our trailer. Our trailer kin fit inside this here gues' house.

"Daddy this a dream house for all the lit'le girls. Oh and lit'le boys too," Tennessee commented.

"Suga, I know what you talkin' 'bout. I feel lack a different woman in here. It somethin' in the air; I don't know what it is. It's a good feelin'. It feel lack when we go to church," Memphis was still overjoyed.

Cousin BJ commented, "Yeah Cousin Rachel and Big shot, they good people. They bless."

Tennessee said, "They don' be lis'enin' to dat rap. They jes' lis'en to gospel and dat uplifin' music."

Cousin BJ was curious. "I know them kids lis'en to dat rap."

"No, they don't daddy, dat is kinda strange," Barry Joe Jr. assured him.

"I believe that son," Memphis agreed.

Tennessee explained, "Daddy, they don' lis'en to dat rap, they always goin' to church and it jes seem lack they have a lit light up over they heads. It almos' lack you wanna step inside they shado'."

Cousin BJ said, "Lit'le girl, I think I kinda know what you sayin'."

A song came on the radio. Suddenly, he thought of his lovely Mother. His Mother was an anointed woman of God and the anointing flowed when she sang. This song was one of his Mother's favorite songs. It brought tears to his eyes. Memphis, Tennessee and Barry Joe Jr. noticed when the song came on, Cousin BJ's entire demeanor changed. Memphis moved closer to Cousin BJ, as she touched him, he trembled as he reminisced on how he loved this song and how his Mother led the song on the adult choir back in their home church. Cousin BJ's Mother was suffering from Alzheimer's.

He thought, *"Momma always say son never fogit you kin do ever'thing when God is in it. Back then I wanted to be somebody so I kin take care my Momma. I can't even take care my fam'ly much less, my Momma. What in the jimmy cricket happen?"*

Tears started trickling down his cheeks. Memphis started experiencing what she felt several times at church. Barry Joe Jr. noticed his parents were very serious at that moment and he knew there was something in the atmosphere. Then he remembered when they were at Mama Lula and Papa Ray's house. Tennessee looked at everyone, one by one and burst out in tears.

She thought, *"Is dat Jesus? This feel lack at Mama Lula and Papa Ray house and at church.*

As the song continued, Cousin BJ started singing. Memphis began singing thereafter. Not long after, the children joined them. Their bodies started moving without them recognizing. Cousin BJ and his family have never had a moment together like this before. For the first time, they all held hands as a family of four and in unity. When the song went off, all of them naturally embraced.

Cousin BJ with tears still running down his cheek

explained, "That bought back a lotta mem'ries, jes lack at Papa Ray and Mama Lula house. That felt lack church. How kin we fogit how the spirit of Jesus feel?"

Memphis suggested, "We gotta get back to church at home."

"Yeah Momma, gra'ma need to go to," Tennessee added.

Cousin BJ replied, "I think Momma will lack dat."

"You mean we not go git to sleep in on Sund'ys?" Barry Joe Jr. selfishly thought.

"Daddy you gonna have to stop drinkin' yo' beer."

Cousin BJ looked away thinking about the challenges ahead.

Memphis remarked, "Ever'thin' is gonna have to change."

"Daddy yo life ain't over." *Little Tennessee gave a little words of wisdom.* "It ain't never too late, Daddy."

Memphis looked toward Tennessee. "Baby, you right yo Daddy still young."

Cousin BJ said, "I might need to go to school. Yo, I ain't never been good in school. School jes ain't fo' me."

He observed the guest house. Then he started thinking about his home in South Carolina.

"I guess I ain't go never have nothin' lack this."

Memphis reacted, "Babe, this a nice place any woman would die fo' it. BJ, it don't take all this to be happy."

"Yeah, but babe you think I don't want somethin' lack this fo' my fam'ly."

He looked around again.

"What a man lack me 'pose to do? I didn't even finish ninet' grade. Momma had need some help wit' bills. Why not help my Momma? I 'pose to help Momma."

Later Rachel went to escort them to the main house. While they were walking to the main house Rachel noticed Cousin BJ was not quite himself.

She looked at him. "Cousin BJ, I don't know how to take you when you're not joking. I can feel that there is something on your mind. Cousin BJ, always remember John and I are here if you need us."

"Yo I ain't no free-loada Cuz."

Memphis glanced at Rachel.

"Cousin BJ, I know that."

When they walked in, their eyes lit up even more; the house was breathtaking. The atmosphere was pleasant, and serene. There were beautiful paintings everywhere you look and right next to, beneath or on top of the paintings were scriptures and words of encouragement. They were totally comfortable in this environment due to all the godly love that Rachel, John and the children possessed. They were no longer intimidated by the materialistic things that surrounded them. Rachel had the table looking exquisite. She laid out her fine china; the table was decorated in bright yellow and blue throughout the dining room. There were candles scattered about on the table. In the middle of the table there was a massive bouquet of fresh cut yellow roses. These beautiful decorations were on a big-oversized walnut dining room set. On the table were: macaroni and cheese, ham, candy yams, dirty rice, potato salad, chicken dressing, fried chicken, green beans, pumpkin pie, strawberry cheese cake and lemon pie.

At the dining room table Rachel told everyone to join hands while John said the grace. After the grace, Rachel, John and the kids took their napkins then spread it on their laps. At the same time Cousin BJ, Memphis, Tennessee and Barry Joe Jr. immediately started using their utensils. They simply were not use to this type of environment at dinner time. Of course Rachel and John were not going to say anything.

Out of nowhere, Charlotte, in the sweetest voice known to man said, "Cousin BJ, everyone is supposed to spread their napkins on their laps."

Memphis was a little embarrassed, "Oh, we sorry."

Everyone laughed.

John pleasantly remarked, "That's fine we are just accustomed to dining a certain way."

Cousin BJ commented, "Cuz, yall eatin' lack yall own

Atlanta."

Everyone laughed.

Man, I know we keep sayin' how nice this house is, it mus' be nice livin' large lack dat."

"Cousin BJ, "Without God none of this would be possible." Rachel made sure everyone knew that God was always blessing.

Barry Joe Jr. said, "Cousin Rachel, that's how them people yall hang out wit' do it to; don't they?"

Cousin BJ immediately corrected, "Boy, watch yo' mout'."

"It's quite alright Cousin BJ." Rachel understood Cousin BJ's reaction.

Charles smoothed out the atmosphere. "The next time everyone should know what the cloth napkins are for."

Cousin BJ commented, "Yeah, now I know how to ac' if we ever go to one of them fantsy rest'rants."

Everyone laughed.

"Yes, you are certainly right Cousin BJ that is what they usually do as well." Rachel said with such humbleness.

John smiled as he inquired, "Memphis I'm very curious about this. How did you get the name *Memphis*?"

"I git dat all the time." Memphis grinned.

"That's my great-gran'ma name."

Cousin BJ loudly and proudly explained, "Yeah when she was pregnant with little Tennessee."

Memphis nudged Cousin BJ. Then they laughed.

"I tol' Memphis it'll be on time to name baby girl *Tennessee*."

Charles and Charlotte look at one another and burst out laughing.

Rachel, without a smile, turned to them and quickly corrected them. "Children that is quite enough."

John turned towards Charlotte and Charles and gave a stern look.

"Cuz, them kids alright, shoot my kids even joke 'bout it. Everybody do." Cousin BJ, did not care.

Rachel explained, "Yes, I can certainly understand where

you are coming from, but my children are not allowed to make fun."

"Ah Cuz lighten up they fine."

"Alright Cousin BJ."

She looked at Charlotte then to Charles with no smile.

"They are off the hook this time; but they still know the difference between right and wrong."

Tennessee remarked, "I git pick on so much at school 'till I done got use to it."

"Cuz, *referring to John*, yo you know ever'body always wonda what's so diff'rent 'bout yall. I'm gonna tell ever'body yall really livin' for Jesus."

John explained, "Cousin BJ when you are truly following Christ, sometimes it's not easy. It is a life that no Christian would want to live without."

Rachel explained, "The main thing Christians need to do is get in position. What I mean by that is you have to be obedient to what God is telling you to do."

"Yeah, Cuz lack wit' me I love my beer ever'day after I get off work. See dat pumpwood is some hard, tough work. Me and da boys always joke and say you ain't a man 'till you pump some wood."

Everyone laughed hysterically.

John said honestly, "I don't know whether I would be able to survive."

Cousin BJ commented, "Yeah, Cuz you the man, but you wouldn't be able to take on my job. Yo hands too pretty."

Everyone laughed.

"Yes Cousin BJ, I'm going to have to agree with you on that." John was quite happy to agree.

Sasha came by to give Rachel some products for her hair from the salon. As Rachel and Sasha walked in the dining room, Cousin BJ almost choked on his food because of Sasha's stunning looks. Cousin BJ could not resist himself. Sasha's skin was flawless. Her skin and hair was a mixture of black and Japanese. The texture turned out to be cold black with deep waves like that of finger waves flowing from the scalp all the way down to the tip ends.

Rachel introduced Sasha to everyone. When she got to Cousin BJ, the only thing he could do was giggle like a monkey out of control. When Rachel realized that he had taken an interest in Sasha, she immediately, but kindly got Sasha out of the door. Of course Sasha was not going to stay very long anyway. But Rachel was always so very polite, kind and watchful.

Everyone was finishing their dinner.

Cousin BJ asked, "Cuz, *referring to Rachel,* all yall friends look lack movie stars?"

She pretended she didn't know what he was talking about.

"I'm not sure of what you are saying."

John pretended purposely as well. "Our friends have successful businesses and they have to carry themselves in a certain manner."

Memphis asked, "So Cousin Rachel what kinda business she got?"

"She owns a salon in the heart of Atlanta."

"Yeah she look lack money."

Cousin BJ loudly interrupted, "Cuz, what dat girl mix wit'? Cause I know she mix."

Rachel quickly answered, "Yes, I think her Mother is Japanese and her Father is black.

Rachel instantly and intentionally changed the subject.

"So is everyone ready to go to church Sunday?"

Tennessee responded, "Yes Mam, we was jes talkin' 'bout that."

Barry Joe Jr. commented, "Cousin Rachel, I can't stan' when church is borin'."

Rachel politely reassured him. "I'm sure you want be bored at all. We have children's church and teen's church for you all. You will enjoy church and most importantly, receive the message that God has for you."

Cousin BJ jokingly shared, "Cuz, I might need to go to dat teen church so I kin understan'."

Charlotte with that Minnie mouse tone tried to reassure her cousin. "Tennessee, you are going to love children's church. I'll take care of you. Sometimes, they don't treat people like Jesus would."

Charles said timidly, "Yes, Barry Joe Jr. you'll be fine with me in teen's church. They act kind of crazy sometimes, but you just have to ignore them."

John said, "Yes, we are going to have to introduce you all to Pastor Patterson."

Memphis said excitedly, "Yeah, I always wanted to go to one of them big churches."

Cousin BJ grinned, "Yall think they gonna let me roll in dat parkin' lot wit' the purple star?"

John said, "Of course Cousin BJ, don't be silly, man."

"Yeah dat what you say. Yo you know that parkin' lot gonna be fill with Beemer's, Benz's, and Jags."

Rachel smiled, "Cousin BJ that is not what it is about. It is about Jesus. You know Cousin BJ not one of those Beemer's, Benz's and Jags are going to get anyone into heaven. If they don't have Jesus, they don't have anything except a temporary high."

Cousin BJ laughed loudly, "Alright Cuz, I hear ya girl."

Everyone was arriving at Sunday morning service. Rachel walked all the children to their classes. Meanwhile, John, Cousin BJ, and Memphis were all sitting in the sanctuary awaiting service. As their friends arrived, John introduced Cousin BJ and Memphis to them. Rachel arrived back just a few minutes before praise and worship. Paul and Sasha came just in time for praise and worship as well. As soon as they walked past John, Rachel, Cousin BJ and Memphis, Cousin BJ's head quickly turned towards Sasha. He developed this great, big smile. Memphis noticed and immediately slid closer to him. She nudged him, grabbed his hand then whispered something in his ear. Instantly and mysteriously Cousin BJ calmed down.

The praise and worship leaders started singing *Thank You Lord For Everything*. Rachel and John immediately stood up. As they stood up, Cousin BJ and Memphis looked at one another not knowing what to expect. As praise and worship progressed, the more people got up in the congregation to sing, worship, and praise the Lord. Along with Cousin BJ and Memphis were people looking at others wondering why they were acting the way they were. These particular people obviously weren't use to this sort of atmosphere, but on the other hand others were use to praising God. When this particular worship leader sung, her voice was like that of rolling thunder. The words of the song seem to leap on hearts that had been hardened for ages. She ministered, "No one knows what the person that is sitting next to you have gone through or is going through. You should praise God, no matter who is around! Why don't you get up and give God the highest praise!" A lady started screaming. Her friends that was with her seemed as though they were afraid or maybe they just wasn't use to their friend reacting in such a manner. When the ushers came to attend to the lady, her friends who were still sitting, were fixing their obviously tailor made suits. At the same time looking down to see if their shoes were free of dirt. Apparently they just did not want this sort of attention drawn to them.

Meanwhile, Ronald got up with his hands in the air knowing that God is going to continue providing the strength for his family. Tressie slowly got up. She suddenly lifted her hands for dear life while tears trickled down her face.

She thought, *"I need all the help that I can to endure this mountain. Thank you for my husband and my children and I do mean my Stacey as well. Someday I will be alright with the word disability. Lord please continue to give me strength where need be."*

When Tressie's hands went up, Ronald began crying like never before. His manner was that of a Mother weeping for her child. A couple rows back Reese was holding Melody tightly as he felt worn in his spirit. Both were thinking of spending time with their children and the stronghold that both of them had been struggling with which was their image. Melody finally stood up; Reese arose immediately afterwards. He ran his fingers through his hair then instantly began crying. When Melody turned her head and saw the way Reese opened his heart, she finally opened her heart, instantly began to weep. These glorious connections between the other couples filled John and Rachel's hearts even more; they continued weeping for their friends because they knew what their friends were battling. John and Rachel began to thank God for what he was doing and continued to do. Without looking, they started holding hands in unity for their friends.

Cousin BJ and Memphis jumped up without knowing what was happening. The only thing they knew is that at this particular moment they needed to be up thanking God for everything. John was standing next to Cousin BJ then grabbed Cousin BJ's hand. The spirit was so strong it flowed through Cousin BJ's hands and before Memphis knew it she was holding Cousin BJ's hand. John, Rachel, Cousin BJ, and Memphis hands were raised giving God the highest praise. Sasha and Paul saw all of their friends crying and praising God. They couldn't help, but stand up and give God all the praise for every aspect of their lives.

Howard sat still for a while until he started patting his feet uncontrollably. Joanne was already sitting while crying. She saw Howard patting his feet. Before she realized it she popped up, both of her hands up in the air. Whatever Joanne was going through at that moment, she forgot all about everything. She praised God for the good and the bad. Howard found himself up out of the seat with his hands up to the most high and tears streaming down his face.

Pastor Patterson spirit was stirred up from praise and worship; therefore there was no need to preach. He had an altar call. Pastor Patterson, the associate Ministers and Deacons prepared for prayer.

One young lady started walking down the aisle with her six children. She had one in her arms and holding one child's hand. The other four looked completely lost, walking slowly behind their Mother and tears streaming down their innocent faces. They knew their Mother was hurting, but they were help-less. This young lady was single, in her twenties, and she had six children ages ranging from a year old to ten years old. This young lady was tired of being sick and tired. As she came up her hair was all over the place from crying, moaning and groaning; her clothes looked as though she tried her best emotionally, mentally and physically. She barely made it to the altar. Her eyes appeared as if she suffered from allergies due to the swelling and gunshot red coloring.

There were some people who thought, *"How could she come out the house looking as such and to allow her children to come out the house looking in such disturbing ways."*

Others thought, *"She probably should have thought about that before she had all of those children."*

One gentleman bowed his head and prayed, *"God bless this young lady. You know her story, it matters! Give her a sound mind and provide her the finances that she need to survive with her children. In Jesus's name, amen."*

Several ministers started praying over the young lady. When they got finished, they escorted her to the Pastor's office.

Cousin BJ and Memphis was still moved from praise and worship. Cousin BJ headed up to the altar. Memphis followed immediately afterwards. As they walked up, Rachel started praising God with the highest praise because she knew in her heart they were about to give their lives to Christ. Then John started giving God the highest praise as well.

When they both made it up to the altar, one of the Ministers quietly asked, "How can I pray for you?"

Cousin BJ said, "We wanna git save."

Memphis agreed, "Yeah, we wanna be...

Before she could get the next word out, she started crying. Before they knew it they were on their knees worshipping God. Minutes later, the minister told the Pastor that they were there to give their lives to Christ. Pastor Patterson went to them. He looked Cousin BJ in the eyes, with all his heart, "Young man, may God bless you and your wife. Thank you for being a man of God by being a leader."

He turned to Memphis, "Young lady may God bless you."

Then he looked toward the congregation and announced, "We have two precious souls that want to give their lives to Christ."

People stood up while they clapped. Rachel and John went up to join Cousin BJ and Memphis.

Pastor Patterson looked to Cousin BJ and Memphis, "Do you believe Jesus is Lord?"

Cousin BJ and Memphis answered, "Yes Sir."

"Do you believe Jesus died on the cross for our sins?"

They answered, "Yes Sir."

"Congratulations, you have just been saved. We will send you all in the back to talk to some of the Ministers and Deacons about your walk with Christ."

The congregation stood up onto their feet while they clapped.

After service, Cousin BJ, Memphis, Rachel, John and Pastor Patterson were in his study.

Rachel was overjoyed, "Pastor Patterson, it does my heart good to see my cousins give their lives to Christ."

Cousin BJ and Memphis looked to one another with a smile.

Pastor Patterson said, "Yes, you all should have unspeakable joy right about now."

Cousin BJ replied, "Pastor Patterson, you got some 'vice fo' us?"

"Certainly son, Salvation is just a start. Now it is time to start serving and spreading the Gospel. Everyone held hands while touching and agreeing."

Pastor Patterson prayed for Cousin BJ, Memphis and the children.

The *Get Together* at John and Rachel's after church.

Rachel and John were awaiting their guests. Chef Hogan was preparing Sunday dinner for this particular Sunday. All of the children were upstairs in the children's area. Cousin BJ, Memphis, John and Rachel were in the entertainment room which was built just for fellowship. There were two sets of custom-made sectional sofas, several huge cherry wood coffee tables and end tables that matched the coffee tables. On the wall in the middle of the room there was this big beautiful painting of God's hands comforting the whole world. The name of this painting was *All God's Children in His Hands*. On the painting, there were millions of people on their knees praying inside of God's hands. On their faces were sadness, frustration, anger, anxiety, confusion, jealousy, embarrassment, humiliation and envy. Covering the entire painting was a soft silhouette of Jesus's face. Whenever Rachel had gatherings, that painting seemed to magically flow into guests' hearts. This painting literally fascinated everyone in so many different ways.

Everyone finally made it, except the Crane family. Rachel and John hired a few young ladies from church to take care of the children.

Rachel commented, "It was a moving service today."

John answered excitedly, "Yes service was definitely moving today, what a blessing for all of us."

He got up, gave Cousin BJ a handshake and Memphis a hug to congratulate them again. Everyone else was motivated by John to do the same.

Tressie tried in her best behavior to start up an honest conversation, "Cousin BJ, what is your job title?"

Rachel and John were on pins and needles. They glanced at one another wondering what in the world is Tressie going to think or say after he gives her the answer.

Cousin BJ loudly and proudly answered, "I work in pumpwood. Yeah, I been doin' dat fo' years."

She appeared totally confused, but she still had an honest question.

Tressie asked innocently, "Cousin BJ, is that some kind of special wood?"

Everyone else was so uncomfortable; they tried to ignore the conversation all together. Cousin BJ replied, "Yeah, it's that sof' wood."

Tressie surprisingly grinned and nicely smiled at Ronald. Ronald gently took her hand to calm her mind down as if she was one of his children. Suddenly the conversation disappeared.

Out of nowhere Sasha said, "Rachel, you know I have been over here and we have sat in this room numerous of times, but that picture is capturing my attention in a different way this time."

Rachel kindly replied, "Sasha you know that picture is captivating to many people. It always stirs up peoples' spirits."

Sasha shared, "Something in my spirit is leaping and I don't feel that way very often."

Cousin BJ asked, "Cuz, is dat what goin' on wit' me right now?"

Rachel innocently asked, "Cousin BJ I don't know. What exactly are you feeling?"

Sasha couldn't help herself. "Cousin BJ, I'm sorry, but don't you just feel like you have to shout and tell everyone about the goodness of Jesus."

Cousin BJ noticed Memphis was staring at the picture as well.

Then he looked back at Sasha in agreement. "Yeah, it's almos' lack somebody touch yo' heart and speakin' to ya."

Memphis commented, "Cuz, dat picture not normal."

John was filled with joy. "Praise the Lord! That picture is always a blessing to our guests."

Melody joined, "I distinctively remember when you had that beautiful baby shower for one of the young ladies at church and everyone felt the need to give their heart wrenching testimonies."

She looked around at everyone.

This stirred up Joanne's spirit. "Rachel this picture seems to have some sort of anointing. I know that sounds impossible, but it has an unusual power."

Rachel answered, "Sister, all I know is the painting is a blessing and captivating. I pray that God continues to use it to glorify His name and His power."

Howard shared, "I remember when Joanne came home from the baby shower. I thought she had been in a fight with someone."

Joanne appeared to be having flashbacks of the baby shower. When Howard turned to her, tears rolled down her face. By this time, everyone's eyes were on Joanne.

Rachel asked, "Are you alright, Sister?"

"I just remembered thinking experiences of this magnitude don't happen like this every day at a baby shower."

Sasha could not help herself. "I feel the need to share a story."

Paul and Ronald at the same time said, "What story?"

Sasha began telling her story. "Sehara and I were at the supermarket the other day. As we browsed through the supermarket on one isle, a woman was counting her money and going through her coupons. I figured she must be frustrated because she may not have enough funds to get all that she needed. I assume the little girl was her daughter. She kept asking for everything that she saw. Her Mother tried her best to ignore her. When I got to the checkout counter, the woman was checking out as well. When the checker got done with adding up her groceries, there was a discrepancy. At this point, I felt ashamed for the woman and her daughter."

Sasha's eyes watered up.

"So, I chose to walk away from that situation. As I walked past, I thought, *"Maybe I should just give her a twenty dollar bill."*

"Then I still proceeded to walk past. When I got in the car, I felt this deep feeling of guilt."

Her voice started cracking.

"Between the guilt and the shame for the woman I just said to myself, *"God loves me so much. He will forgive me for this.*

"I wondered what would happen to the woman and the little girl. Why did I automatically assume she did not have enough money? I don't know why I shared this story because it is such an embarrassment to me. Clearly, I was being selfish which is not of God. We have to do better."

Sasha looked to everyone for comfort and validation.

Rachel gave her insight, "Sasha it sounds like you were convicted by the Holy Spirit."

Cousin BJ asked, "Cuz, you mean yo' conscience?"

Reese joined, "Yes Cousin BJ you know when people say *something told me*. That is the Holy Spirit and to be honest I need to follow the Holy Spirit more often myself."

Tressie joined, "Do you have to be saved in order to have the Holy Spirit?"

Rachel replied, "Yes, you receive the Holy Spirit when you get saved. And with all my heart, I believe even when a person isn't saved, somehow, they are still guided by the voice of God."

"We got the Holy Spirit in us?" Cousin BJ asked excitedly and proudly.

"Yes Cousin BJ, the Holy Spirit is there to guide us in every step of our lives. It is up to us to follow."

Cousin BJ had to tell his story. "I don' know why, but I gotta tell this story. I never told this to nobody lack yall before."

Rachel and John were moved because they know his story.

He continued, "My Momma got bad off sick when I was in nint' grade. I was tear up when I quit school. In another way, I was happy 'cause ever'body picked at me 'cause I was in a special class."

This statement struck a chord with all the ladies. Cousin BJ and Memphis caught each others' eyes and instantly started weeping.

He choked up, "I always wanted to be good in school. Lot of times I wonda, why me?"

At this point the ladies were weeping as well as Cousin BJ and Memphis. The other men were very attentive. The men tried their best to hold back the tears.

"My daddy had died when we was li'le so Momma was already bringin' us up by herse'f. I was the oldes' of six kids. Yall, I know this sound crazy, but I was mad wit' God fo' years."

Cousin BJ buried his face in his hand. Rachel and John got up, stood next to Cousin BJ, and gently touched him.

"Now I feel thangs go change fo' me."

Everyone cheered him on for support.

He continued, "All yall livin' lack the stars do. I feel a li'le mo bette' 'bout myse'f thanks to yall. Ah… Yo look at me I'm cryin' lack I'm a li'le punk. What wrong wit' me?"

Everyone got up and formed a circle around Cousin BJ and Memphis. Rachel didn't waste time when moments like this arrived. She ran upstairs to get all of the children so they could partake in the divine moment as well. When Rachel ran upstairs, Chef Hogan joined the circle. Although Chef Hogan rarely went to church and was not a *Christian*, he knew he had to join. Everyone was down stairs. For a moment or two everything was quiet. Afterwards the adults and children grabbed one another's hands. Cousin BJ and Memphis came out of the middle then united with the circle. They knew this prayer was for everyone that was there. Unexpectedly, seven-year- old Samone wanted to say something apparently a burden was on her heart for a very long time. It was as if she was longing to express her feelings, but something kept her silent. Everyone stood there waiting and watching Samone for a few minutes. As they stood there everyone was curious as to what she had to say.

Melody was a little nervous. "Spit it out sweetheart. What's wrong? Cat got your tongue"

Reese appeared to be a little disturbed.

Samone finally said, "I'm ready to tell everybody what I wanna say, daddy."

She went around the entire circle and watched everyone's

expressions, didn't realize it, but she was standing in the front of this beautiful painting. Samone looked up at the painting.

"Everybody knows my Mommy and Daddy have all these businesses."

Everyone looked at one another wondering.

Samone continued, "But I think they don't need to work that much. I love my Nanny Abby, but Nanny not my Mommy or my Daddy. I get so mad when we out with Nanny Abby and we see the other families where ever we go."

She continued, "Yeah it's cool to have every little thing a little kid could ever ask for."

She turned to her parents.

"But that stuff I would just throw away for some time with my Mommy and Daddy. Mommy and daddy, I know Nia and Tremaine feel the same way."

She looked at Tennessee then turned to her parents again and pointed to Tennessee.

"Her family always spend time together even on the week days. Mommy Daddy, will you ever be able to spend more time with us?"

Melody with her head slightly down, "Honey you know we have to work to earn a living, not just a living but an extravagant living. Your Dad and I want to provide the very best life for you, your brother and sister."

Samone seemed to get a little agitated. Her Mom simply didn't want to get it.

"Mommy, you not hearing me."

Reese with a swiftness said, "Honey you know that we have to work long hours."

Samone was as humbled as she knew how. "Daddy, the hours are too long. You and Mommy always talk about our lifestyle but me, Nia and Tremaine don't care about all these things that we have."

She started weeping then her brother and her little sister starting weeping.

Tremaine said what was on his mind, "Samone they don't

hear us. Don't you get it?"

Reese and Melody immediately went over to where their children were in the circle. Their eyes were so desperately speaking to Rachel. Everyone looked at one another not knowing what to do or say. Rachel kindly went over to them, then gently took each hand of the Ford family and put them together as though she were linking together chains.

Meanwhile, everyone in the circle was touched by how the children cried out to God in perfect time. Rachel quietly went back to her spot. Everyone else reverenced themselves to the prayer that was to come. Rachel prayed for each person.

Cousin BJ, Memphis, Barry Joe Jr. and Tennessee were looking as if they found something new that was so spectacular it was worth sharing with the whole world.

Howard, Joanne, Amira, Ashton and Ashley were feeling like things were looking up even more that God had allowed them, as a family, another precious moment together.

Paul, Sasha and Sehara faces were facing Heaven. They held on to one anothers' hands for dear life hoping and believing God was going to answer their prayers. They were thanking and praising him for all of their blessings.

Chef Hogan bowed his head as tears came streaming down his face, but he did not care because he knew he needed to be a part of this amazing prayer.

Alicia, one of the young ladies from church, always was a positive example for her peers. As she bowed her head, she poured out her heart for them.

Marsha, another young lady from church had seven siblings and was always searching for ways to help her parents out. She looked toward heaven, thought about her parents and siblings. She believed her parents finances will one day soon be stable and her siblings will one day be able to go to college.

Tammy, another young lady from church, longed for a better life because she grew up dirt poor. She strived for the best because she knew there was a better life than what she has had thus far. She stood there with her head bowed and with all her heart believing God would continue to keep her family in His care.

Some of the adults were either eating in the dining room or the *Get Together* room. Marsha, Alicia, Tammy and all of the children were eating in the children's dining area in the children's area upstairs.

Downstairs in the dining room Sasha, Paul, Rachel, John, Tressie, Ronald, Cousin BJ and Memphis were having a conversation.

Sasha asked out of concern. "Rachel, are you and John going to venture off and start having new friends?"

Rachel and John looked to one another. The both turned to Sasha and gave her the friendliest smiles.

Rachel explained, "Sasha honey, it sounds to me you are concerned about our next season in life. You know God does put everyone in your life for a reason and sometimes for a season. It is up to us to follow what God has for us. As for everyone in here, we are always going to be here for anyone of you."

Tressie anxiously asked, "Rachel, I'm kind of worried. What do you mean by seasons?"

"You shouldn't be worried about anything because God is here for everyone whether John and I are around or not. Tressie seasons refer to a length of time."

Tressie was uncomfortable. Ronald sensed this deep emotion from Tressie. He grabbed her hand.

Ronald reassured her, "Honey you know John and Rachel isn't going anywhere."

He caught Rachel and John's attention hoping and praying that the statement he just made stands true.

Cousin BJ eagerly jumped into the conversation. "Cuz, look how yall got yall friends feelin' 'bout yall. Yo, yall got some of dat Jesus power?"

John gave Jesus the Glory. "Cousin BJ, it is because of Jesus who lives in us that people gravitate towards and sometimes deter people away."

"That's deep. Yo I know some people dat 'pose to be save

and they still go to clubs and drink lack it ain't no t'morra on Sat'day and back in church on Sund'y."

Ronald turned towards Cousin BJ then to John, "No one is perfect. That's something all of us have to remember. Everyone fights their flesh daily."

Cousin BJ asked, "Yo, you mean when we do somethin' dats not right, but sometimes we do it anyway. That can' be right. I'm guilty of dat one myse'f."

John explained, "God knows our hearts. It really bothers me when Christians use that statement just to sin that one more time. We must repent and turn from our wicked ways."

Memphis joined the conversation.

She nervously hesitated, "So Cousin John, I have to give up my liquor."

She looked around at everyone who was in the dining room with the biggest grin ever. "I lack to go out sometimes wit' my home girls. That ain't no harm, is it?"

John thought, *"Lord she just got saved a few hours ago. But she has to know the truth. She asked the question. Guide me Lord, God."*

"Memphis you have to have the desire to want to change your ways. We all know you and Cousin BJ just got saved. You are going to have to start reading the Word and start going to bible study wherever you all decide to join church. Memphis, it is not ok to go out partying without your husband. The devil is busy and anytime he sees fit he is going to find his way in your household. As for alcohol, you cannot drink until you are drunk. The question is who is going to have just a little alcohol when they are out drinking or at home?"

Cousin BJ seemed confused. "Cuz, you mean to tell me we can't have, but one drink?"

"Cousin BJ, God knows your heart. You have to remember God also sees and knows everything. You are going to have to have the desire to want to stop drinking. There are lots of Christians who drink and find that there is nothing wrong with it."

Paul jumped into the conversation, clearly feeling some

sort of guilt. "John, you know we drink when we are out. I know you and Rachel don't. Does that make us wrong?"

"Paul man, you know that I am going to tell you what is in the Word. If I have made some of you a little uncomfortable, forgive me. The Bible does say, "Do not drink until drunkard."

Reese and Melody felt convicted again. Both still chose to ignore the advice.

Cousin BJ jokingly commented, "Yo, yall look lack yall seen a ghost."

He noticed Reese and Melody looked directly to John.

"Yo Cuz, *he pointed at Melody and Reese*, I think you scared 'em."

Everyone laughed.

Reese and Melody laughed, but still felt conflicted and convicted in their spirits.

Although Cousin BJ and Memphis was laughing, in their hearts they wanted to change their ways.

A couple of hours later as everyone prepared to leave, Rachel stood back in order to observe her precious friends. She began to think of their upcoming trials and how will they chose to handle their trials? When she thought about Cousin BJ and Memphis getting saved, tears came to her eyes. Everyone looked around for Rachel in a ripple effect. As Rachel looked up, all of her family and friends were staring and smiling at her. The children ran over to her to give her a cuddle and say good-bye. As she embraced the children, tears stream down her face at the same time she smiled at the adults.

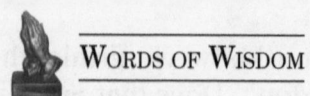

Brothers and Sisters, who have we walked alongside to salvation? Whether we know it or not, we are constantly being watched by unbelievers. What will our lives say to that precious soul that longs for Jesus, but is too immature to realize He is all he or she needs? Our lives speak volumes. We should always acknowledge and recognize that we are ambassadors of Christ. We should allow our Sunday gatherings to account for something. There is always a family member or friend going around that same mountain over and over again. There are times we do things that we know are not good for us, but yet we yield to the situation. Yet our God is so gracious, we get through and we still stand. Will we truly be the one who prays for the hurt or the lost? Will you be the one who will immediately pray? We should always remember we were not always saved. We are here to be the light of the world like Jesus. I don't know anyone who wants to be knocked down when they are already down, besides lost souls are suppose to be able to come to church to find love and guidance and ultimately find Jesus!

CHAPTER 19

Isaiah 61: 1-3 The Spirit of the Sovereign Lord is on me, because the Lord has anointed me to preach good news to the poor. He has sent me to bind up the brokenhearted, to proclaim freedom for the captives and release from darkness for the prisoners, to proclaim the year of the Lord's favor and the day of vengeance of our God, to comfort all who mourn, and provide for those who grieve in Zion- to bestow on them a crown of beauty instead of ashes, the oil of gladness instead of mourning, and a garment of praise instead of a spirit of despair. They will be called oaks of righteousness, a planting of the Lord for the display of his splendor. (N.I.V.)

It was Christmas time! The ladies went to New York City on a long weekend shopping trip.

Rachel, John and the kids were finishing Christmas decorating.

John asked Rachel, "So honey do you have everything planned out for you ladies' *New York City Shopping Trip?*"

"Yes, and I am going to take the ladies with me to one of the homeless shelters so that they can have a chance to give back.

John laughed, "Honey, did you speak to the ladies about this?"

Rachel also laughed, "Of course I did. But, I don't think they were thrilled about the idea. John, you and I know God works in mysterious ways. He is certainly working on each one of those ladies and yes, Scarlette as well."

"You are definitely right. God is working on them day by day. We should never give up on anyone because God has never given up on us. God is working even when we think He isn't. Honey, I am sure you all will have a great time in New York."

Charlotte commented, "Mommy, I bet those lights are going to be so pretty."

"Yes Sweetheart, I bet they are going to be pretty."

She embraced Charlotte and observed Charles and John. "I feel guilty for leaving you all."

"Mommy, you are always taking care of me, Daddy and Charles. Don't feel guilty. Daddy knows how to take care of us."

Charlotte looked at John then she started giggling. "Mommy, I have it covered just in case Daddy doesn't know what to do."

Charles commented, "Yeah, Mom you always think of everybody. You think of people no one else thinks about."

John watched Rachel as she finished the Christmas decorations. When she looked up she caught John's eye. She immediately walked over to him. Cozy Christmas music was softly playing in the room. The children conveniently were upstairs. John asked Rachel for her hand to dance. Rachel laughed; then she took his hands. They were softly and gently swaying to the music in front of the cozy fireplace.

When Sasha arrived from work, Chef Joe was finishing up dinner. Sehara ran in the kitchen when her Mom arrived and gave her a great, big hug. Chef Joe felt the need to share some concerns with them.

"Christmas is near and there are so many people who are in need and people who are hurting beyond belief. My next door neighbor has three children and they will not be able to get their children anything for Christmas. Instead of Christmas this year they have no choice, but to pay their mortgage. On top of it all, one of the children has this incurable disease. I can't wait until I am blessed to be a blessing to other people. I barely have enough for my own family for Christmas, much less someone else's family."

Sasha heard Chef Joe, but her mind was on her long weekend with the ladies in the city that doesn't sleep. Paul heard Chef Joe's concerns, but still chose to ignore the magnitude of the story.

Sehara asked while her eyes brightened, "Mommy can we help that family? Mommy Daddy, the little girls want have baby dolls and the little boys want have little cars. That's sad."

Sasha remarked, "Sehara that is not what Christmas is about."

Paul agreed, "Yes honey, Christmas is about Christ not gifts from your parents."

Chef Joe noticed little Sehara. "Thank you for your thoughtful feelings, but I did not mean for your Mother and Father to buy my neighbors gifts sweetheart. My heart was just speaking."

Little Sehara's heart was sincerely broken.

She went to Chef Joe with a loving and compassionate heart, "Christmas is about Jesus. Chef Joe I betcha Jesus would help your neighbors."

"I'm sure they will be fine."

"Chef Joe, Jesus is gonna take care that family."

She pointed her little finger toward Chef Joe.

"You just watch and see."

After dinner, Sasha and Paul were upstairs in their master suite. Sasha started thinking about the story Chef Joe told.

"Paul, sometimes I wonder if I am a child of God. I was so excited about the New York trip with the ladies, I just blew Chef Joe's story off. And how sad is it that our little girl realized how important that moment was when Chef Joe needed someone to really listen to his story. I need to call Chef Joe."

Paul replied, "Sweetheart, you are right. I am no better than you. I did not speak up either. God uses children to do some of the simplest things but huge at the same time."

Sasha and Paul's spirits were convicted. They looked up and said, "God please forgive me."

Both looked at one another and shook their heads up and down signifying what they needed to do for Chef Joe's neighbor.

Tressie was preparing for the trip to New York City. Everyone was finishing their dinner.

Stacey asked, "Mommy, you go to da cidy? Mommy, it breauthiful thar."

"Oh sweetheart, it is going to be fantastic in New York City at Christmas time. That should be every woman's dream."

Nanny Nellie fantasized, "Yes, Mrs. Ivy maybe someday I will be able to afford to go to New York City."

She gently smiled.

"As long as I have Jesus, my family, and my health… what more can a woman ask for?"

Tressie looked toward Nanny Nellie with her artificial sympathy. "Oh Nanny Nellie, I do pity a woman who simply doesn't have, but in her heart she feels like she is just as happy as anyone else."

Steward was a little annoyed, "Mom that is not at all what Nanny Nellie was saying."

Ronald felt the need to explain for Tressie. "Son, you know your Mother loves shopping in New York City. She is just excited son."

Melinda was agitated, "Dad, it doesn't take a lot of money for anyone to be happy. I agree with Nanny Nellie as long as you have Jesus, your family and your health, anyone should be satisfied."

Ronald as kind as they come, "Yes sweetheart, *referring to Tressie*, I understand what you are saying. It is also a blessing when money is not a problem."

Tressie got excited again, "You guys I can't wait for our shopping trip. New York City is absolutely gorgeous at Christmas time."

Melinda out of spitefulness said, "Oh Mom, I have a great idea. Why don't you take Nanny Nellie with you?"

All of a sudden, Tressie's face looked as though she ate a lemon and a lime at the same time.

Nanny Nellie immediately reacted. "Melinda honey, Nanny Nellie is fine. Besides I will miss my family terribly."

Little Stacey commented, "Nanny Nel I miss you thu. I love you Nanny Nel. Mommy when you leab?"

Stacey gave her Mommy an innocent smile. All of a sudden Tressie left the table. Ronald excused himself thereafter.

Ridge and Scarlette were in the family room watching television. Ridge received a phone call from Meriah's birth Mother *Marley*. When he received the call, he left the room immediately.

Marley was burdened, "Ridge, will Meriah have Christmas this year for the first time. I feel like she is missing out. Not believing in Christ is your belief, not mine. For years I have respected your beliefs, but I feel it is time for her to know about Christmas."

Ridge was a little uncomfortable. "Marley, why do you insist on this every year? You know what my belief is."

Scarlette came in the room. When she gestured to Ridge, he immediately cut the phone's speaker off.

Ridge whispered, "I'll talk to you later about it."

Scarlette loudly commented, "Oh Ridge, not that again."

Scarlette immediately left the room. A few minutes later Ridge was off the phone.

Right afterwards Scarlette was back in the room with Ridge. "Ridge, she pulls that crap every year this time and she knows our belief."

As soon as she made that comment, Little Cassidy Arnasia came in the room. Ridge and Scarlette instantly felt uneasy. She looked at both of her parents.

"Mommy Daddy, I hear that song, that song in the car Mommy."

They immediately knew what song Little Cassidy remembered.

Scarlette asked, "Are you alright honey?"

Little Cassidy Arnasia tried to assure her parents. "Mommy, daddy I feel strong. A change Mommy! A change!"

Meriah came in the family room without any prompting.

"Daddy, I had to come down, what is going on?"

"Honey, everything is fine."

Meriah sat next to her Dad.

Little Cassidy Arnasia went to her big sister. "Meriah, a change!"

Ridge and Scarlette's feelings were conflicted. They both looked toward the girls. The girls were so peaceful and happy. It was as if they knew a change was on the way. Ridge and Scarlette, at the same time, look at one another then turned away.

Joanne was packing for the New York City trip. Nanny Nora was in the family room with Ashley, Ashton, and Amira watching a Christmas story on television. As they were watching television, they all were packed together, on the sofa, like sardines. The love Nanny Nora gave these children was indescribable. As they ate their popcorn and sipped on their drinks, she guided the children through the story.

Joanne ran downstairs. She caught a glimpse of Nanny Nora and the children. Joanne felt an overwhelming feeling of guilt. She thought, *"Why is this bothering me? I make sure my kids are taken care of. They have everything in the world any child would want. How many people can say they have a great nanny like Nanny Nora? Have I ever sat down to watch a kid's movie with my children and really truly be there?"*

All of a sudden she decided to join them while they watched the movie. She squeezed her body unto the couch among everyone. The children were thrown by her sudden unusual behavior.

Little Amira innocently asked, "Mommy, it feel funny you sit wit' us. You alright Mommy?"

Joanne played it off by smiling. "Amira don't be silly."

Ashley was annoyed, "Mom, you don't usually watch our kind of shows; you are usually out having lunch with whomever or doing whatever."

Nanny Nora quickly and seriously chastised, "Now Ashley, you respect your Mother. You know that is no way to talk to your Mother."

Joanne tried to hide her crushed feelings again. Although Joanne knew Ashley was out of place, she could not chastise her because in her heart, she knew Ashley was telling the truth. She attempted to reassure Nanny Nora and shielded her shame.

"You're right Nanny Nora. Ashley knows her mouth is too big for her body."

Ashley, with an attitude immediately got up and stumped her way upstairs to her room.

Ashton was aggravated as well, "Man, we was having a

good time."

He went upstairs as well.

Nanny Nora smiled as nicely and genuinely as she could said, "Mrs. Stone, you know they are at that age."

Little Amira tried to explain. "Sometimes Mommy they have to say, they can't help. You know Mommy, in a way they can say."

Little Amira gave her Mommy an innocent smile. She hugged her and then she was back in Nanny Nora's arms, a safe place.

Reese and Melody were both coming in from work. Nanny Abby was eating dinner with the children. As they come in from work, both tried to rush upstairs. Before they knew it, Little Nia caught a glimpse of them before they reached the stairway.

Little Nia got excited, ran up to her parents, desperately wanting her parents' time. "Mommy, Daddy, Santa Claus is coming soon. I been a good girl all year!"

They both were tired and exhausted from work. On top of everything else, both were feeling guilty and at the same time disappointed.

Melody said, "Sweetheart, you are exactly right. Santa will be here soon."

Reese immediately afterwards said, "Baby girl, what did you tell Santa you wanted for Christmas?"

As soon as Reese asked this question, it seems as though angels escorted Samone and Tremaine in at this very moment. Out of nowhere Samone and Tremaine answered at the same time, "Time!"

Reese and Melody pretended they did not know what their children were talking about.

Tremaine spoke for himself and his little sisters, "Mom Dad, how many times do we have to tell yall?"

Reese replied in his authoritative voice, "Son, you watch your tone with me."

Samone was as respectful as she knew how, "Daddy, why are you raising your voice? We're only speaking from our hearts. We love yall. Daddy, are we even allowed to love our parents?"

At this point Melody was in tears. "Kids, we only want the best for all of you."

Little Nia with all of her sweet little heart replied, "Mommy, we want best from our Mommy and Daddy. Yall, give yo' bes'?"

At that moment Nanny Abby came in because she knew in her spirit that it was time for her to minister to the children. She went into the hallway.

"Now children it's time for bed."

As soon as Nanny Abby spoke, the children followed her upstairs. As the children rush upstairs, Nanny Abby gave Reese and Melody the eyes to let them know she will talk to the children for them.

On her way upstairs, Nanny Abby prayed silently. *"Lord, comfort these precious children and change their parents' corrupt minds. Now Father, I am waiting for you to let me know the exact time to talk to Mr. and Mrs. Ford. Father, I feel for these innocent little children. Put your hands on their little hearts right now precious Father. In Jesus's name, Amen."*

Several hours later, Melody was packing for the New York trip. Reese was finishing paperwork that he didn't get finish at work. Melody was excited about the New York trip with the ladies. Everything she pulled out of the closet she asked Reese's opinion.

Out of the blue, Reese said, "Honey, we are going to have to face that giant one day."

"Reese, what are you talking about?"

Reese pulled Melody closer to him, "Our children are hurting."

"Honey, they just don't realize how much we love them. We have a prosperous and fulfilling life. Our home is a home that everyone dreams of; they will realize it when they are grown."

Reese desperately asked, "Honey, do you think we will still have their hearts?"

Tressie arranged for a beautiful, winter white limo for everyone. When these ladies arrived at the airport in their limo, they captured everyone's attention. Of course Tressie would not have it any other way. Scarlette, Joanne, Melody and Sasha were riding Tressie's coat tail and loving every minute. Rachel was content and would feel the same if someone dropped her off at the airport, but she was also grateful to Tressie for the ride.

The driver of the limo greeted and helped all of the ladies out of the limo. Tressie got out of the limo sporting her long fur coat and an animal print scarf to accent everything. As she swayed from side to side, her stiletto boots told her story. Her hair was freshly done; sharply cut dirty blonde bob, round brushed, straight from the salon.

Sasha followed. She stepped in all red wearing tights with an oversized elegant red cashmere sweater. To make everything pop, she strutted in a pair of red and black stiletto boots. Her hair was natural on this day, which cascaded down her back like deep beautiful black waves against her clothing, walking as though she could stop traffic.

Scarlette was next to step out of the limo. She was dressed in these beautiful dark jeans, which resembled dark slacks tailor made. She sported a pretty, winter white leather jacket with the boots to match. To set everything off, her hair was pulled back in an elegant, long blonde ponytail accented by a bit of Italian jewelry.

Next, Melody got out of the limo. She wore a fitted sweater dress that accented every little perfect curve she possessed. To accent her already small waistline, she sported a cropped leather jacket. Along with everything, she stepped in some sharp stiletto leather boots which was specially designed in Italy.

Joanne was the next to step out of the limo. As she slowly walked, she sported a pair of winter white slacks and a silk top to match. For cover she threw on a long wool winter white coat with some four inch heel boots. Her brunet straight hair was freshly styled from the salon.

Lastly, Rachel got out of the limo wearing chocolate from head to toe. She stepped with her chocolate brown cropped stiletto boots. Her hair was as sharp as they come. Just freshly relaxed and cut from the salon and not a hair out of place. The cut accentuated her beautiful features. Rachel's walk was just as confident and sharp as the haircut she wore.

As they walked through the airport, heads turned, some stopped, conversations stopped, conversations started, newspapers were lowered and shades were lowered. Young women were tucking and pulling as if they were making sure their clothing was in the right place. Young men were looking to make sure everything was in place. Then all of a sudden they stood taller. Little girls stared until the ladies were out of sight. Little boys grinned while they watched the ladies walk through.

The ladies took their first class seats and got comfortable before the flight. Of course the adrenaline had all of them pumped up to shop, explore and see off and on broad way shows.

The ladies were reading, looking at magazines or just enjoying their first class flight.

Sasha was flipping through a glamour magazine. She looked out of the window with eyes as teary as a baby wanting attention. She thought, *"There are so many needy people in the world. I would be in the same boat if I helped everyone who is in that predicament. I know I have a heart. Oh God, I need to call Chef Joe."*

Right after this thought, she overheard two ladies that were going to New York City to shop for people who just wasn't as fortunate as they were. As these ladies carried on their conversation, both of them had tears that rolled down their faces representing the families that they were so excited to help for the holidays.

Tressie was reading a book. She suddenly ran across a sentence that reminded her of Nanny Nellie. As she looked down at her beautiful stiletto boots she thought, *"What lady would not want to wear these? Nanny Nellie is always there for me.*

She is even taking my place now. Why wouldn't I bring her with me? But I am with my friends. She will certainly feel out of place with my classy friends. Oh, but Rachel will easily take her under her wing. That is just not my calling."

Rachel was excited! She turned to Tressie and then to everyone else and suggested, "What would truly be a blessing is if all of you bring your hardworking nannies with you to New York City at Christmas time one year." The ladies were reluctant to comment. They all laughed, but they couldn't respond.

Scarlette was reading a story in a magazine, titled *Step Child*. This story touched her heart in a way that it has never been touched. The child in this story was hearing impaired. Her Stepmother always thought this precious child was a burden to the family. She thought the child's handicap made them less than other families. One day this very child saved her Stepmother's life. This hearing impaired child saved her Stepmother from these would be *murderers*. The article explained that the child was hearing impaired, but she also had a sense that no one could explain. This sense was the key that saved her Stepmother's life. After the incident, the Stepmother got saved and her whole life was changed for the good. Now the Stepmother tells her story to all families who consider themselves a *step family*, her life changing testimony. Since the Stepmother has been giving her life changing testimony, there have been so many people that have changed their perspective about being a part of a step family. Scarlette had tears flowing like her heart flowed at that very moment. As she sobbed Rachel came to console her.

"Scarlette, are you alright?"

"Just read that story." She gave Rachel the magazine.

Melody was flipping through a parenting magazine. She ran across a page with a family that resembled her family. She read their story. This family was totally different. They did not have much money, just enough. What they did have was love, time and everlasting life. The Mother and Father were Pastors of a small church. The children's testimony about their parents was outstanding, to say the least. The children boasted about their parents who always spent time with them, made sure they knew the Word of God, and most of all their parents taught them about salvation. On top of everything, these precious children were saved. At Christmas time, these children would take their presents and give them to children who were less fortunate than they were. They accredited their personalities and character to, first of all, to the Almighty God then their parents. When Melody finished this short story, her stomach was in knots. Conviction was all over her. Rachel felt this in her spirit. She went over and gently touched Melody's hand. Melody quickly squeezed Rachel's hand. She quietly went back to her seat.

Joanne was observing a couple that was sitting across from them. She felt their spirits which were intertwined. The couple may have been the same age as she and Howard. She overheard the couple excitingly telling another couple that they were celebrating their twentieth wedding anniversary in New York City that weekend. As she observed this particular couple, she started reminiscing on how she and Howard's marriage were before children. She thought about how her body was before having children. As she daydreamed, the couple caught her eyes and gave her the friendliest smiles. Joanne felt so comfortable. She immediately started talking to them.

"I know you all probably are wondering why this crazy woman is staring at us. You all are like a magnet to everyone around you because of your relationship."

The lady had lots of energy, "Thank you, everyone tells us that."

Her husband was looking and smiling the entire time.

The lady continued, "I think, I would marry him again."

Her husband's smile turned into this obnoxious grin.

Although Joanne was thrown by this man's obnoxious grin, she kindly asked, "If you don't mind me asking, how do you both keep your marriage so contagious?"

The lady responded with no hesitation, "Everyone else

asks that question as well and we always say, Our God Almighty. You have to respect one another. Honey, when God sees that you are trying your best, of course He is going to reward you for just that. All these years that we have been married, we always try to iron out anything that is not of God. It has not always been easy."

Joanne shared, "I know that I just met you, I love my husband and I have everything any woman would want to have, but I wish things were different. What couple wouldn't want to genuinely be happy in each other and with each other?"

The lady firmly told Joanne, "Honey, always follow what God tells you. It wouldn't hurt being submissive to your husband as long as He is following Christ. Everyone seems to be against marriage counseling, but for us it has been a fantastic tool for our marriage as well."

Joanne was thrown again because she thought a couple such as this particular couple shouldn't need counseling.

"Why would you all need counseling?"

The lady replied, "Honey, it keeps our marriage fresh. Yes, every year around our anniversary we schedule counseling with our Pastor. Trust me it has truly been a blessing in our lives and those who surround us."

The only thing Joanne could do was tell the woman and her husband, "To God be the Glory."

Instantaneously the couple lifted their heads; lifted their hands to glory while tears of joy trickled down their cheeks. Joanne felt the tears of joy and began rejoicing as well. God reminded Joanne of the blessing that she had in her life. Without realizing it, she turned toward Rachel. She thought, *"God planted a couple into my life. They are the couple that is the ideal couple among all of us. I need to take advantage of this blessing."*

Rachel woke up from a nap, while the other ladies were asleep. For some odd reason, out of the blue Rachel began to weep. Then she began to silently pray, *"Father, I don't know why I'm crying, but you know all things. Whatever is in my near future, my family's near future and my friends near future, Lord, give us a double portion of perseverance if need be. Father, give us peace that surpasses all understanding. As my friends and I vacation in New York, give us safe travels wherever we decide to go. If there is something that we need to get out of this trip, Father, open our hearts and give us the ear to hear your voice. Father, we love you and we are thankful for everything you have done for us. I know these ladies don't realize your omnipotent power, but I do. In Jesus's name, Amen."*

As soon as she finished praying, all at once the other ladies awoke from their naps. As they all turned to Rachel, she was wiping her tears of unwanted affliction. Rachel began to put on her beautiful smile, but the ladies, Scarlette as well, felt deeply in their spirits that something was going on with her.

Sasha nervously asked, "Rachel, what is wrong?"

Tressie commented, "Rachel, this isn't like you. Of course we all are use to you with tears in your eyes as you pray, but I have to say something is strangely different."

Joanne insightfully commented, "Rachel all of us woke up the same, exact time."

A tear dropped down one of her cheeks.

"That is scary. Are you alright?" Joanne nervously replied.

Scarlette said, "This is going to sound like my Little Cassidy Arnasia, but something is not right."

Melody was on edge, "Rachel, the ladies are right. There is something about you that is not adding up. You have to be alright!"

Rachel tried her best to calm the ladies down.

"Ladies, I am fine. You all don't have anything to worry about because all of you know who I serve and who I believe in. Therefore, I am blessed and always will be blessed. You ladies should worry about nothing and pray about everything."

The ladies arrived at their hotel which was *The Grande Exhibit Hotel.* Their maitre'd met and greeted them at their limo. The exquisite hotel resembled those old buildings on the streets of Paris and London. As the ladies entered the hotel, there was a spectacular entrance. There were many small exhibits of art throughout the hotel. There were marbled floors, live plants; beautiful sculptures of Jesus and angels. To top it all off, there was a Chaplain on board twenty-four hours a day. When they arrived to their suite, which was literally the size of a six bedroom spacious, elaborate home especially made for queens. Each woman had her own luxurious bathroom; attached to that there was a splendid powder room. In the center of all the mini suites, there was a spacious sitting room. The lamps were sculptures of angels. When they were turned on, the angels' eyes and wings lit up. In the middle of this huge embellished coffee table sat an enormous Holy Bible. This bible was a bible like no one had ever laid eyes on before. This extraordinary bible was enveloped with soft gold leather. The pages were an ivory color; the letters were blue-black ink. The words that were spoken in the bible by God were in pure solid gold; it literally took one's breath away.

The next day, the ladies were having breakfast in *The Grand Dining Room*. All of them noticed this gentleman that each of them saw the day before. The strange thing about this is none of the ladies said anything about him to one another. This man was a *Distinguished Gentleman*. He stood about seven feet tall, his salt and pepper hair flowed all the way down his back touching his derriere. He wore a suit that looked as though he slipped it on at the dry cleaners on the corner. Apparently, his shoes were just shined by the best. His complexion was flawless, but anyone who had eyes could truly tell he was an old wise man. The white shirt underneath his suit was as white as snow. His top hat simply reminded one of Abraham Lincoln.

While the ladies waited for breakfast, Rachel decided to ask the gentleman to join them. As Rachel approached the distinguished gentleman, she felt this anointing that was indescribable. When Rachel came face to face with him, she offered her hand for him to shake. He kindly shook her hand.

Rachel said, "Hi, my name is Rachel."

The distinguished gentleman replied with this deep voice, sounding like James Earl Jones and Barry White all in one. "Hi, young lady my name is Steadford Grey."

"Please to meet you Sir. Would you like to sit and eat breakfast with us? *She laughed.* I promise we want bite."

Rachel and Steadford went back to the table where all the other ladies were sitting. The ladies spirits were accepting of this distinguished gentleman. This took the ladies by surprise. Otherwise they just would not have been acceptable. He mesmerized the ladies. Rachel introduced Mr. Steadford Grey to the ladies. Sasha was first to be introduced.

Rachel as happy-go-lucky as they come, "Mr. Steadford Grey, this is Sasha. Sasha, Mr. Steadford Grey." Sasha felt this indescribable anointing that embodied this gentleman. She shook his hand and just could not stop staring at him.

Rachel introduced Tressie, "Mr. Grey, this is another friend Tressie. Tressie, Mr. Grey." When Tressie got ready to shake his hand, it was like she was getting ready to shake the President's hand. Tressie was giggly and excited. "Hi Mr. Steadford, I am very pleased to meet you Sir."

Now it was Scarlette's turn to meet him. Rachel introduced him, "Mr. Steadford this is another friend and her name is Scarlette. Scarlette, Mr. Steadford." Scarlette looked at him while she was shaking his hand and felt this strange feeling like the times at the salon and in the car on the way back to Atlanta from Ridge's friend's house. She was amazed by this moment.

It was Joanne's turn to meet him. Rachel introduced him, "Mr. Steadford this is another one of my friends and her name is Joanne. Joanne, Mr. Steadford." Joanne gently smiled and admired his stunning voice.

Rachel said "Now Mr. Grey last, but not least this is my other friend Melody. Melody, Mr. Steadford Grey." Melody gave Mr. Steadford this big smile. She gasped as she shook his hand. He reminded her of Reese's family, but of course Reese's family could not grow that tall in a million years.

Mr. Steadford Grey, being the ultimate gentleman, pulled the chair out for Rachel to sit down first. Before he sat down, he gently pulled his chair out a little bit further to allow for his seven foot body to sit as any distinguished gentleman would. As he sat down, all the ladies watched his every move. Mr. Steadford Grey treated his top hat like a woman treats her five hundred dollar purse. When he sat down, he immediately signaled for a servant to take his sharp, vintage top hat that was in immaculate condition. Directly after he took his seat, he crossed his long legs that went on for miles and miles.

Their breakfast finally arrived. Everyone except Scarlette held hands in order for Rachel to say grace. After Rachel finished saying the grace, Mr. Grey looked directly at Scarlette.

Mr. Grey intuitively wondered, "Young lady, I noticed you did not say your grace. If you don't mind me asking, what is the story behind such bold behavior?"

Scarlette not quite as nonchalant as she always were answered. "Mr. Steadford, to be frank, I don't believe in God."

He paused then sighed. "I see."

Rachel asked, "So Mr. Steadford, are you going to any shows today?"

"Angel, I don't usually attend the shows. Where ever I am supposed to be, I will be there."

Tressie curiously asked, "Mr. Steadford, are you the owner of this fabulous hotel?"

He slowly turned to Tressie. "Young lady, no, I am not."

She giggled, "I was just a little curious. You look as though you just might be the owner. I don't know too many people who walk around as sharply dressed as you are."

Mr. Steadford nodded his head. "Thank you, young lady."

Sasha excitedly asked, "Mr. Steadford, do you mind if I asked you this one question?"

He turned to Sasha, as cool as a cucumber, "No young lady, you can ask me anything you desire."

Sasha as polite as she possibly knew how, "Mr. Grey, is there a Mrs. Grey?"

He paused then gently answered, "No, young lady, there is no Mrs. Grey."

"A young man as handsome as you with no wife, how do you keep the ladies off?"

All the ladies laughed. He looked at every lady that was at the table.

He gave insight to them. "When I observe you ladies and observe this magnificent hotel, I automatically think about all the other women that would love to be in your shoes. You ladies are some of the most beautiful ladies I have ever laid eyes on. But you all know and I know that if your heart is not right, the outside does not matter. I pray you pay it forward."

He turned to Scarlette.

"Young lady, I know you don't believe in our Almighty God. But, it want be very long."

Then he started talking to the other ladies.

"Young ladies, think about Jesus's heart. His heart was infectious. We should try to immolate him every day of our lives. Besides you wouldn't be here if it weren't for Him."

He turned to Scarlette again.

"Yes, even you young lady."

He quickly turned to Rachel.

"Angel, keep obeying Christ. You are definitely on your assignment. You other ladies get serious about our Almighty Father, because He is certainly serious about you and His kingdom."

As he spoke it was like Jesus speaking. The ladies felt his loving spirit pouring out into their hearts. By the time he was done, all the ladies were up and out of their seats shaking his hands and thanking him for his words of wisdom. Soon after, Mr. Steadford Grey was gone. The ladies finished their breakfast.

The ladies went sightseeing, ice skating and their last stop was the homeless shelter. As the ladies entered the *New York City Family Center for the Homeless*, everyone that saw where they were going thought that they were lost. Own each side of the streets, homeless men and women thought that the ladies were movie stars. They literally cheered for them as they entered the building.

They entered the front desk. Of course, Rachel articulates how they wanted to help. The lady at the desk had a warned out mean look that would stop a pit bull in his steps.

Rachel was nice as she always were explained, "Hi, my friends and I wanted to know what time is your feeding?"

The lady at the front desk obnoxiously and unprofessionally burst out laughing at the ladies. Rachel acted promptly because she knew the other ladies would probably give attitude back to the lady.

"We come to be of assistance to you all."

The lady at the front desk foolishly commented with that strong New York accent, "Oh, you're not joking."

Rachel introduced herself and the others.

The lady at the front desk, finally answered her question, "The feeding starts at four-thirty in the evening."

It was evident that the ladies did not like the smell, the attitude from the workers and the volunteers. Rachel noticed how uncomfortable the others were. She went over to encourage them, since this was their first time volunteering at a shelter.

As they prepared for the people to arrive, everyone was whispering and wondering what their motives were. The ladies were even more uncomfortable. They started complaining to Rachel. She pulled all of them to the side and reassured them that they will be blessed if they just persevered.

Rachel expounded, "Scarlette; you know I love you. Now to you other ladies…Jesus went everywhere to heal the sick. What makes you think it is going to be any different for us. Ladies, just this morning Mr. Steadford Grey gave us a word from the Lord. If you had not realized it, his presence is in our favor. We should consider his presence a blessing from God. I know you all notice the power Mr. Steadford Grey possesses. Think about it ladies, a human being with an anointing as strong as Mr. Steadford is one in a million."

Scarlette was still stunned, "Rachel, I've never experience power such as his in any human being. I was blown away by this man's presence."

Sasha remarked, "I have never seen a man with such great prestige before."

Melody commented, "Ladies, we just could not keep our eyes off of him. And it wasn't an attractiveness that we see in our husbands. This distinguished gentleman carried an attractiveness that cannot be described."

Joanne immediately afterwards said, "I hope I don't sound crazy, but Mr. Steadford is Heaven sent. Rachel, you know exactly what I mean."

Tressie was staring. Then she looked at all the ladies. "I don't know what it is that we need to grasp on this trip, but it is powerful."

She looked at Rachel.

Tressie continued, "I feel it in my spirit. It is up to us to follow."

All the ladies agreed. Rachel looked upon Tressie as a Mother would her child and grabbed Tressie's hand to let her know just how proud she was of her. Of course, Scarlette agreed along with the other ladies, but did not realize she was also going to be used by God.

As everyone was serving, this family of six came through the line. The children were so beautiful underneath all the helpless filth. The Mother and Father's hurt that saturated their faces bore every minute of this dinner. Their mannerisms were to be expected. The Mother carried her position in spite of the odds that were against her family. She made sure her husband and children had everything they needed before she was mentally able to sit down and enjoy her meal.

The seating was limited at the shelter because there were so many people in need. When the family sat down, there were elderly ladies and men slowly coming through for food. Their faces were worn from worry, and brutal comments that were thrown at them every day. If they could live off of the comments and rude treatment that they endured day after day, they certainly would not be in such predicament. Somehow they had the energy to say thank you and truly thank God for yet another meal.

The ladies were oddly surprised, but at the same time, realized they were also being blessed because they were helping in a small way, in their eyes. They felt an overwhelming sense of guilt in their spirits. Sasha, Tressie, and Joanne all at the same time looked up, thrown by surprise. There was this entire family with tears streaming down their faces. They carried this moaning and groaning which consumed their distressed spirits. This family had just gotten kicked out of their apartment thirty minutes prior. The husband lost his job several months ago and had not been able to find anything that would compare to what he had been making before. All of their bills had gotten behind and they weren't able to catch up on their rent. To ignite everything, their landlord would not let them take any of their belongings due to prior eviction notices.

After these unfortunate, impoverished people were done eating, they were having conversations with one another. Rachel advised the ladies to go around to the tables and talk to our sisters and brothers because this might be the only love they get for a very long time. She explained that this was the lowest point in our sisters and brothers lives and we need to be that shoulder for them to cry on. Rachel also warned them that they may be that seed that need to be planted in their lives at this very moment.

Scarlette childishly commented, "Excuse me Rachel, but I have never seen these people before in my life. How can we be related?"

"Scarlette, I know your belief. Listen one day you will realize why I said they are our brothers and sisters. And I believe it will be soon."

Reluctantly, Tressie acted like a child who was about to get punished. She knew in her spirit that she needed to talk, but truthfully did not want any part. After several minutes, she finally got over herself and started talking to this Mother and Father who had several children with special needs. Both of them had great paying jobs which were more than comfortable for years, but when the economy took a dive so did their jobs. All of their children needed special attention due to their learning disabilities. They wanted the best for their children just like any other family. They paid out of pocket for everything. As these beautiful parents pour out their story, Tressie, out of her comfort zone, sympathized with them because of her sweet little Stacey. She embraced everyone in the family one by one.

She whispered, "God has a blessing waiting for you."

As she whispered, tears rolled down her cheeks. Tressie could not help, but think about her late nights up alone praying about her little Stacey.

Rachel was talking to these two ladies who became friends when they met each other on the streets. They believe God brought them together in order to endure being on the streets. Their children abandoned them due to inevitable aging; they moved to other states in order to avoid caring for their Mothers. These were two of the happiest women Rachel ever came across in spite of their situation. The women's smiles brought Rachel to tears. She wrapped her arms around them both, standing between them. One arm went around one lady and the other goes around the other lady.

Sasha was having a conversation with this interracial couple who were newlyweds. In order to get married and live in peace they felt they had to leave their home state completely. They thought *The Big Apple* was where dreams come true. They started struggling the minute they got married. Both of them had jobs, but they barely got by. The strong relationship they had before was nonexistent. As the young man told the story, the young lady sobbed the whole time. The last statement the young man made startled Sasha. The young man, with the last bit of pride in his body said, "But through it all, every Sunday we find it in our hearts to attend church."

Melody chatted with this family who was actually from

Italy. They had always had a dream in their hearts to have an Italian family business in *New York City*. They sold everything in Italy and came to America; they put up their house for collateral. When their business crumbled, they also lost their brownstone. Everything went great for about five years then everything went downhill and so did their dream. Melody started holding back her tears. The children reminded Melody of her own children. She pictured her children sitting where these children were. Their story all of sudden hit Melody like a ton of bricks. Rachel immediately went over to comfort Melody. As Melody sobbed, the family just held their heads down with nothing else to say.

Joanne was talking to these two men who had been on the streets for years. These two men lived on the streets and walked the streets so long that they accepted this lifestyle with open arms. Apparently, they had developed some sort of mental instability. They didn't think they were worthy of anything else. They actually took pride in coming to the shelter to eat any chance that they could. One of the statements these guys made really stood out to Joanne.

They said, "We live on the streets. And we may not know much, but the one thing that we do know is God loves us."

The two guys joked and laughed the entire time Joanne talked to them. Joanne was in awe of their attitude.

Scarlette was so hesitant to talk to these people who so desperately needed help from anybody. In her eyes, they were not worthy of a conversation.

Scarlette thought about Mr. Grey, *"Mr. Grey said we should pay it forward. His presence was like no other I've ever met."*

She finally got up the nerves to approach this one person that was sitting alone at a little table in the corner. When Scarlette entered the table, the woman moved over and turned her head. Scarlette suddenly left herself mentally. She gently touched the lady. The lady began to burst out in tears. Scarlette knelt down and put her arm around the lady as the lady sat and wept.

The ladies were helping with the cleanup; and still experiencing negative attitudes from the workers. Rachel went to the restroom and there were two employees that worked in the shelter who was there just to chat about the ladies and why they were there. Rachel entered the restroom.

As soon as Rachel went in, one of the employees said, "Here's one of them now."

Rachel smiled knowing that God had her back at all times.

"I'm sorry, are you referring to me."

Rachel kindly held out her hand and introduced herself. The employees' spirits were so mean and evil, but there was something about Rachel's pure and loving spirit that forced these two employees to give her the time of day.

One of the employees slowly said, "Reign."

As she shook Rachel's hand, she looked at Rachel as though she had never seen such kindness.

As the other employee shook Rachel's hand, without any hesitation she responded, "Sadie, yeah Sadie."

She looked at Rachel, and suddenly she was eager to have a conversation.

Sadie asked, "Rachel so are you some Pastor or missionary or something?"

Rachel proudly, "No, I am a servant of God."

Reign commented without editing asked, "I thought so, some Jesus freak. Are you filthy rich or just rich?"

"First of all, I am rich in the Lord."

Before Rachel could say anything else, Sadie interrupted Rachel. "Just answer the question."

"Yes, we are."

Reign and Sadie blurted out, all at once, "We knew it."

Sadie laughed, lit her cigarette, puffed then finally blew it all out. "Do you mean your *Barbie Doll* friends are rich as well?"

Rachel moved away from the cigarette smoke.

She answered, "Yes."

Reign then lit her cigarette. She watched Rachel as though she was totally out of her league. Rachel quickly went to use the restroom. When she finished, the employees were finishing their cigarette break.

Before Rachel left the restroom, she quickly looked back at the employees, with all the love in the world, "Ladies you all have a blessed Christmas and a blessed New Year."

Reign and Sadie with their cigarettes between their fingers just blew the smoke out of their mouths in awe as Rachel walked out.

When Rachel came out of the restroom, all of the others were at a table discussing the stories that they heard. Rachel knew these ladies had an experience of a lifetime. None of them had volunteered at a shelter before and just never took the time out to hear someone else's story that was truly in need.

Tressie was sitting at the end of the table. She slid over to make room for Rachel.

Sasha wondered, "Is this what you deal with when you are volunteering? How awful!" Rachel, this is depressing. We all are sitting here, knowing the lifestyles that we live. How can we not feel guilty?"

Rachel knew the guilt the ladies were enduring.

"Sisters listen, I don't feel guilty because I know that I always give my time and my love. Yes, my heart goes out to these beautiful families. Ladies, I pray for our sisters and brothers all the time. And yes, I have prayed for them without even knowing them. When you truly live for Christ, this is the heart that you acquire."

She looked over to Scarlette.

"You know that is what I believe. I am not going to apologize for being a child of God. Ladies you have to have a desire to give your all to God!"

As they sat there, the oppressed people that they talked to and even the ones that they didn't have a chance to talk to came over to their table. One of the men touched Rachel's hand so gently; he silently spoke to Rachel's loving spirit. As Rachel kindly turned toward the desperate old man, she looked this old soul in the eyes and then she looked at the others that were behind him. The manager of the shelter came rushing over.

The manager asked, "What is the problem?"

The old man with a weak tone, but with great confidence responded, "This lovely lady was just about to pray for me and my friends. I know you all could care less because this is plainly a paycheck for you all that work here. I feel so strongly that the good Lord is telling me she has a *true heart* for the homeless and the unfortunate."

He looked at Rachel then he looked at his friends behind him, paused, then looked the manager of the shelter directly in her eyes, "We are people too."

The manager asked Rachel, "Are they bothering you ladies? They can be troublesome and annoying at times."

She looked down at Rachel, glanced at the other ladies; then she whispered, "Not to mention the smell is not all that great."

All the other ladies felt a deep sympathy for these poor, unfortunately souls that so desperately wanted to know a way out of the darkest place that they could ever encounter. Rachel's heart cried out for the manager's heart and soul.

She kindly but carefully commented, "Ma'am I mean no harm, but they deserve to have a conversation, just like you and I have. They are not bothering me in any way. As a matter of a fact, I would love to pray for them right now."

The manager looked at Rachel as though she lost her mind.

"I'm surprise you all are still here. You've helped serve today and your job is done. You all can leave because they usually go back on their streets. Do you really want to pray for them? We have Preachers and Pastors that come here all the time, but they never take the time out to pray for them."

Rachel got out of the seat. She said, "Ma'am."

When Rachel started to speak, a little six-year-old boy came running to Rachel. He grabbed her hand.

"Mrs. Lady,"

He formed his little hands into praying hands.

Pray for Mommy, my Daddy,"

He looked back at everyone else and pointed to them as well.

"them too."

He looked over to the manager with the saddest eyes anyone would ever see.

"We sleep out there. *He pointed his little finger to the manager.* She don't pray!"

The little boy's statement brought the manager to tears. Immediately afterwards all the other ladies were up prepared to pray; Scarlette was ready to listen as well. The few of the shelter workers, who really cared about the unfortunate homeless souls, were the first to come up. Nosiness brought the other shelter workers up to the front or so they thought.

The manager's hands went up; ready to pray. "You do what you are led to do."

She grabbed Rachel's hand.

Everyone formed a huge circle.

Rachel gave thanks. "I am so thankful for you all to give me a chance to pray for all of you and your future."

One of the women wondered, "Why is she thankful? We are the ones who need any and everybody's help. She needs no one. She has to be sent by "The Almighty God!" You don't find people like her every day."

Soon afterwards, Pastor Leon Wolfe walked into the shelter. He was one of the Pastors who visited regularly. When he walked in, he felt the beautiful spirit of Jesus upon all of these people who were in unity for the first time. Pastor Wolfe's eyes instantly gravitated towards the ladies; he grabbed Sasha's hand to join this first time unity. Pastor Wolfe experienced this overwhelming, unexplainable feeling that he had never allowed himself to feel before. In order to relieve it, all of a sudden he said to everyone, "If you all don't mind we are going to pray."

All of the homeless precious souls started looking at one

another in agreement.

One of them commented, "He has never said anything to us."

Another person said, "Yes, the only thing he ever does is eat, look at us and nods his head like he is answering a question."

Another said, "He always shows up in his three piece suit smiling as though he is doing us a favor."

Rachel was as godly as she knew how, "I'm sorry Pastor, but I am about to pray for my brothers and sisters. You can certainly join us, but I will be leading the prayer."

"Oh, of course I'm sorry for my intrusion. You go right ahead."

"Thank you Pastor."

Rachel announced to everyone, "None of you know me or my friends, but I can say this. I am led by the Holy Spirit. I believe with all my heart, God answers prayers instantaneously when his children pray in powerful unity. My friends and I have been touched by your stories. Our hearts intertwined with yours, and brothers and sisters when that happens, Jesus Christ is all over it. Now as we pray, I would like for you to individually talk to God as if you were talking to me or anyone else in here. I know this is my first time meeting all of you, but I love you and want the best for you. I believe in my heart that if you all believe that God can do any and everything, He will certainly move on your behalf."

By this time, these beautiful souls longed for more of God's presence. Everywhere you look, there were tears of joy and hope. The employees were in just as much need as the homeless, if not more.

Rachel began to pray. *"Lord, God hear our prayer. My brothers and sisters need your divine guidance. We pray for jobs, homes, people that you will divinely put in our lives for our good. Father, I pray that they always feel your love even when things seem like they are not working out for the good. I pray for these precious little children who have their whole lives ahead of them. I pray that you give them divine wisdom. When the parents lose their sense of self, give them renewed strength. I pray for miracles in my precious brothers and sisters lives.*"

Someone cried out, "Yes, Father we need you!"

She continued, *"Father, I pray for all the Pastors, missionaries, and all the leaders of the church. Show them exactly how we are supposed to love."*

All of a sudden, Pastor Leon Wolfe helplessly was on his knees blurting out a cry from the depths of his soul. By this time, Rachel wept as she prayed.

"Father, I feel my brothers and sisters' hearts crying out for you. We long for your continued presence in our lives. Wrap us in your arms like never before. We need you in every aspect of our lives."

By this time, there was not a dry eye in the house. The chain of hands, were out of sorts. Now, they were in groups holding one another. A shoulder was there for someone. An embrace was there for another. Pastor Leon Wolfe embraced the precious souls that longed for someone in the body of Christ to recognize them. As Pastor Wolfe embraced everyone, a stream of tears became his inviting best friend. All of the ladies' spirits shone as bright as a star. For the first time, the employees made an instant connection with these precious souls. They realized that people are people whether they are on the streets or not. *Oh, how God smiles when we are at our best.*

It was the latter part of the day; the ladies were feeling alive from the experience at the shelter. They decided to walk a few blocks before calling for their limo. As they were walking, Joanne noticed a group of young men she caught a glimpse of before. She kept quiet because she did not want to startle the other ladies.

Rachel's attitude changed, "Ladies, lets hold hands like we are little girls again."

Scarlette joked around, "Now, how old are we?"

The other ladies noticed Rachel was not smiling. Somehow they walked into a dark alley. Joanne stomach dropped as though she was on a deathly rollercoaster. Sasha started crying frantically.

Melody asked, "Rachel what is going on?"

Tressie was frightened, "Where are we?"

All of the ladies' stomachs joined Joanne's. There was a loud shout from the group of thugs that was following them. All of them wearing the same article of clothing which signified *GANG*. They walked as fast as their stilettos would allow them. They ran into another alley that led to nowhere. As the leader came up to the ladies, he grabbed a switch blade. The other gang members followed the leader.

The leader said, "Um, we got some rich, fine meat today partners." The others cheered, sounding like a pack of ferocious dogs that caught their prey. The ladies were all crying and praying to God. The leader turned around to the other members of the gang to crack another joke. Out of nowhere, Mr. Steadford Grey appeared on the scene.

He shouted with that stunning voice that was a mixture of Barry White and James Earl Jones, "Boys, what are you doing to these beautiful ladies? What are you going to do with those weapons?"

When he spoke, it sounded like heaven opened up just for these ladies. Mr. Steadford Grey went up to the leader of the gang with his sharp suit, top hat and every bit of his seven feet slim body.

"Now give me the weapon that is in your hand."

Like a two year old, the leader handed over his toy frantically, "Yes, Sir!"

The others were so frightened of Mr. Steadford Grey, they ran as fast as they could. A couple of them were so scared. As they looked back they ran into some of the buildings. The leader of the gang ran as though he was dodging a bullet. Mr. Steadford Grey turned around and looked at the ladies. They were relieved and so thankful that he was there at the right moment.

Mr. Steadford Grey took the role as a Father figure for the ladies. "Ladies, you all need to be in a taxi or limo. What made you want to walk? I know you all can afford a taxi or limo. You ladies are making me frantic for you. God loves you, but you always have to be wise in all the decisions that you make."

The ladies were so shock because Mr. Grey appeared out of nowhere.

All of them asked, "Where did you come from?"

"Young ladies that doesn't matter; please don't do that again. Use wisdom in all things!"

He turned around and the ladies followed him like he was the Mother duck and they were his ducklings. He led them out to the main street and there was their limo. Mr. Grey rode in the limo back to the hotel.

There was silence all the way back to the hotel. Mr. Steadford Grey was sitting on the back seat of the limo. The ladies were sitting on the side seats of the limo. They looked worned out and also relieved by this point. They all sat with their legs crossed with their stilettos, as quiet as they have ever been. Rachel glanced at Mr. Grey with a smile. She looked at the other ladies. Scarlette stared at Mr. Grey in awe of what just happened. Joanne admired him even more because he just saved her life. Sasha looked at him as though he was beyond human. Melody looked to him wanting to be a part of his being because no human being could possibly be this cool and smooth. Tressie watched him as though she was in a dream. He sat there; watched over the women, as clean cut and as sharp as he was at the breakfast table with his top hat.

When they arrived at the hotel, Mr. Grey got out first. As they got out one by one, Mr. Grey silently escorted them one by one.

When they all gathered in the lobby, Mr. Grey kindly dismissed his presence. "Good night ladies. I am sure we want be going anywhere else at this hour." All of the ladies replied, "No, Sir!"

After the ladies call their families and got cleaned up, they gathered in the sitting room of their suite. For a moment they sat there in silence.

Rachel broke the ice. "Ladies, you know we are blessed to be alive."

Tressie and Joanne were thankful and relieved all at once. They asked, "Where did Mr. Steadford Grey come from?"

Scarlette admitted, "Now, you all know I don't believe in off the wall things that are not explainable, but I have to admit this distinguished gentleman is one of a kind. Yes, he came out of nowhere."

Sasha's eyes watered as she thought about what happened. When Rachel looked down she touched the enormous, beautiful Bible that sat on the coffee table. The conversation became mute again. As Rachel gazed at the Bible, the others started staring as well. The atmosphere in the room changed. Then there was a heavenly scent that filled the room. Rachel, Tressie, Joanne, Sasha and Melody praised God for saving their lives and allowing Mr. Steadford Grey to be their *Angel* on earth. Scarlette cried with conflicted feelings. Rachel went over and held her as she silently prayed for her salvation.

The next morning the ladies were just happy to be alive. They were getting ready to go shopping. Someone knocked at the door. Sasha carefully opened the door.

The butler had a message for the ladies, "Mrs. Richardson, I have a message from a distinguished gentleman for all of you ladies. He would like to escort you ladies while you shop in the city today."

The other ladies heard the message as the butler delivered. All of them smiled because each of them knew the message was from Mr. Steadford Grey. Of course, they would not refuse his offer. All of them laughed. The butler joined them.

The butler asked, "Ladies, is he a fairy God Father to you?"

They suddenly thought back to what happened the night before. Their demeanors changed as they thought about what could have happened.

The butler noticed then he kindly apologized, "I'm sorry

ladies, I didn't mean to..."

Rachel interjected, "Sir, you are fine. Last night Mr. Stead-ford Grey literally saved our lives. And it is ironic that you said *Fairy God Father*. Now, I don't know how this is going to sound, but I believe in my heart and so do the other girls that the *distinguished gentleman* is our earth angel."

The butler commented, "Mrs. Richardson, while talking to him there was a power that surrounded him. That is the only way I can explain it. I have never had an experience like that before; and we only talked for maybe a minute or so. Ma'am I have escorted and served for the richest and finest of this world and none of them hold a candle to this man's presence."

"Yes, the ladies and I know exactly what you are saying when you say his *presence*."

The butler glanced at the ladies then turned to Rachel.

"Ladies, I better get back on the job. It was really nice talking to you. Be careful and have a blessed day."

When the ladies' limo came Mr. Steadford Grey, dressed in his three piece burgundy suit which looked as though he just got dressed at the cleaners, got out of the limo allowing the ladies to get in first. Mr. Grey wouldn't have it any other way. As the ladies got into the limo, one by one, Mr. Grey greeted and complimented them with the most charming disposition.

When everyone was in the limo, they all were like little girls that surrounded their Father not knowing when or what to say because of their recent misbehavior. Rachel could not keep silent for very long.

"You know Mr. Grey you really didn't have to waste your time with us today."

Tressie agreed, "Yes, Mr. Grey you will only get bored with us girls."

Sasha cracked a little smile, "Mr. Steadford, we don't want to be a bother."

"Young lady, you all don't seem to understand, this is my assignment for today."

Scarlette had that smirk look on her face curiously and

sarcastically, "Mr. Steadford, I can't imagine you being in school. Just what do you mean by assignment?"

"Young lady, I have to watch out for you today. You are on my watch. Believe it or not ladies, this day was always on my watch and destined for this exact time."

A dramatic chill came over the ladies. The only thing they could do was observe one another. Mr. Steadford Grey sat there with his long legs crossed, as if moments like this happened every day. He got even more interesting to the ladies.

Joanne was very curious, "Mr. Grey, we just met you yesterday, but for the life of me, it feels like I have known you for eternity."

Mr. Grey slowly shook his head up and down, agreeing with Joanne's statement.

"Young lady when you get that prophetic feeling about someone, it is supposed to happen. It is already written."

Scarlette was fascinated, "Mr. Grey you are like no other person I have met before. Being around these ladies, especially your angel Rachel, your presence is quiet familiar."

Mr. Grey slowly shook his head up and down, "Young lady people tell me that all the time. They can never figure me out. There is nothing to figure out. I'm just like any other person who is assigned to help a human being."

The driver stopped at the first store.

Rachel looked at the ladies wondering, "Did any of you tell him where to stop?"

All of them answered, "No."

Mr. Steadford Grey with a little smirk on his face admitted, "Oh, I'm sorry young ladies. I gave the driver the schedule for today."

The only thing the ladies could do was smile at each other because they knew this distinguished gentleman was there to protect them.

The first stop was at the *Top Shop*. Heads turned while Mr. Steadford Grey escorted the ladies out of the limo.

The ladies were all browsing the beautiful *Top Shop*. After a while, all the ladies had items in their hands to take into the dressing room.

Tressie had this beautiful long gold and black sequenced jacket with the black slacks that had the sequence design cascading down the sides.

Sasha picked up a gorgeous silk crème skirt suit; paired with the wide belt for the jacket which was embellished with soft gold sparkles which really set the suit off.

Joanne grabbed this long chocolate sweater dress. The sweater dress had beige and brown embroidery around the neck area which set the whole dress off.

Melody, of course, found this pretty silk, burnt orange mini dress with the wide belt to accentuate the waistline.

Scarlette found a red, leather cropped jacket and the leather bottoms to match.

Rachel grabbed an exquisite off the shoulder sequence, winter white party dress.

They were all in the dressing room trying on their outfits.

Rachel was taking off her bra in order to try on the party dress. As she looked down to take off her jeans she noticed something that looked somewhat like a bruise on her left breast.

She thought, *"It is just a bruise. I must have somehow hit it without knowing it."*

She totally ignored the bruise. She was in the process of slipping on the party dress. Something in her spirit would not let her continue without checking her left breast again. She proceeded to check to ensure everything was alright. As she was making the circular motions with her fingers, low and behold she found a lump. Immediately Rachel fell on her knees and prayed like she had never prayed before. All the other ladies were out of their dressing rooms complimenting one another and enjoying the moment. The longer Rachel prayed, the louder she became. The other ladies began to quiet down.

As soon as they heard Rachel, they immediately ran to her dressing room and all at once they asked, "Are you alright?"

Rachel got herself together. Then she opened the door.

Tressie was in an uncomfortable state, "Rachel, I hate to ask. Why were you praying and crying?"

Rachel didn't have a chance to answer.

Sasha immediately afterwards said, "Rachel, I don't like this feeling I have."

Joanne had a worried look on her face. "Sweetheart, tell us everything is alright."

Melody anxiously commented, "Rachel you are the strong one. There can't be anything wrong."

Scarlette was unsettled, "Rachel, I'm starting to feel like my Little Cassidy Arnasia. Something is not right."

As Rachel came out of her dressing room, the ladies made room for her. They anxiously waited for an answer. There was total silence for about thirty seconds.

Rachel wiped her tears, turned to the ladies and clearly announced, "Ladies, I found a lump in my breast."

The ladies were shocked at that moment. The sales assistant came to the dressing room with a message.

"Is everything alright? I have a message from a distinguished gentleman name Mr. Steadford Grey."

She had a note card in her hand. It read, *"All things work out for the good of them who love the Lord. God promises that He'll never leave us or forsake us. I am right outside if you need me."*

Instantly after the message was delivered the ladies got very emotional. They all embraced Rachel. Rachel had peace that surpassed all understanding. The ladies spirits were so crippled they left the *Top Shop* without buying anything.

As soon as they all entered the limo, Mr. Steadford Grey reached over and touched Rachel's hand. "Angel, everything will work out for the good."

A tear fell from her face. "Mr. Grey, I know it will and thank you for your godly encouragement."

"Angel, find privacy and call your husband when you get back to the hotel."

The other ladies were crying their eyes out. They all were thinking the worst.

Rachel gave insight to the ladies, "You all know my faith is strong. I am here to tell you it is still strong. I will take the necessary precautions. Ladies dry up your tears. I am the same Rachel that walked into the *Top Shop* and the same one who flew on the airplane with you. Believe me ladies, God has always taken care of me and He always will."

As Rachel talked to the other ladies, Mr. Steadford Grey shook his head up and down in agreement.

He looked toward Rachel with admirable eyes, "Angel, you have always been a light for Jesus. Your marriage is beautiful. Remember what our Father has already done for you."

Mr. Steadford Grey leaned forward towards Rachel.

"Angel He will not stop blessing you."

The ladies have questions for him.

Tressie nervously said, "Mr. Grey, I felt relief when you were speaking to Rachel. Sir, can you be sure she is going to be alright? Your spirit is so strong and pure. Your spirit is the closest we will ever come to Jesus."

"Young lady there is no comparison. We can only try our best to be like Him every day."

Joanne commented, "Mr. Grey, she is our angel. She is always there for us. We don't deserve to have her as a friend."

Scarlette was still weeping, "Mr. Grey, the ladies are right. You are like no other I have seen. I know I don't believe in you all's Jesus, but from what they are always saying, you fit the description."

Mr. Grey looked at Scarlette, "Young lady, you can know Jesus for yourself. I don't want to see you lose your soul. This is why, *he turned to Rachel*, angel can stand strong knowing God has already worked everything out for her."

Scarlette was as respectful as she knew how, "Mr. Grey, I have been an *atheist* all my life."

He stared at Scarlette not blinking an eye, "Young lady, you need *Jesus*. Trust me, He is already there. It is up to you to make the greatest and best decision of a lifetime."

Although Rachel was tearful she smiled as Mr. Grey counseled Scarlette.

Melody expressed her concerns. "Mr. Grey, Rachel has to be alright. She is our rock. The entire family is Heaven sent. Her husband is just as angelic as she is, believe it or not."

As Melody expressed, Mr. Grey shook his head up and down in agreement, as if he had known Rachel and her family all of their lives.

Mr. Grey responded, "Young lady, I know she will be alright. She has favor and she is covered."

Sasha looked toward Mr. Grey with sad eyes, "Why do horrible things happen to good people?"

"Trust me doll, she is healed."

Sasha's head dropped with a little relief.

"Young lady, don't stress about anything. Our Almighty already has it worked out; watch and see."

Rachel smiled as she wiped her tears. All the ladies, all at once, looked at one another as they hovered over Rachel. Each of the ladies laid one hand on Rachel. Mr. Grey waved his hands over all of them. As He waved his hands it was like wind rolling through in a split second. The ladies felt the power of God.

As soon as the ladies got back to the hotel, Rachel went to her private room to call John. Rachel dialed John's cell number.

As John answered the phone he sensed in his spirit that something was wrong. "Hello honey, Is everything alright?"

"John, are the kids around?"

"Honey, is there something wrong? I feel awkward in my spirit."

Rachel got herself together. "John, I found a lump in my breast. Honey, I immediately fell on my knees."

There was complete silence.

"John, are you there?"

John finally answered, "Sweetheart, we have to make arrangements to get you seen immediately. I'm sure Dr. Manny will give us an appointment. This is definitely an emergency."

Rachel was as calm as ever before, "John, you and I both know I am already healed."

"Of course you are."

WORDS OF WISDOM

Brothers and Sisters, God always give us warning signs of what is to come. Often times the message is delivered through our spirits. We must pay attention as God speaks. It feels like a million dollars when we develop the ears to hear Him speak and the eyes to see what he sees. To explain furthermore, when we connect with the Holy Spirit, we will be able to see and hear as the Holy Spirit reveals. If we feel in our spirits we are suppose to be at a convention, seminar, or whatever the case maybe, we must make it our business to be there. We must be aware of His soft, beautiful whispers.

Brothers and Sisters, often times we will hear stories of Angels on Earth. I believe God place certain people in our lives for His purpose. Many times, these people are protecting us and we don't even know it. We must learn from awkward situations and times that seem unbearable. When we put Jesus first in our life, there is no way we can lose.